END GAME

A MASON SHARPE THRILLER

LOGAN RYLES

INKUBATOR
BOOKS

Published by Inkubator Books
www.inkubatorbooks.com

ISBN (eBook): 978-1-83756-180-3
ISBN (Paperback): 978-1-83756-181-0
ISBN (Hardback): 978-1-83756-182-7

For Brian, Garret, and the Inkubator Books team...
Thank you for believing in Mason.

1

The driver was dead before the van stopped spinning.

I saw it all from a hundred yards away, a deluge of rain obscuring the windshield of my '67 GMC pickup. Only one wiper worked, and my headlights were dim in the inky blackness of Alabama midnight.

The first vehicle was an old panel van, something built twenty years ago, unmarked and puttering along just ahead of me, driving slowly to manage the rain. The second was some kind of small sedan, topping the next hill and racing toward the two of us at a rate of speed inadvisable in perfect conditions. The road dipped at the bottom of the hill, and I could see the wide pool of rainwater built up there, like a small pond.

The driver of the sedan never saw it, not even braking before he made impact. The sedan hydroplaned, spinning instantly out of control and hurtling into the median. I marked its progress by the flash of headlights bucking upward as tires bounced over grass, then dipping toward the pavement again a moment before bumper met bumper, and the sedan smashed headlong into the oncoming van.

Both vehicles spun, hoods buckling and glass shattering. The sedan hurtled back toward the median, and the van left the pavement, rocketing into the right-hand ditch and rolling toward a line of trees like a tumbling toy.

I smashed the brake, wrestling the wheel as I felt the back end of my truck start to fishtail. A barrage of rain beat down on the metal roof, flooding my ears with roaring chaos as I slid to a stop. I hit the emergency flashers, wondering if they even worked, and threw the door open.

The air hung thick with the heavy stench of burned tires, the pavement littered with broken glass and mangled metal. I broke into a run for the sedan first, resting nose-up in the ditch, twisted beyond any recognition of make or model. The windshield was blown out, and I could see a body resting behind a detonated airbag, but it didn't move. As I slid across sodden grass and reached the door, I knew he was dead. He lay head-back in the seat, his face covered in blood, his mouth hanging open. I checked for a pulse and felt nothing.

The other seats lay strewn with the usual car clutter—empty Coke bottles and fast-food trash, but no humans. I clawed my way back to the blacktop and looked for oncoming traffic. There was nobody. The highway lay black and wet, lost someplace south of Columbus, Georgia. The middle of nowhere.

I ran to the far ditch and found the van resting upside down, pinned between hardwood trees, now rotated so that the driver's door was fully exposed as I approached. The sedan had made impact just forward of the door, and that entire section of the van was caved in. As I reached the smashed window, I saw a torn and bleeding arm dangling from a body still belted into the inverted driver's seat. I reached for his wrist, shouting into the darkness, but long before I touched bloody skin, I knew he was dead also.

The collapse of the driver's compartment had rammed the steering column right into his chest. Frozen dead eyes stared out into space, blood trickling from his lip, and he didn't move.

It was ghastly, but nothing I hadn't seen before. My combat-jaded mind tuned out the gore, and I shouted into the van.

"Is anybody in there? Can you hear me?"

No answer, but I thought I heard a dull whimper. I staggered in the mud-slicked grass, fumbling through my pockets in search of my flashlight. Then the stench reached me, penetrating the rain. An acrid odor I would recognize anywhere.

Heat and burning grease.

My attention snapped back to the smashed nose of the van, and in the blackness I thought I saw a soft glow. An electrical fire, probably. A ruptured battery, a torn cable, or just pure engine heat collided with combustible debris. It could be any one of a hundred things, but the prospect of a vehicle fire cut my opportunity for a rescue attempt in half.

Grabbing the mangled door, I gave it one desperate tug before knowing the effort was useless. The door was distorted beyond any hope of opening. I looked to the rear end of the van only to find it driven against an oak tree, blocking the back doors. There were no rear windows, and the windshield was barricaded by the buckled mass of the van's hood.

I made for the passenger's door, slipping and sliding through the mud, smelling growing heat and melting rubber. I felt the warmth on my face as I circled the front bumper, spitting rainwater and reaching the passenger door. It was smashed also, but not as badly. I hit my knees and ducked to look through broken glass into a darkened interior. More of the car clutter I'd seen in the sedan littered the upturned ceiling of the van, joined by a trace of blood and an abandoned shoe.

And then I saw the second passenger. It was a woman stretched out on the floor, clutching her arm and moaning softly. I couldn't see her face—only her torso up to the chest, visible as vague shadows in the near perfect dark.

"I see you!" I called. "Lie still. I'm coming!"

I grabbed the door handle and jerked. It was plastic and decades old. My adrenaline-charged yank tore the handle clean off with a brittle snap, but the door didn't open. I ripped my shirt off, peeling soaked fabric over my head and wrapping it into a makeshift boxing glove to smash away the remaining glass.

The growing fire was more than a smell now. Light leaked out of the engine bay and around the mutilated hood, offering limited illumination of the interior. I pounded away the remnants of the passenger window and saw the woman drag herself backward, crying out in fear at the sight of fire. She reached for the back doors.

"There's a tree!" I shouted. "You can't go that way. Come toward me!"

I yanked on the door. With the passenger-side A-pillar smashed in, the window space alone was too narrow to force my bulky frame through, but the woman looked petite enough.

"Come toward me!" I called.

An unintelligible cry answered from the van, but the woman didn't turn.

I forced my head and one shoulder through the gap, wincing as sharp metal bit into my bare chest. The dangling arm of the dead driver smacked me in the face, and I forced it aside, twisting to look backward.

Growing light flooded the interior, and I saw the woman. She was indeed small—not more than a hundred pounds, curled up against the back door, her arm clamped at her side, her face obscured by a mass of blonde hair. She didn't turn as I pressed inside, and I called into the van again.

"I'm here! It's okay. Just come toward me."

The woman turned, the hair falling away, firelight flashing across her face. The breath caught in my throat, and I did a double take, blinking hard. Certain that I wasn't seeing what I thought I saw.

And then I pushed the thought away because it didn't matter.

"Come toward me!"

She didn't move, shaking in the back. I beckoned with an outstretched arm, my back tingling as the fire grew hotter behind me.

Still, she didn't move. I could see it in her eyes. She was shell-shocked.

I wriggled out the window and tried the door again. It was caught on a mutilated latch, but as I tugged, I felt it give a little. I needed more force. I needed leverage.

The tire iron.

I fought to my feet and raced to my truck still parked in the rain with both headlights blazing. Leaping into the bed, I tore through my stacks of camping gear, tearing lids off plastic bins and ripping past propane bottles and cooking implements. A quick glance to the van confirmed that the fire was growing, and my heart rate spiked. I could see flames licking out of the engine bay, flickering taller as they ignited more combustible components. Gas lines fed that engine bay, and there was a good chance one or more of them was ruptured.

From there it would be a short path for the fire back to the fuel tank suspended almost directly above the shell-shocked woman.

My fingers touched the tire iron, and I sprinted for the van. I smelled gas as I circled the nose and reached the door, shoving the implement into the doorjamb. I threw all of my two-hundred-pound frame into the bar, heaving and tugging. Metal popped, and my face burned with the rising heat. I slung the iron down, grabbing the door through the busted window and wrenching backward.

The door shrieked open. A rush of heat from the engine bay signaled the ignition of fuel. I threw myself down and pressed inside, pushing the driver's dangling arm aside again. The heat on my back was intense enough to scald skin. I rotated left and looked backward, already calling into the van.

The woman was gone.

2

I sat on the open tailgate of my pickup as the first responders arrived. A fire truck was joined by two cop cars—a Chevrolet Tahoe and a Ford F-250 Super Duty, both painted in sheriff department whites and tans. The Tahoe's light bar blazed, while subdued blue and red LEDs flashed behind the Ford's sprawling windshield.

Fully saturated by the downpour, I didn't even notice being wet anymore. The rain helped to soothe my singed back as I watched the van burn. It was fully engulfed in a gasoline fire now, consuming the body of the crushed driver within it.

There was nothing I could do about that.

"Did you call?"

A short, stocky cop appeared from the Tahoe, dressed in a full sheriff's deputy uniform with an actual star pinned to his chest. An LED flashlight blazed across my face, and I held up a hand.

"One body in the van, one in the sedan. Both DOA. There was a woman, but she's gone."

The guy lowered the light, his flushed face puckering in suspicion as he turned to the van. Already the firefighters were engaging the blaze while paramedics surrounded the sedan. They would know shortly what I'd known from the start. There was no saving the guy. If the head trauma hadn't killed him, the snapped neck would have. But they had to try.

The driver's side door of the Ford popped open, and a second cop dropped out. He wore boots and jeans paired with a simple black T-shirt. A Glock rode his hip, but I saw no star or badge. A black baseball cap adorned with an American flag patch shielded him from the rain as he approached, walking calmly with dark eyes darting from one scene to the next and coming to rest on me.

He was young. Early thirties, I guessed, and probably ex-military. He had that look about him—that quiet confidence that spoke of trauma worse than this in his recent memory.

I also knew he was in charge.

"You call?" the new guy asked.

I wiped rain from my forehead. "I did what I could. Both drivers were dead on impact. There was a woman in the van, but while I was getting my tire iron to force the door open, she must have slipped through the window. She's gone."

The stocky cop narrowed his eyes. "What do you mean *she's gone*?" He spoke with a heavy Southern accent, a little different from the Georgian drawl I'd become accustomed to over the last few months. A little whinier. A little higher pitched.

But maybe that was just his current state of mind.

"It's a pretty self-explanatory statement," I said. "She isn't here."

The stocky cop drew breath. His companion cut him off. "We'll figure it out, Owen. Assist the EMTs."

Owen marched off dutifully, leaving the new guy to extend a hand.

"Luke Rakow, Delamar County sheriff. And you are?"

His accent was gentler than Owen's. Less redneck. A little more traditional. I took his hand and was met with a confident but not overbearing grip.

"Mason Sharpe," I said simply. I didn't have a fancy title to add to my name.

Rakow glanced beneath my tailgate, probably looking for a license plate. Maybe wondering who I was and where I was from. In a county this rural, I assumed the local sheriff would be reasonably familiar with most faces.

But not mine.

"You look like you could use a cup of coffee, Mr. Sharpe. Why don't you join me at the station? We can take your statement in a dry office."

I looked over my shoulder, back toward the unfolding carnage. The firefighters were already bringing the blaze under control, the paramedics negotiating with them about the best way to remove the body of the sedan's driver. The other body—the charred one—would require more careful attention. They'd probably leave that to the coroner.

I sighed. I didn't want to go to any station. I could just as easily give my statement here. But I was sopping wet, exhausted, and had no idea how much farther I'd need to travel before reaching suitable accommodations for the night. I should have stopped in the last town.

Besides. Coffee sounded good.

"All right, Sheriff. Point the way."

THE SHERIFF'S station consisted of a series of metal buildings built together alongside a county jail, sitting all alone next to a two-lane state highway. After waiting long enough to ensure the situation at the crash scene was under control, Rakow led me in his oversized Ford, my GMC struggling to keep up while one windshield wiper contested the continuing downpour.

The county he led me through was rural to the point of appearing desolate. I noted neither houses nor streetlights along our path to the station, which itself seemed to sit in the middle of nowhere. A compound on the edge of a frontier. Or at least, as much of a frontier as a state like Alabama could claim.

Once inside, Rakow was true to his word, leading me past a desk sergeant and down a wide hall straight into his office, where I was offered a chair across from his desk and handed a piping hot cup of coffee. He didn't seem to care that we were both dripping water on the smoothed concrete floor. A quick inspection of the decor in his simple headquarters confirmed what I already suspected—he was military. I saw it in the folded American flag framed behind his desk, and the U.S. Army ball cap resting on top of a metal filing cabinet.

Otherwise, the office was bare. No family photographs, no personal trinkets, no sports memorabilia. Just a map of the region on one wall, and an aging computer set on the desk alongside a stack of documents. Rakow removed his hat and mopped water from his short brown hair, and I modified my initial judgment of his age. He was closer to late twenties than early thirties. Very young to be a sheriff.

I wondered if he had family in the business. Maybe his old man had been sheriff and passed the job down. Maybe that was how it worked in Alabama.

"Mind if I see some ID?" Rakow asked.

I dug my Arizona driver's license from a damp wallet and surrendered it without complaint. Rakow scanned it carefully, rubbing his thumb over the surface to check for the inlaid seals that marked a genuine state ID.

Good instincts, I thought. He was experienced for his age.

"Mason Lewis Sharpe...of Phoenix?"

The statement carried the tone of a question.

"I guess so."

Rakow looked up from my driver's license. "What does that mean?"

I shrugged. "I'm from Phoenix."

"But you're not *of* Phoenix?"

"I don't currently reside there."

"Where do you reside?"

Another shrug. I wasn't intentionally being evasive. I just didn't know how to answer the question. I didn't really have any place to call home at the moment. I'd spent the last three months sleeping in the bed of the GMC at campgrounds scattered across central Georgia, slowly improving my camping stove culinary skills, nursing gentle melodies out of my violin, and doing my best not to think.

Or to feel.

"You live on the road?" Rakow prompted.

"Something like that."

Rakow seemed to accept that answer as he returned my driver's license. I sipped coffee.

"Why don't you tell me what happened?"

Rakow took notes on a clipboard as I recounted the events on the highway, interrupting with simple questions now and then to clarify the when, what, where, and how of it all. He was a good interviewer. He knew how to get to the heart of the matter without fixating on extraneous minutiae.

"Talk to me about the woman in the van," he said. "Any identifying traits?"

I squinted. "Your guys still haven't found her?"

Rakow didn't answer, but the silence was an admission. It was odd, I thought. It had been well over an hour since the first responders arrived on scene. I had used my flashlight to search the woods after the woman disappeared, and failed to find her. But I didn't think she would go far. Shell-shocked and disoriented, she probably stumbled into some ditch and collapsed, semiconscious and helpless until the paramedics arrived.

I would have expected them to find her quickly with their high-powered lights and additional manpower.

"She was small," I said. "Petite, I'd say. Ninety or a hundred pounds, slender. Long blonde hair."

"Age?"

"Tough to say. Mid-twenties, maybe late twenties. About your age."

Rakow made a note, completely ignoring the curiosity in my last comment. "Any other identifying characteristics? Tattoos? Scars?"

I hesitated, playing back those tense moments in the van. The heat on my back. My heart pounding as adrenaline dumped into my veins. Clawing my way through the tight window space and peering into the darkened interior.

There was something. Something I hadn't wanted to

believe at first, and couldn't quite believe now. But I had seen it.

"You're going to think I'm crazy," I said.

Rakow offered a tired smile. "Humor me."

"She had different-colored eyes."

The smile faded, and Rakow sat suddenly very still. "What do you mean?"

I motioned to my face. "One blue eye, very bright. Like crystal. And one brown."

Rakow sat with the clipboard resting in his lap, staring without blinking. There was something in his face—something between disbelief and raw recognition.

But it wasn't disbelief of what I had said. It was something deeper.

Without comment, he set the clipboard down and pivoted in his chair to the file cabinet. Drawers rattled and documents fluttered. After a long moment, he returned, holding a single sheet of paper, that gray look still covering his face.

"Was this the woman you saw?"

He laid the sheet on the table. It consisted of a single photograph, the body of which was occupied by a lone figure. Not a woman, but a child. Thirteen or fourteen, maybe. Petite and slender, with long blonde hair, a bright smile...and two different-colored eyes.

Crystal blue and rich brown.

"That's her," I said, looking up. "Definitely."

Rakow sat back, folding his arms and growing quiet. He still faced me, but I had the feeling he had forgotten I was in the room. He stared at the wall, jaw moving slowly as he chewed his tongue.

I frowned. "Who is she?"

Rakow snapped out of it, looking back to the picture. He shook his head slowly.

"Her name is Delia Crawford," he said at last. "And she's been missing for over a decade."

3

Rakow had me repeat the events at the van, asking more questions this time. Taking more detailed notes. I recounted everything I could remember, but the detailed version of my story was pretty much the same as the summary. Other than that brief moment when I'd registered Delia's striking eyes, I hadn't focused much on the woman in the van. Only on getting her out alive. It was all a blur of adrenaline and noise and supercharged action. A little like combat, but Rakow's questions had the cadence and organization of an after-action report.

Yes, he was definitely military.

Near the end of his notes, a commotion erupted outside the office, someplace down the hall. Something shattered against the tile floor, and the desk sergeant I had observed on entry shouted for backup. Rakow dropped his clipboard and bolted to his feet.

"Stay put. I'll be back."

He left me in the office, the door half open, the picture of Delia still staring up at me. The commotion from down the hall sounded familiar. Slurred, irate speech. A heated argument, punctuated by grunts and animalistic growls. Somebody was dragging in a contentious drunk—something I'd done plenty of times during my years as a Phoenix beat cop.

Not an enviable job.

"I tell ya, Sherruff. I weren't doin' nothin'! Mindin' my own business."

"Bullsheet, Lamar. You were busting bottles in the street. Don't you know how dangerous that is? Somebody could blow a tire!"

I recognized Owen's whining drawl and nudged the door closed. Standing, I turned to the wall-to-wall map pinned behind me. It displayed the entirety of southeast Alabama, with Delamar County highlighted in bright yellow, its borders drawn in red.

The county was of average size for the east coast, but irregular in shape. Its entire eastern side bordered Georgia, with a substantial lake riding the state line for the entire length of the county. There was a city sitting near the top of the lake—a midsized-looking town, labeled *Muscogee.* But the star marking the Delamar County seat sat nearer to the heart of the county, alongside a mark a mile or two down the road that signified the sheriff's station.

The town was called Able, and it looked to be little more than a dot. A collection of short streets. Right in the middle of nowhere.

I sighed, shoulders slumping, and turned from the map. When I left central Georgia the previous day, I hadn't planned on stopping in Alabama. Were it not for the rain, I probably wouldn't be in Alabama at all. US Highway 431 cut across the southeast corner of the state, crossing through a city called Dothan before Highway 231 led the way into Florida.

It was Florida I was trying to reach. There was a beachside concert in Panama City I wanted to see. The Zac Brown Band was playing. I'd been practicing a few of their songs on my violin all spring, and hearing them live sounded fun.

Or at least…it sounded like a reason to get out of bed.

The door swung open, and Rakow returned, his black T-shirt semi-untucked, looking tired and irritated. A quick glance at the clock confirmed what I already knew—it was nearing one a.m.

Owen marched in after him, his face flushed. Under the fluorescent light of Rakow's office, I got a better look at him, immediately noting the scripted title on his fresh sheriff's department shirt: *Chief Deputy*. He was a burly guy, shoulders bulging beneath his shirt, his hair close-cropped and turning gray. It wasn't a military haircut. More like the haircut a military wannabe gets. I estimated him to be in his early forties, in good shape, with all the usual gear a cop carries loaded onto his waist, including a full-size Glock handgun with a Punisher logo emblazoned onto the base plate.

A bona fide badass.

Rakow resumed his seat and motioned for Owen to close the door. I remained standing as Owen scooped up the picture of Delia and surveyed it with disbelieving eyes. Then he shook his head.

"There ain't no way, Sheriff. This girl's dead."

"She wasn't two hours ago," I said simply.

Owen flushed, his gaze snapping toward me. "You calling me a liar, son?"

I didn't answer. Rakow motioned Owen back with a tired, semi-irritated wave.

"Chill out, Owen." He turned back to me. "Mr. Sharpe, why don't you tell us a little bit about yourself."

I restrained an exhausted sigh, mentally kicking myself for ever agreeing to return to the station. It always went like this. No good deed unpunished. I couldn't blame Rakow for wanting to know more about me. After recovering from the initial shock of my claims, it was natural to question the credibility of a lone witness turned up out of nowhere. Claiming to see a woman nobody had seen in over a decade.

Maybe I was some kind of attention junkie, parking alongside a random wreck. Chasing my fifteen minutes of fame. Maybe I was a true crime addict, familiar enough with Delia's case to know what to say.

It was a logical train of thought, but I wasn't about to dive into who I really was, or what I was doing here. I'd recounted that story far too many times since the previous November, and it never got easier.

"I was driving," I said. "I saw the wreck and rendered assistance. I saw the woman, but then she disappeared. That's all I know."

"What are you doing in Delamar County?" Owen demanded. His tone carried an undertone of suspicion, but I was too tired to care. It was a reasonable question, after all. What was anybody doing here?

"I'm headed to the beach. There's a concert I want to see."

"Late to be driving," Owen challenged.

"Not a lot of hotels around here," I said.

Owen shot his boss a blustery look, still laden with suspicion. A few months ago, it might have been enough to justify a snarky barb from me, but I had learned the hard way that small-town cops could be suspicious of outsiders, and maybe they had a right to be. Regardless, I was simply too tired to care what Owen thought.

Rakow held up a hand, calming his deputy.

"Owen, why don't you go book Lamar and finish out your shift? We'll circle the wagons tonight and work on this in the morning. I'm beat."

It wasn't the order Owen wanted, but there was no debate in Rakow's tone. The chief deputy retreated from the office, closing the door behind him, leaving Rakow to descend into his sagging chair and stare me down for a moment that lingered closer to a minute.

Not suspicious. But probing. His next question didn't surprise me in the least.

"How many tours?"

I didn't answer immediately, looking again to the Army hat atop the file cabinet. Recalling how he'd inspected the ID. How young he was to be sheriff, yet he'd managed Owen's bluster with ease.

He'd been a military cop, I was sure of it. And one of the good ones, probably. A guy who had learned the hard way that de-escalation was a far greater tool than the weapon on his belt.

"Three," I said. "Afghanistan. You?"

"Two. Iraq. 42nd MP Brigade. Guardhouse duty, mostly. But I know the look of a guy who's been downrange. You're dripping with it."

There was a question at the end of his statement, but I didn't answer it. He motioned to the chair across from him, and I reluctantly took a seat.

"Infantry?" Rakow asked.

"Seventy-fifth," I answered simply. Civilians called us Rangers, but Ranger can mean a lot of things in the Army. Sometimes it can mean as little as a jackass college grad with lieutenant bars who overcame Ranger school, but has never been shot at.

Being a member of the Army's Seventy-Fifth regiment is something else. More than just a patch, it's a job.

A job that gets you shot at.

"Impressive," Rakow said. He didn't sound impressed, but I didn't need him to be. I simply wanted him to take me seriously enough to accept my statement and cut me loose. It was another two or three hours to Panama City. If I pushed, maybe I could make it before crashing for the night.

"You got a place to stay?" Rakow asked. It was the question I'd been dreading, and I chose not to indulge it.

"Actually, I'm about to hit the road. I'd really like to make it to Florida before I stop."

Even as I said it, I knew I was kidding myself. My body was rebelling against a long day behind the wheel paired with the stressful attempted rescue. I'd be lucky to make it to Dothan, but judging by the map on Rakow's wall, that town looked large enough to offer plentiful accommodations.

"I'll walk you out," Rakow said. He guided me back down the halls, past offices and file rooms, acknowledging the sleepy desk sergeant with a grunt and a nod.

Outside, the rain had slackened considerably, reduced now to a light spray. My old GMC sat gleaming under the parking lot lights, the hood a mottled pattern of faded green paint and growing rust splotches. The truck needed a full paint job, a new windshield wiper motor, and half a dozen other minor repairs, but for all its idiosyncrasies, I really enjoyed it.

It was simple. At this stage in my life, I needed simple.

Rakow followed me to the truck, hands in his pockets, and surveyed the plastic bins lying in disarray in the bed. I regarded the lidless containers I had ripped open during my desperate search for the tire iron and held back a frustrated groan. Most of my gear was now soaked, and some of it probably ruined.

No good deed unpunished.

"So you just...live out of your truck?" Rakow asked. There was an undertone to his voice. It sounded like surprise mixed with just a hint of concern.

"I camp," I clarified.

"I don't see a tent."

"I've got a hammock. I sleep in the truck bed pretty often. I've got an air mattress."

Rakow nodded thoughtfully, and I knew what he was thinking. Combat ranger, three deployments, Afghanistan. A battered war vet with a load of PTSD. Homeless, and in denial about it.

I couldn't deny it was a tough picture, but the source of my broken lifestyle had little to do with PTSD. At least not the combat kind.

"I tell you what," Rakow said. "Why don't you crash at my place tonight? I've got a spare bed in back. Tomorrow morning, we'll whip up some pancakes. Send you off right."

The concerned tone was gone from his voice, replaced now by an easy-going warmth. He gestured toward his truck, but I shook my head.

"Thanks, but I should really hit the road. I'll get a hotel."

"It's over an hour to Dothan," he said. "And it's already late. Come on—one vet to another. You helped us out tonight. Let me show you some Southern hospitality."

He turned for his parked Ford, and I hesitated alongside my truck. I hadn't expected an invitation, and I didn't really know what to do with one now. I wasn't used to sleeping at other people's houses. But if I had observed one thing about the Deep South since traveling out of Atlanta, it was that people were generally laid-back. The edgy suspicion and nervousness I had become accustomed to living in big cities was nowhere to be found in the rural countryside.

Maybe it was culture; maybe it was naiveté. Either way, it was certainly welcoming.

Rakow stopped at his truck, one boot on the running board. "Relax. I'm no serial killer."

"How about your wife?" I asked.

"Haven't got one."

I surveyed my camping gear, wondering whether or not it would all fit in the cab. Probably not.

"You're parked at a sheriff's station." Rakow laughed. "It'll be there in the morning."

He swung into the truck, and the big diesel fired up with an angry growl. I lingered next to the truck, contemplating another hour behind the wheel along dark Alabama highways, cold and wet.

Or a climate-controlled cab, followed by a warm bed and a hot meal in the morning.

It was an obvious choice.

Ducking into the cab of my GMC, I retrieved my backpack and double-checked its contents. Then I turned for the Ford.

4

Rakow's F-250 was an absolute beast. It dwarfed my GMC, all shiny white and lined with chrome, four doors and four-wheel drive with oversized all-terrain tires. The seats were leather, and the dash was equipped with all the fanciest bells and whistles, but it wasn't hard to tell that this was a working man's truck. There was mud on the floorboard, dust on the dash, and tools littering the back seat. A pair of military dog tags hung from the rearview mirror, and a Mossberg 590 shotgun rode in a window rack.

As a police vehicle, it was a far cry from my unmarked Ford Taurus back in Phoenix. The truck was more comfortable. More customized.

Rakow piloted back onto the two-lane state highway and punched the gas, the turbos kicking in as the diesel inhaled air like a yawning dragon. In mere seconds, we left the sheriff's station and all its lights behind and were lost in a pitch-black world of rural countryside.

"I'm a little surprised," Rakow said.

"By what?"

"You haven't asked me about Delia. It's a pretty intriguing case. I figured another cop would be interested."

I paused, long and thoughtful. "How did you know I was a cop?"

"I ran your name through a criminal database when I stepped away to help Owen. Pulled up a note about the Phoenix PD. Beat cop, then homicide detective..."

He trailed off, and I wondered if he had investigated further, and knew what had happened next. Or maybe he was simply letting the subject float, in a hope that I would elaborate.

It really didn't matter. I didn't want to elaborate. I didn't want to discuss Phoenix...or why I left.

"I am a little curious," I said, pivoting the conversation back to Delia.

Rakow settled into his seat, one hand riding the bottom of his leather-wrapped steering wheel. The highway rose and fell, winding around low hills, with bright headlights casting a momentary glow over open fields and groves of planted pine trees.

It looked a lot like central Georgia.

"There used to be a summer camp not far from here," Rakow said. "Pretty popular place back in the day. Usually hosted eighty or a hundred kids every year. Delia was there the summer she turned fourteen. They put her to bed one night in one of the dormitories, and she wasn't there the next morning." Rakow shrugged. "Simple as that, really. Nobody has seen or heard of her since...until tonight, I guess."

He shot me a sideways look, and I suddenly wondered if he shared Owen's suspicions. If he thought I had manufactured my story, maybe for attention.

I decided to steer away from the car crash.

"What's the deal with her eyes?" I asked. "Why are they different colors?"

"There's a scientific name for it, but I forget what it is. It happens sometimes. Like a one-in-one-million type of thing. Delia's case was stronger than usual—her blue eye was especially bright, so the condition was more obvious."

"She was a local girl?"

"As local as it gets. Her family is from Muscogee. Pillars of the community, actually. They were big in the bauxite industry before its decline."

"I'm not sure what that is," I said.

"It's a sedimentary rock mined for its aluminum content. Used to be a big deal around here, but most of the mines have shut down. The industry moved overseas, like everything else."

Rakow slowed, turning the truck off the highway and onto a wide dirt road packed tight with orange clay. The pines were now joined by hardwoods, their drooping limbs at times scraping against the roof of the jacked Ford. Rakow kept his foot on the gas, plowing along with the familiarity of a man who'd driven this route a few thousand times.

"Didn't they launch an investigation?" I asked. "To find Delia."

"Of course. Big one. The whole region was involved. FBI came down at some point. It was quite a circus, actually. A lot of debate over jurisdiction, a lot of red tape. There's a guy down in Dothan who wrote a book about it. True crime writer...I forget his name. But anyway, there was nothing to go on. People always think there's all this invisible evidence lying around, and no crime goes unsolved. But sometimes that's just not how it works. Sometimes you've got nothing."

He trailed off and glanced sideways again. "I guess I don't have to tell you that."

He didn't. My tenure as a homicide detective in Phoenix had been relatively short, but I'd solved several cases and left a few dozen more in process. Sometimes the answer was painfully obvious, requiring my services as a detective as a mere formality. Other times, it was like a person had been struck dead by an invisible hand.

No evidence. No leads. Just heartbreak and loss.

After another two miles or so, Rakow steered onto a wide gravel drive, small rocks popping beneath the heavy tires. We crossed a culvert and a small creek, the forest around us growing thicker. I had the sudden thought that I was very trusting for a complete stranger. Were Rakow not in uniform, I never would have gone for this.

Maybe it was still a dumb idea. Maybe I'd wind up rotting in a shallow grave someplace amid these pines, struck dead by an invisible hand.

"Got a little land way out in the sticks," Rakow said, as if he could sense my unease. "It ain't much, but it's home."

On cue, the trees fell away, and the Ford's high beams cut a wide swath over an open clearing three or four acres in size, with a pond on the left-hand side. On the right-hand side, a cabin-style house was built beneath a single oak tree, its walls clad in cedar plank siding with a metal roof and a full-width front porch. Behind it, I noted a slouching barn nestled next to the tree line, and as we neared the house, a dog barked over the growl of the diesel, loud and territorial. I located the K9 on the front porch, loping down the steps with a stiffness that contrasted the formidable bark.

Rakow parked the truck underneath the oak tree and cut the engine. "Welcome to *mi casa,* Sharpe."

I grabbed my bag and dropped to the ground, immediately accosted by the dog. It was a border collie, mostly black with irregular patches of white and a toothy grin that again contradicted the bark. I braced myself for a lunge, but instead the dog leapt up and placed two muddy paws on my chest, its tongue dropping out of its mouth as it panted.

"That's Mossy," Rakow said. "She's harmless."

I scratched the collie's neck, smiling as she closed both eyes, her mouth dropping open another half inch. Instantly consumed by bliss. Completely at ease with a new friend.

"Hey, Mossy," I whispered. "You're a pretty girl, aren't you?"

Rakow kicked his boots off on the deck and whistled. Mossy abandoned me, rushing to join her master as I pushed the truck door closed and cast a glance around the yard.

There were faded wind chimes hanging from the porch, and an overgrown garden bed beyond the home. A sign by the door was scripted with the family name, and a little iron cross hung in the window. Ragtag pillows rested in rocking chairs and the swing suspended at the end of the porch. The figurine of a hummingbird sat atop a stake in a long-forgotten flower bed.

They were elegant, feminine touches. But they were long outdated and uncared for.

Rakow caught me staring. His voice dropped. "My mother. She died when I was fourteen."

"I'm sorry," I said, and I meant it. I lost my mother young also. It's the kind of thing you don't really heal from.

The silence between us became uncomfortably long, and Rakow unlocked the front door. "Breakfast at oh-five-thirty, Sharpe. Military hours. Don't sleep in."

THE GUEST ROOM that Rakow showed me into was small but comfortable. A very old bed was fit with a sagging mattress and surrounded by dusty bedroom furniture and walls hung with family photographs. I picked out Rakow almost immediately. He was a miniature version of himself today, cradling the head of a whitetail deer, a rifle leaned against his shoulder.

All the photos were old. There was nothing beyond his early teenage years, leading me to believe his mother had been the photographer of the family. He offered me a bottle of water and a blanket, then informed me where the bathroom was, and left me to myself. I thought it was a little strange at first, to be so at ease with a total stranger in your home. The more I thought about it, the more I wondered if his father was also dead. Rakow lived alone in this place, and he wasn't married. There was a story there, but I wasn't going to pry into it.

I locked the door and settled onto the sagging bed, my back still tingling with the sensation of the burn marks. They weren't bad, but I would feel them for a day or two. Peeling my shirt off, I ran a hand through my hair to mop out residual rainwater, then turned to the backpack.

All of my most personal items were kept inside. A toothbrush, a razor, and two pairs of fresh socks—something any self-respecting soldier would never be caught without. There was a book also, a collection of short stories by Hemingway that I'd purchased at a secondhand shop in Macon. I'd read about half of it and was enjoying the distraction.

But buried in the bottom in a compartment sufficiently sheltered from the elements was the only item that couldn't be replaced. Mia's Bible was leatherbound and worn, with her name written in elegant script on the cover. It had sustained a little moisture damage during my recent travels, and I now kept it in a plastic bag to prevent any further deterioration.

Tucked inside the front cover was the only photograph I still had of her. Also a little worn and now a little faded from the hours I'd kept it pinned to the dash of the GMC. Her gorgeous smile radiated up at me, and like I did every night, I tried to imagine that she was still there. That we were still engaged, still marking off the calendar on our way to the big day. That I was simply on a lengthy deployment, aching to be shipped home, where I could wrap her in my arms again.

It was a routine I had practiced every night for nearly ten months, but the warmth it had brought me only weeks prior was beginning to cool, and that terrified me. I had to stare longer at the picture now to remember her smell. To recall the way her voice cracked when she was telling a joke and couldn't stop laughing. To imagine her touch on my bare skin, tangled beneath the sheets.

All of those memories, despite my most desperate efforts, were starting to fade. I could feel them slipping slowly through a sieve at the bottom of my mind, fading into blackness. Leaving behind their basic structure, but losing their color. Losing their feeling.

I swallowed hard and pressed the picture back into the Bible, snapping it closed and clutching it. I stared at her worn name on the cover and thought about how many times I'd watched her read those crinkling pages, curled up on the couch with a cup of tea, not a trace of makeup on. Looking as gorgeous as the rising sun.

The memory felt fresh and brought just a little of the

warmth I craved. But as I switched the lights off and lay back on the bed, another memory took its place. The hollow sound of gunshots echoing down a hallway, mixed with panicked screams.

The slick stickiness of blood on my hands. The blackness closing in.

Mia slipping away.

And not a damn thing I could do to stop it.

5

Rakow reneged on his promise of pancakes the next morning, rattling my door at a quarter after five. I was awake anyway, already dressed, reading from Psalms in Mia's Bible. It was her favorite book, and reading it made her feel a little closer.

"Sorry, bud. The state sent a trooper down to have a look at the crash site. We gotta roll."

I didn't complain, grabbing my bag and scratching Mossy behind the ears on my way to the Ford. Rakow worked his radio during the drive, communicating with deputies and talking the trooper out of a nervous panic about the crash site. Apparently, the rain had intensified during the night, and the trooper was stressed about losing evidence for his accident report. The sky was clear today, with an orange crest rising behind pine trees, illuminating a cloudless Alabama sky. Aside from Rakow's relentless barking into the radio and the growl of his diesel, it might have been peaceful.

"There's a diner on Main Street, just down from the

square. Good biscuits and gravy. Why don't you head that way, and I'll meet you in a minute?" Rakow jabbed his thumb over one shoulder, in the general direction of where I remembered the town of Able lying on his wall map. I nodded my acknowledgment and folded myself back into my old GMC. It sat right where I'd left it, not an item missing from the bed, and feeling like a sardine can after riding in Rakow's Ford.

Able lay just over a mile down the state highway, and it was every bit as shabby but quaint as I expected. A post office passed on my right, followed by a filling station with an attached service garage. Then a row of old homes, mostly wooden, mostly of an early twentieth-century architecture.

The square was aptly named. A courthouse sat along the north side, tall and bleak, built of concrete and in need of a thorough pressure washing. Across the street lay a small park, with three massive oak trees sheltering a handful of picnic tables and a concrete pedestal with the statue of a soldier standing atop it. He looked weathered and old, cradling a nineteenth-century-style rifle. A civil war infantryman, I thought. A Confederate.

Turning right along the loop that ran around the park, I noted an insurance agency, a local law firm, a hardware store, a laundromat, a Mexican restaurant, and half a dozen empty storefronts, the peeling letters of businesses now long out of business sticking to their glass doors.

The diner sat half a block down Main Street, just off the square, with a long row of dirty pickup trucks pulled against the curb. A red awning overshot the sidewalk, with a yellow sign advertising the establishment's name: The General Store Restaurant.

I parked the GMC and enjoyed a warm summer breeze

wafting down the street, smelling of pine trees and dirty concrete. It was going to be another brutally hot day in the South—not as hot as Phoenix, maybe, but twice as humid. I had endured a few weeks of such weather as spring gave way to summer, and I couldn't say I had enjoyed the experience.

I was hoping Florida would be better—maybe not cooler, but at least there would be water.

Pushing inside the diner, I was greeted by a welcome wash of air conditioning and the clamor of three or four dozen people devouring breakfast. The diner consisted of one room, narrow, with a row of tables and booths stretching down the right side and a long counter stretching down the left. Flattop grills sat behind that counter, piping hot and sizzling with rows of fresh bacon and eggs.

The smell was overwhelming.

I found my way to a table and was quickly greeted by an attractive young woman with a messy head of red hair and a grin altogether too enthusiastic for so early in the morning. She took my order for eggs, sausage, and a plate of the biscuits and gravy Rakow had bragged about, leaving a water glass next to a napkin. I relaxed in the booth and watched the street through a foggy glass door, contemplating the three-hour drive to Panama City under a cloudless sky, my windows down and my overworked wiper blade mercifully turned off.

It sounded a lot better than battling my way through the monsoon of the night before.

The redhead with the happy grin brought my food, and my morning got even better. I'd heard a lot about biscuits and gravy in the South, something that I was familiar with but never would have eaten in Phoenix. Past experiences with cold, congealed gravy and dry biscuits at Fort Benning had forever turned me off to the idea, but the General Store Restaurant's rendition of the dish was altogether a cut above. I chowed down like I hadn't eaten in a week, mopping up the last of the gravy with a piece of buttery toast before packing in the eggs and sausage. It was the best meal I'd eaten in weeks.

The waitress came back to check on me, and this time I didn't mind her boisterous cheeriness, requesting a cup of black coffee and the check at her convenience. She bounced off, and I relaxed into the booth again, pushing the plate away and watching the sun gleam across the chrome trim on my GMC's tailgate.

And then I saw something else. No, not something. *Somebody*. He was tall and rail thin. A kid by the look of it, but the glare of the sun left me unsure. I made out a mass of pale blond hair, dark black jeans and a black T-shirt. He stood on the sidewalk in front of my truck, and as I watched, he hopped into the street and tried the door handle.

I sat up, craning my head for a better view. He tugged on the door, but it didn't open. It was locked.

I looked for the waitress, but she was lost behind the counter. Standing, I dug a twenty from my pocket and pinned it beneath my water glass, then jogged for the door.

A pickup truck rolled down the street as I stepped onto the sidewalk. Jet black, built on an elevated suspension atop beefy mud tires, it was one of Ford's Raptors—an off-roading racing truck, not more than a year old. I caught sight of the skinny kid with the blond hair standing behind my GMC, just on the other side of the Raptor. His arms were extended, cradling a cell phone. He snapped a picture of my license plate, then turned for the truck.

"Hey!" I shouted, stepping into the street.

The kid heard me, turning sharp blue eyes in my direction. Then he jumped into the Raptor and slammed the door. The driver hit the gas, and tires ground. As the truck passed, I looked through tinted windows to see another kid behind the wheel—a lot bigger than the first, a real muscle mass—but with the same bright blond hair and piercing blue eyes.

The Raptor's motor howled, spitting out a storm of aggressive exhaust, and then it was gone. Down the street and over a low hill, racing out of town.

I stood in the street, hands in my pockets, and watched it go. I pictured the beefy kid and fixated on the moment our gazes met.

He hadn't looked afraid. He hadn't looked like a kid caught screwing around with somebody's antique truck.

He'd looked smug.

I rolled my shoulders to loosen a stinging back, then turned for the restaurant. Maybe the spunky waitress had my coffee ready. But then I heard the now familiar growl of Rakow's diesel snarling around the square and turning onto Main Street. The big Ford rolled up to the restaurant, the driver's window dropping as Rakow approached.

"Hey, Sharpe! You eat?"

I nodded.

"Hop in," Rakow said. "Local guy just called the station. He found a girl in his barn this morning—blonde hair. Different-colored eyes. I need you to identify our Jane Doe."

6

I gave only momentary thought to refusing before swinging aboard Rakow's F-250 again. Maybe it was the sunshine, maybe it was the biscuits and gravy, but whatever the reason, I felt better than I had in days and more agreeable. I figured I could spare a couple of hours if Rakow needed a positive ID. It was the right thing to do, and anyway, I felt like I owed him something for welcoming me into his home.

The ride took us out of town, but not toward the highway. I knew by the digital compass mounted into the Ford's rearview mirror that we were headed southwest, deeper into the county. Rakow drove with his emergency lights off but his foot buried in the gas, topping low hills and crashing over potholes like a Marine charging into battle behind the wheel of a Humvee.

"I think you should fire your road crew," I quipped.

Rakow offered a dull smirk. "It's a rural county. We don't get a lot of state funding, let alone federal. We do what we can."

Alongside the winding road, I noted packed groves of planted pines, joined occasionally by small pastures and compact fields. It didn't look like farming country. More like a very subdued version of north Georgia. Untamed forests closed tightly over the road in places, with short bridges crossing narrow creeks.

We reached a driveway ten minutes later, and I pinched my fingers across the dash-mounted GPS unit to obtain a larger view of the county. Tracing the space between our blue locator dot and US Highway 431, where the crash occurred, I measured with my fingers and frowned.

"Long ways to walk on foot," I said.

"I know," Rakow said. "I thought so too."

The driveway was dirt, rutted and flooded with rainwater. The Ford's rear tires slipped, and Rakow locked the beast into four-wheel drive, grinding ahead with the same aggression as he had barreled down the country roads. I noted a barbed-wire fence running between the trees on either side, with numerous metal signs nailed to stakes facing the drive.

NO TRESPASSING.

PRIVATE PROPERTY.

SECURED BY SMITH AND WESSON.

TRESPASSERS WILL BE SHOT — SURVIVORS WILL BE SHOT AGAIN.

"Who is this guy?" I asked.

Rakow grunted. "Who, Palmer? Moonshiner. Small-time weed dealer. Does a little meth on occasion."

I turned to face him before I could stop myself, and Rakow laughed. “He’s just an old jackass. Vietnam vet. Got more than his share of action, I think. Doesn’t like visitors.”

“So I gathered.”

The Ford rumbled out of the trees into a rolling clearing mostly overgrown with tall weeds and brush, the metal roofs of a house and barn barely visible ahead. Two rusted-out tractors and a panel van sat parked amid the weeds, long lost to time and now slowly consumed by the undergrowth. A dog barked somewhere ahead, and as Rakow turned in behind the house, the windshield displayed a yard crammed with junk—old appliances, rotting furniture, and a pigpen constructed out of shipping pallets.

The dog was a pit bull, chained to a rusting refrigerator and snarling with glistening white teeth.

“Stay cool,” Rakow advised, cutting the engine.

He dropped out of the truck and shouted toward the house, “Hey, Palmer!”

A screen door groaned on a rusted spring, and Rakow scrambled for cover behind his door, one hand dropping to the Glock strapped to his hip. I saw the guy appear on the back porch—an old crow, just as Rakow described, shirtless and wielding what appeared to be an M16—and threw my door open, rolling for shelter behind the Ford’s engine block.

“Dammit, Palmer!” Rakow shouted. “You can’t call the cops, then turn out with a gun. We’ve talked about this!”

“Sorry, Rakow. You startled me, is all.”

“Put it down!” Rakow demanded.

“Okay, okay. Imma just leave it on the porch, then. Hey, Booker! Shut up! Shut up, now! Damn dog.”

I peered over the hood of the Ford, watching as the old man laid the rifle down, then shuffled down the porch steps.

He wore a handgun on his hip, his bare chest a nasty tangle of gray hair, his scalp mostly bald. Early seventies, I figured. A big Eagle, Globe, and Anchor tattoo on his shoulder.

Rakow slammed his door, and I straightened. The two exchanged a handshake; then the old Marine turned suspicious eyes on me.

"Who's this?"

"This is Mason Sharpe," Rakow said, his voice calm again. "He thinks he may have seen the woman in a car accident last night. He's here to provide a positive ID."

"He a fed?" Palmer demanded.

"No, Palmer. He's not a fed. Chill out."

Rakow turned toward the house, slogging through mud and giving Booker the dog a wide berth.

"She ain't up there, Rakow," Palmer called. "She's in the barn."

Rakow stopped, frowning over his shoulder. "What?"

"I told you I found her in the barn."

"You didn't take her inside?"

"She was all crazy! Wild eyes, like I told you. I thought she might be on something. Like that LSD stuff. Acid! You know the CIA used to experiment on soldiers with that shit? I had a buddy—Booker, I named the dog after him—he went crazy, man. Shot Charlie all to hell. Saved my life, but then he gets home and blows his brains out. Who does that, Rakow? Drug victims, that's who. The CIA dosed him hard. Put it in his coffee, damn sure of it!"

Rakow held up a hand, frustration and semi-exhaustion playing across his face. "Palmer, where is she?"

"In the barn! I locked her in—she's still there."

"You locked her in? Are you out of your mind?"

Rakow marched for the barn, and I fell into step behind

Palmer, keeping the old guy—and the 1911 on his hip—well within view.

The barn was older than the house, built of rough-sawn lumber now long dried out by the sun, with a double door held closed by a chain and a padlock. Palmer stopped at the door, fiddling with the lock, then shot Rakow a hesitant look.

"Now...about the stuff inside..."

Rakow rolled his finger impatiently. "I'm not worried about that, Palmer. I just need to see the woman."

Palmer tore the chain out, then dragged one door open on sagging hinges. Rakow drew his duty light with his left hand, keeping his right resting on the Glock.

"Sheriff's department! Anybody in here?"

The light cut a swath through the interior of the barn, illuminating dirty hay and aged timbers and then the largest moonshining still I'd ever seen. Standing eight feet high with a mess of tangled copper pipes, electronic upgrades, and a tank large enough to inebriate the crew of a battleship, it glistened under the flashlight while Rakow completely ignored it.

I stepped in just behind, tracking Palmer with my peripheral vision as he gestured toward the back of the barn. There was a stack of wooden crates there, all loaded with glass bottles and rubber stoppers. More moonshine—a metric ton of it.

Rakow flipped the retention strap off his Glock and took a cautious step forward. The crates shifted, and bottles rattled.

"That's her!" Palmer said, one hand dropping to his 1911. Rakow glared, and Palmer released the weapon.

"Sorry, Rakow. Old habits."

Rakow took another two steps forward. The flashlight

blazed. I followed, rolling right to expose the space behind the crates. I saw white skin and a small foot snatching quickly out of sight as we approached.

Rakow lowered both the light and his voice, speaking calmly into the darkness.

"Delia?"

Two more steps, a pivot to the right.

And then I saw her.

7

It wasn't a woman, it was a girl. And it wasn't Delia—or at least, it wasn't the woman I saw in the van.

The figure curled up in the back of the barn, her shoulder blades pressed against the rotting interior of the rough-sawn wall, was barely a teenager. Frail, with long blonde hair, pale skin, and torn clothes. She was missing a shoe, and one eye was bloodshot, leaving her with a crazed look.

Wild eyes, just like Palmer said. But not different-colored eyes.

Rakow released his handgun and dropped immediately into a crouch, lowering the light. I stepped back, leaving him to speak softly to the girl in a slow, gentle drawl.

"Hey there. I'm Sheriff Luke. What's your name?"

The girl didn't answer, but her good eye darted from Rakow to me and then to Palmer.

When she saw Palmer, she began to shake, scrambling back against the wall. Rakow looked over his shoulder and spoke through gritted teeth.

"Get back, idiot."

I ushered Palmer back. His face flushed red, and as I neared him, I smelled liquor on his breath.

"I think you should step away," I said quietly. His lip trembled, and both eyes rimmed red.

"Whall...she ain't nothing but a squirt!"

I led him out of the barn, leaving Rakow to sit on the floor cross-legged, talking calmly, both hands held open in his lap. He was good at this—even I felt a little calmer as I left the barn, pushing Palmer ahead.

"What happened?" I demanded.

Palmer looked confused, scrubbing the back of one hand over his weathered face.

"Booker was barking! I thought it might be the feds tryin' to poison my well, so I went for my gun. But then I seen this woman run across the yard and into the barn. When I got there, I only got a glimpse, see. Just her face, just a moment. I never realized she were a kid!"

The stench of moonshine was overwhelming. I turned my face away and watched the barn as Rakow appeared. He walked slowly, head down, clasping one of the girl's hands in one of his own. She walked on shaking legs, clutching her body and drawing back when she saw Booker.

Rakow motioned angrily to Palmer, and the old vet hurried to calm his dog. Rakow led the girl toward his truck while I watched in semi-detached confusion. I wasn't sure what I'd expected to find in Palmer's barn. After meeting the old coot, I had been ready for almost anything.

But this still felt wrong. Like I was missing something.

Rakow motioned me over, and I met him at the front bumper of the Ford. He kept his voice low, still gently holding the girl's hand.

"You speak any other languages, Sharpe?"

"A little Spanish. What's up?"

Rakow shook his head. "I don't know. I don't think she speaks English."

I dropped into a crouch, offering the child my gentlest smile and mimicking Rakow's relaxed tone. "*Hablo Español?*"

She stared at me blankly, not evening squinting in the morning sunlight. I noted her pale skin and the brilliant sapphire blue of her eyes. Bright hair, and narrow, strong features.

The girl certainly wasn't Hispanic. If anything, she looked European—Eastern, or perhaps Scandinavian.

"I'm out," I said, rising to my feet.

"Okay. I'll call social services. There's a whole procedure for this." Rakow turned for his truck. "Stay with her."

He circled toward the door, and I crouched next to the girl again, returning to my smile. I scrambled through my mind for what to say—what to do. I knew nothing about kids beyond the scant child management training provided by the Phoenix Police Department during my years as a beat cop. I've never had kids. Never been an uncle. Never really spent time around them at all.

I decided to go with my gut and just be friendly.

"You like butterflies?" I asked, motioning to the butterfly embroidery on the outside thigh of her blue jeans. It was emerald green, crafted with tiny threads strung with little beads. The girl followed my gesture, and the flicker of a smile passed across her lips. So brief I almost thought I'd imagined it, but her eyes brightened a little.

"*Fluture*," she said.

My smile widened. "That's right. *Fluture*."

I had no idea what the word meant, or even what

language it was, but her smile flickered again. From behind the driver's door, I heard Rakow calling into his radio, communicating with the station about social services and an ambulance. I wasn't sure what the procedure would be for a rural sheriff's department, but I knew back in Phoenix there would be an entire domino chain set off by an event like this. All kinds of departments and agencies at play.

"Are you from Europe?" I asked.

The girl's face remained blank.

"*Europa?*" I tried Spanish again. No dice.

Then I heard the crunch of tires from somewhere behind me, sliding through mud under the pressure of a big engine. I looked over my shoulder to see Owen's Tahoe roll out of the trees, its brush guard gleaming in the morning sun, the tires and fenders caked with mud.

Owen stopped twenty yards behind Rakow's truck as Booker went nuts, baying and yanking at his chain despite Palmer's best attempts to calm the dog. The girl began to shake, her frightened gaze darting first to Palmer, then to the newcomer. Owen stepped out of the Tahoe, already shouting to Palmer.

"Shut that dog up!"

"I'm tryin', dammit! He don't like visitors!"

Booker lunged at the chain, dragging the heavy refrigerator two inches in the mud. Palmer yanked him back, and the dog yelped. The girl took a half step back, jaw trembling. I held up a hand, keeping my voice calm.

"It's okay...it's okay. *Fluture?*" I motioned to the butterfly again.

The girl ignored me, still fixated on the developing chaos. Owen approached from the Tahoe, then stopped when he came level with Rakow's Ford, and pulled his sunglasses off.

"Who's that?" he said, pointing to the girl.

Panic crossed the child's face, and I reached for her hand. I was too late. She turned and bolted, heading straight for the woods behind the barn, bare feet pounding the ground like her life depended on it.

8

"Sharpe!"

Rakow shouted from the truck, but I was already on my feet.

"I've got her!"

By the time I broke into a full sprint, the blonde cloud of the girl's head had already disappeared into the trees, still hurtling on at a mad dash. Despite the bare feet and whatever state of shock we'd found her in, she ran like hell, weaving between dense clusters of pine trees and waist-high brush. I crashed along with a lot less grace, tearing through the low-hanging limbs and gasping for breath.

I've always been in good shape. From scrabbling on the streets of Phoenix as a kid, to powering through boot camp and Ranger School, to passing physicals for the police department. Physical fitness was just a part of life.

But now that life was behind me, and I'd let myself slip a little. My muscles burned and my heart pounded as I tore through a thicket of briars, one arm bleeding, throat raw as I shouted after the girl.

She wasn't stopping. Her slender form disappeared behind a tree, then became momentarily visible between two pines. She looked back, face flooded with fear, mouth half open.

We made eye contact, and I slid to a stop, holding up a hand.

"I'm not going to hurt you. I just want to help."

She hesitated, eyes darting, chest heaving in panicked little gasps. I heard Rakow and Owen thundering toward us from over my shoulder, and her gaze snapped in that direction. The terror returned, and she twisted, hurtling forward.

And then she simply vanished. A shrill shriek was followed by a crunching, tumbling sound—then silence. I fought between the trees and reached the edge of the gully fifty yards ahead. It was hidden behind another tangle of briars—a twenty-foot drop down a sheer wall, ending in a dry creek bed littered with smooth stones and piles of dry leaves.

The girl lay motionless at the bottom, one leg twisted beneath the other, her face buried in the leaves. My heart pounded, and for the first time in a long time, I felt genuine fear.

God, no.

I swept the length of the gully, quickly identifying a stretch of forest floor that dipped toward the creek bed at a hikeable angle. Rakow shouted behind me as I crashed ahead, pushing branches and undergrowth aside without care for my bleeding arms or whiplashed face. Stones crunched under my tennis shoes as I reached the creek bed and tore up it, back toward the girl.

Military training kicked in as I slid to my knees alongside the motionless child. Hours spent in classrooms and out in the field, learning the best techniques to keep wounded people alive long enough for the choppers to arrive. They called it MARCH—an organized sequence of priorities to address in order.

First, Massive Hemorrhage. Nobody lasted long while dumping blood.

I found the girl facedown in the leaves, arms splayed out, one leg twisted at an unnatural angle beneath her. Almost certainly broken, but I saw no trace of blood.

Check.

Airway Control was next. No oxygen, no life. I hurriedly scooped leaves away from her face, clearing her nose and mouth to intake oxygen before I cupped a hand beneath her face to feel her breath.

It was still there, coming in ragged little gasps, but she was out cold.

Airways. Check.

Respiratory Support, Circulation, and Hypothermia came next. All quickly addressed and dismissed. Her respiratory system was still functional, and her heart was still beating. No danger of hypothermia in the blistering Alabama heat.

Check, check, check.

"Sharpe!"

I looked up to see Rakow and Owen stopped at the top of the gully, peering down.

"She fell," I said. "Where's that ambulance?"

"En route," Rakow said. "What do you need?"

"I don't want to move her—I don't know what's broken. Go back and get the paramedics."

Rakow sent Owen for help, then went to work kicking brush aside with his heavy boots, making a path for a stretcher. I turned back to the girl, reaching down to her skull and probing gently with my fingers.

The *H* in MARCH doubled for both Hypothermia and Head Trauma, and it was the latter I was most concerned about. A broken skull, a fractured spine. Things that could cause instant and permanent damage.

I couldn't see into both her eyes to check her pupils, a first alert of spinal damage. I didn't want to roll her over, either, in case there *was* spinal damage. So I checked her ears and nose instead, looking for blood or spinal fluid. I probed her skull gently, feeling for fractures or collapsed sections of bone.

The skull felt good. I saw no spinal fluid. Moving behind her ears, I reached her neck and probed the vertebrae, sweeping aside the tangle of blonde hair to inspect the base of her skull.

My fingers froze, and my blood ran cold. Just beneath her skull, buried under the cloud of pale blonde hair, was a black tattoo. About an inch long and half as much high, completely invisible except under careful inspection, but now crystal clear in the morning light.

It was a barcode, complete with a series of small black digits inscribed beneath the vertical lines.

I drew back my hand and sat motionless next to her. Rakow called down from someplace in the trees, shouting to let me know that the ambulance had arrived. I looked up, heart thumping, then reached into my pocket to dig out the burner phone I had been carrying over the past few months. I'd bought it in Atlanta, and I almost never powered it on, let alone made a call on it.

As the device slowly awoke, I placed a hand on the girl's wrist, checking again for a pulse. It was still strong. I deployed the phone's camera and focused on the tattoo, snapping one picture before returning the device to my pocket.

I could hear the paramedics now, crashing through the forest toward the gully.

"Over here!" I called. "Hurry. She's still breathing."

THE PARAMEDICS DEPLOYED into the gully, and I stepped back to let them work. They repeated my procedure of inspecting the girl for spinal damage before gently rolling her onto the stretcher and hauling her to the ambulance. Five minutes later she was wired in, an oxygen mask over her face, a monitor measuring the beats of her little heart.

The ambulance doors slammed, and the lights flashed. Then the heavy vehicle navigated back toward the road, its thick tires slipping and sliding up Palmer's rutted driveway.

Rakow wiped sweat from his forehead and replaced his hat, squinting in the morning sun. Owen had cornered Palmer and was grilling him about the girl—where she came from, what Palmer remembered about the night before.

None of it was important. I already knew where she'd come from—and why she was here.

Stepping close to Rakow, I retrieved my phone and called up the single image. I passed it to him without comment, and he squinted at the screen.

"What's this?"

"Tattoo. Base of her neck."

"Barcode?" He frowned.

"It's more of a trademark," I said. "I've seen it before—in Phoenix. Traffickers out of Eastern Europe use it."

Rakow looked up, still confused, but starting to understand. I took the phone back.

"It means she's a human trafficking victim," I said. "And by the look of her, she's on the run. You've got a lot bigger problems in this county than a missing woman with different-colored eyes."

9

I rode with Rakow back to the sheriff's station, hurtling down the winding county roads with even more aggression than usual. Owen trailed us in his Tahoe, and Rakow worked the radio to communicate with his department, leaving me to watch the trees roll by and puzzle over what I had seen.

I remembered a case, not long into my tenure as a beat cop in south Phoenix. I was fresh out of the Army and struggling to understand the difference between bad guys in Afghanistan and bad guys in Arizona—something I still struggle with, I guess. My lieutenant was losing patience with a series of public complaints involving my use of force, ordering me to dial it back or look for another job.

When I pulled over a guy late one Friday night for a broken taillight, I almost ignored the smell of liquor wafting from the sedan's cabin. I almost ignored the shiftiness in his eyes and his excessive compliance.

"Write me a ticket, Officer. My bad."

He wanted the ticket, and he wanted me gone. Every

instinct in the back of my mind told me there was more to this story. Something he was hiding. Something that worried him a lot more than the fifty bucks for a busted taillight.

I thought about my lieutenant and the thin ice under my boots. I thought about what kind of complaint this guy would file if I hauled him out of his car and completed a search only to find nothing.

And then I hauled him out anyway, because if Afghanistan had taught me anything, it had taught me to trust my gut.

There was a girl in his trunk. Maybe twelve years old, small and skinny, bound and gagged. Bright blue eyes and deep brown hair. She didn't speak English, and she barely blinked when my duty light flashed across her face.

She was doped, subdued and compliant. And she had been raped. Many times.

They found the barcode tattoo when the paramedics arrived, and nobody questioned my report that the driver had tripped while exiting the vehicle, smashing his face against the curb. The ice under my feet thickened considerably that night. But I didn't feel like a hero.

I felt like a failure. Because a good cop would have saved her before she was raped...somehow.

"Hey, Sharpe." Rakow broke into my thoughts with a snap of his fingers. "You with me?"

"Yeah." I tore my gaze away from the window, my stomach twisted with nausea. Thoughts of the blonde girl at the bottom of that creek bed wouldn't leave my mind.

Nor would the image of that barcode. Like a brand on a cow. A mark of ownership.

It made me sick.

"You good, man?" Rakow asked.

"I'm fine." I sat up in the seat, stretching my back. It still stung with the kiss of the vehicle fire, reminding me of the other blonde woman in the back of the van. The one with different-colored eyes.

Delia Crawford? A woman missing for over a decade. Two wild events in the same rural county in under twenty-four hours.

A coincidence? I didn't think so.

"Look," I said. "I'm gonna stick around a few days. I'd like to help."

Rakow eyed me, one hand on the wheel, the other cradling his radio. He nodded slowly, then replaced the handset in its rack on his dash.

"I wouldn't refuse the help. We're gonna be hopping for a few days. But this is a law-and-order county, okay? You're not a cop. You can consult, but you can't get in the way or stir anything up."

"Don't worry," I said. "I'm not looking for trouble."

We arrived back at the police station, and Rakow pulled the monster Ford into a parking space near the front door. There was a crowd of vehicles in the lot now—half a dozen sheriff's department Chargers, a silver-and-blue state trooper's sedan, and a knot of personally owned vehicles. Rakow and I barely made it through the front door before he was assailed by deputies, the desk sergeant, and the state trooper, all speaking at once. He whistled loudly, and that killed the chatter from the men and women wearing brown and tan, while the trooper kept going.

"Sheriff, I *told you* I needed you down by the highway at six a.m. sharp. We're losing evidence, here! Now what am I supposed to—"

"Dammit, Kyle. Will you chill out? We've got more than

an accident at play here. Head on down to my office, and I'll be there in a minute."

Rakow proceeded through his deputies one at a time, answering questions and giving orders with calm but commanding firmness. I liked the way he handled his people. He listened, indulging their overboard energy without feeding it, then gave clear and concise directions, without at any point coming across as impatient or condescending.

His people listened, too, and they didn't argue. A token of respect for their boss.

When the crowd finally cleared, Rakow turned to the desk sergeant—an old guy with a handlebar mustache and a head full of white hair.

"Willis, this is Mason Sharpe. He's a retired Phoenix police officer and witness to the accident. He's going to hang around and consult for a few days. Make him comfortable, will you?"

Willis nodded, and Rakow retreated to his office, leaving me with my hands in my pockets in the suddenly quiet department lobby.

"So you saw Delia?" Willis asked.

His voice was as old as his face, rattling a little with the trademark of a smoker and carrying an undertone of good humor. I liked it, and I liked the look of him, also. He was a little overweight but not obese, wearing a standard sheriff's department uniform with a Smith and Wesson .357 Magnum strapped to a leather belt alongside a badge.

Old school. Classic. I had the feeling he'd been wearing that badge for longer than I'd been alive.

"That's what they tell me," I said.

"Hell of a thing," Willis grunted. "I remember when that

kid went missing. Feels like yesterday. I had just retired again."

"Again?"

Willis grinned, exposing a row of tobacco-stained teeth. "I retired from this joint 'bout three times, I reckon. Spent six or eight months at the house dealing with the missus...then come running back."

"Police work will do you that way, won't it?"

He laughed. "You never been married, have you, son?"

I didn't answer, and he must have detected the slight dip in my shoulders. He sipped water and sighed.

"I do enjoy the work. Rakow is a good sheriff. I wouldn't come back for anyone else."

"What's his story?" I asked.

"What do you mean?"

"Isn't he kinda young to be a sheriff?"

Willis cast a sideways glance down the hall. Phones rang in the distance, and Owen was busy arguing with a deputy three or four doors down. Nobody was near enough to eavesdrop.

"Luke's father was sheriff," Willis said. "Spent the best part of twenty years working the job. Most everybody loved him. He was a fair man. Tough—but fair. And honest."

"What happened?" I asked. I already thought I knew.

"Luke was in the Army when it happened. He was stationed someplace outside the country...or maybe he just came back. I don't remember. Anyhow...it happened right here in Delamar County. Sheriff Rakow was murdered. Hell of a thing. They pinned the guy they thought done it, and Luke came home for the funeral. Got to sniffing around, and figured we pinned the wrong guy. So he did some digging of his own...and he was right."

"And then he ran for sheriff," I finished.

Willis nodded. "Not right away. But yeah, he come around. I guess folks figured, hell, the first Rakow done them right. Maybe Luke was cut from the same cloth."

"Is he?" I asked.

"No doubt. Maybe better cloth. Luke's more patient than his daddy. More even-tempered. And he don't drink so much."

I looked down the hall toward Rakow's office and thought back to the night prior, standing next to my GMC. At the time, I thought Rakow must have assumed me to be a lost veteran stricken with PTSD. In need of a hand.

Maybe he had. Or maybe Rakow knew loss, and he recognized its signature.

"I'd like to help him," I said. "I was at the crash scene. I saw that woman they say is Delia. I'd like to look into it."

Willis shrugged. "If the sheriff says you're consulting...I guess you're consulting. What do you need?"

"You got some place where I can use the internet?"

10

Willis led me to an unused office at the end of the hall, where a rickety metal desk hosted an outdated desktop computer. He logged me in and advised me that all searches could be tracked by the department's IT service, then asked if I'd like coffee.

"I'm good," I said. "I won't be long."

Willis shot me a two-finger salute, then waddled off down the hall. I turned back to the computer and navigated to a search bar. Then I input Delia Crawford's name.

The events at Palmer's place deep in the Delamar County hills had shaken me. I didn't want to admit it, but seeing a terrified child with a brand tattoo on her neck bothered me a lot more than two dead men alongside the highway the night before. What had happened to them was tragic and not necessarily anybody's fault. But at least they had lived a few decades. Experienced life. Maybe been married and had some kids. Taken some vacations. Read some good books.

Loved some good people.

None of that could be said for the blonde girl with the barcode tattoo. Barely a teenager, and a long way from being a woman, she had clearly been deprived of even the most basic comforts of childhood. Robbed of her innocence, taken from her home, and now lost in an alien world where nobody understood her.

It was something beyond evil. It was depraved in the most absolute sense of the word. Yet when I considered a place to start my investigation, the first thing that came to mind was Delia.

If Rakow was to be believed, and this woman had been missing for over a decade, it was an impossible coincidence that she should reappear so many years later at the same moment as a human trafficking victim was discovered inside a crackpot moonshiner's barn only a few miles away. In a big city, or even a medium-sized city, the two events could be dismissed as unrelated.

But in a county the size of Delamar, with a sheriff's department boasting only a dozen personnel, and a county seat the size of a movie set? No way. I couldn't deny the likelihood of a link, and that was why I wanted to start with Delia. Rakow and his people would fixate on the girl, processing her through their system of social services and state investigators, locating a translator and searching for her kidnappers.

I would dig into Delia. A cold case, long abandoned and relegated to a stack of permanently unsolved mysteries. Likely, a dead end. But if I had really seen her, then she wasn't dead, and she wasn't even missing. She was hiding—because she had fled the scene of that car accident. And that piece of information, while small, could be enough to turn the whole case on its head.

My initial Google search produced plenty of results. Outdated news articles were joined by a Wikipedia page dedicated to her disappearance, which offered a succinct summary of the event, correlating perfectly with Rakow's account.

Delia was the only child of Mr. and Mrs. Thomas Crawford, of Muscogee. Thomas was involved in the bauxite industry as something of a logistics specialist, arranging the export of the mineral via bulk carrier ship to all the third world countries that actually produced aluminum. His wife, Cecilia, was a schoolteacher and small-time artist.

The condition Rakow had forgotten the name of was called congenital heterochromia and involved a genetic mutation that impacted the development of pigments in the irises. Delia's case was particularly striking—childhood photos pasted into the news stories about her disappearance depicted a happy girl with that corn silk blonde hair, her left eye brilliant blue, her right deep brown. It was the kind of thing you couldn't miss, even if you only saw her in passing.

She was absolutely the woman I had seen in the back of that van.

I spent an hour digging through the next articles, but they generally repeated themselves, recounting what I already knew. Delia had been sent to the summer camp for two weeks of fun and adventures, only thirty miles from her childhood home. She had just turned fourteen, and was obsessed with Taylor Swift. She wanted to be a rock star, and she played guitar.

The night of her disappearance, according to the camp manager, was like every other. A communal dinner was followed by two hours of liberty, during which the kids were free to play in the common areas; then the boys and girls were split and escorted to their private dormitories at opposing ends of the camp.

Delia slept on the bottom level of a bunk bed, near a window that faced into the woods. The window was locked —or it was supposed to be, but the next morning it was found open.

None of the other girls remembered a thing. Nobody heard any disturbance or scream, leading investigators to initially conclude that Delia had simply snuck out, maybe to meet a boy, and then become lost in the woods.

After three days of canvasing the county, however, those suspicions began to change. Sheriff Rakow—Luke's father, I presumed—suspected foul play and requested assistance from the FBI. The Alabama Bureau of Investigations intervened, claiming jurisdiction. Then the state police became involved, and in short order a red-tape nightmare ensued, with almost everyone except Rakow convinced that Delia had snuck out and died in the woods.

Rakow and some guy named Eli Keen. A resident of Dothan, no less, living only fifty miles away.

I found Keen's page on my third Google search and quickly identified him as the true crime writer Rakow had mentioned. Well, true crime might be a bit of a stretch, in the strictest sense of the term. Keen verged a little closer to conspiracy theorist, with four books published about governmental cover-ups and political corruption across the southeast.

His book about Delia was entitled: *Through Her Eyes — The Disappearance of Delia Crawford, and the People Who Covered it Up.* It was his only book about traditional crime and had been published by a small press in Birmingham seven years after Delia vanished.

I navigated to an online bookstore and ran a few searches for the title. Most stores didn't carry it, and those that did featured a scant number of reviews. The book was far from a bestseller. But one retailer offered a sample of the first chapter, and it was the opening few lines that captured my attention.

> *A vanishing girl. A statewide search, mired by mistakes and corruption. A mountain of evidence, swept under the rug. And one sheriff whom nobody believed, following trails that may lead right to the heart of a human trafficking conspiracy.*
>
> *This is the story of Delia Crawford.*

I hovered over the page, fixating on that fourth line. The line about human trafficking.

Clicking back to Keen's website, I found his *Meet the Author* page and scanned the bio. Buried beyond a collection of obscure credentials was a single line of personal information tossed in almost as an afterthought.

> *Eli lives with his dogs in his hometown of Dothan, Alabama. For media inquiries or speaking engagements, please visit our CONTACT page.*

I followed the link and input my email address, then hesitated over the box. I decided to keep my message simple, typing only a couple of lines. Then I hit *send.*

Knuckles rattled against the office door. I looked up in time to see Rakow poke his head in.

"Find anything?"

"Not really," I said. "I was working on Delia."

"I'm headed out to Muscogee to see her parents. Ride with me. I wanna talk about that barcode thing."

11

The ride out to Muscogee was mercifully straight and level, rendering Rakow's aggressive driving style a lot more bearable than it had been on the winding back roads around Able. He still kept his foot in the floor, blowing past 45 MPH speed limit signs doing at least seventy, kicked back in his seat and sipping coffee from a thermos.

"Did you learn anything interesting?" he prompted.

Judging by his darting eyes and the way he fidgeted with the worn bottom of his steering wheel, I assumed the question to be a polite one. Maybe an ice breaker. He had the look of a man operating on too little sleep with far too much on his mind. I wondered how often any significant crime took place in Delamar County—let alone a deadly car accident and a potential trafficking victim all in the same twelve-hour stretch.

Not often.

"A little," I said. "I found Keen's website."

Rakow snapped his fingers. "Keen. That's his name."

"Is he crazy?"

Rakow hesitated, then made a noncommittal shrug. "He's eccentric. And obsessive. He used to come up to the sheriff's station three and four times a week when he was working on his book. I remember hearing about it when I came home on leave. I only met him once."

"I guess that was when your father was sheriff," I said quietly.

Rakow stopped mid-sip, cradling the thermos. Then he swallowed and replaced it in the cupholder.

"Willis told you?"

"Yeah."

Rakow shrugged. "He was a good sheriff."

"A good father?"

Rakow stiffened, and I regretted the question. It was both needlessly personal and unrelated.

"Sorry. I was just curious about his work on the case. Keen seems to think he had leads on a human trafficking connection."

Rakow exhaled a semi-irritated sigh. "That was one theory—one among dozens. My father knew the Crawfords personally. He went to high school with Delia's father. Played football with him. So of course he tried everything. But there was no evidence—literally nothing. Dad was throwing spaghetti at the wall. Nothing ever stuck."

"Keen wrote about buried evidence?"

Another irritated grunt. "He'd like to think so, I'm sure. That's the kind of stuff that sells books. I wasn't part of the investigation, obviously, but Dad never mentioned anything like that. Granted...we didn't talk much."

Awkward silence filled the cab, and I decided to steer

away from the subject of Delia. It wasn't why Rakow invited me along, anyway.

"So the thing with the barcode."

"Right." Rakow reached for his thermos again. "What do you know?"

"I only saw it once, in South Phoenix. Found a girl in this guy's trunk. The paramedics found the tattoo—I was otherwise engaged. But I saw the pictures later. Heard about it."

"What does it mean?"

"It's kind of like a cattle brand. Gangs in Eastern Europe tattoo girls as a way of marking them. Claiming property. But it has the added benefit of making them *feel* like property. Brainwashing them, I guess. Apparently, they like to start with kids. Break them early, and groom them into prostitutes. It's a whole trade. Import, export. Just like...gasoline."

"The girl you found in Phoenix. What was her story?"

"I was out of the loop before that was determined. I remember she couldn't speak much English. She was definitely European. Serbian, maybe. Or Hungarian. Something like that. Probably kidnapped young and exported to the United States for use in underground brothels."

"In *Phoenix?*" The disbelief in Rakow's tone was a little telling. I already believed him to be a good cop, but he was a rural one and somewhat sheltered. Maybe a little naive about big-city brutality.

"In any number of big cities. It happens everywhere, but it's worse in large travel hubs that connect to international borders or ports. Southern California, Texas, New York City. Phoenix isn't great either. The guy she was with was...a customer."

Rakow said nothing, but I caught him glancing sideways at me. I knew what he was thinking, and it made me remember the drunk guy in the sedan, again. How he'd had that girl tied up in his trunk like an animal. How he had stepped out of his car and tripped. And then kept tripping.

He was damn near unconscious by the time backup arrived. My lieutenant asked to see my knuckles, but I was smart. I'd worn gloves and promptly lost them. Maybe it made me a bad cop, but it didn't make me a bad guy. A part of me still wished I had buried him in the desert.

"We've already contacted the FBI field office in Montgomery," Rakow said. "They're gonna send down an agent to interview the girl just as soon as we can find a translator. She's gone quiet, so we still don't know what language she speaks."

"She's in shock," I said. "And she's probably terrified of her captors coming around to punish her for talking. The same thing happened with the girl in Phoenix."

"Does the barcode mean anything?" Rakow asked. "Is it... I mean...scannable?"

He flushed a little as he said it. I shook my head.

"I don't think so. I think it's mostly a humiliation thing. But talk to the FBI, I'm sure they know a lot more than me."

Rakow slowed as we rumbled into Muscogee. The town wasn't large, but it absolutely dwarfed Able. Grocery stores were joined by fast-food chains and hotels, with a lot of traffic crowding in around us. We crossed a bridge that skirted what looked to be the lake I had noted on Rakow's office map. Lake Muscogee—named after the town. Or maybe the town was named after the lake.

It was a nice place. Not fancy, and not especially remarkable, but clean and obviously appreciated by the local residents. As we progressed toward the heart of town, the homes grew older. A lot older. Oak trees leaned low over the street, shading the front lawns of antebellum-style homes that might qualify as mansions. Two stories, sprawling, with tall columns painted in clean white, and ornate landscaping surrounding them.

I felt like I was suddenly being transported back to the nineteenth century. If I blocked out the cars and ignored the wide street, I could picture women in ornate dresses relaxing in rocking chairs on the sprawling front porches. Men smoking pipes and reading newspapers. And yes...probably some slaves tending those flower beds.

A different time, but a time that had left its mark.

Rakow slowed the truck and pulled to the side of the street in front of a particularly fantastic two-story antebellum with a circular driveway looping through the front yard. A Range Rover sat in that driveway, and both the vehicle and the house behind it seemed oddly...out of date. Unmanaged in the context of the exquisite homes surrounding them.

The SUV was dusty, and I noted peeling paint on the house's columns. Weeds in the flower beds. Gunk on the white plank siding that begged for a power washer, but clearly no power washer had touched this place in years. The mailbox facing the street leaned a little, with a three-digit street number missing the middle numeral, and faded gold script reading *Crawford*.

Rakow cut the engine, but he didn't get out of the truck. He sat with the keys in his lap, studying the mailbox, but not speaking.

"You didn't bring me along to talk about the tattoo, did you?" I asked.

Rakow faced me but didn't comment. I knew what he was thinking, and I tried to put myself in his shoes. Not just a cop, but a sheriff. A law enforcement officer, yes, but also a caretaker of his community. A public figure. An elected guardian.

And probably a friend of the Crawfords. His father had played football with Mr. Crawford, after all.

"I saw her," I said. "It was Delia."

"You're certain? Because I have to ask them if they've seen her. And that's going to dig up...a lot of emotions."

"I'm sure."

Rakow nodded slowly. "Okay. Can you be professional?"

"I've worn the uniform, Rakow. This isn't my first house call."

"Right."

He dropped out of the truck without another comment, and I straightened my shirt and ran my fingers through my hair. I hadn't showered since leaving my campground in central Georgia, and I suddenly wished I had shaved that morning. I looked rough.

On the sidewalk, I followed Rakow through the open gate of a picket fence and around the Range Rover. It was several years old, with a University of Auburn license plate on the front bumper.

Up the wooden steps to the porch, I quickly tucked my shirt in and allowed Rakow to take the lead. He rapped on the door with official but not overbearing strength, then stepped back and scooped the American flag patch hat off.

Somebody answered almost immediately, but it wasn't one of the Crawfords. This lady was Hispanic and wore yellow rubber gloves. She smiled and beckoned Rakow in as if she expected him. Maybe he had called ahead.

"They're in the sunroom, Sheriff. You can head on back."

Dusty hardwood paved the way through a foyer, with tall

walls lined with vintage wallpaper and antique furniture. There was a coat rack next to the door, and an oil painting of a cotton field in fall, looking like a field of snow. A staircase led upward to a second-floor landing, and cobwebs clung to the high corners of the ceiling.

Despite the presence of the maid, the home felt somehow very still, as though visitors were a rare occurrence. Rakow followed her down a hallway and through a kitchen to a glass door framed in tarnished brass. It was a sunroom, built against the back side of the house, and the moment he opened the door, a wash of June heat collided with my face like a fist.

Who sits out here in June?

Rakow stepped down, hat in hand, and two people rose from couches near the back of the room—a man and a woman, both in their late forties, both dressed in casual summer wear. The man was mostly bald, with a semicircle of gray hair running around his head, and tired brown eyes. The woman's hair was dyed deep black, her eyes the same crystal blue of the girl in the van, her face caked in too much makeup. They both greeted Rakow with handshakes and polite smiles, thanking him for driving out.

Then they turned to me, and they didn't speak.

"Mr. and Mrs. Crawford, this is Mason Sharpe. He's visiting town from Arizona. He responded to the accident."

So Rakow had called ahead, then. The Crawfords knew why we were here. I wouldn't have played it that way, as a homicide detective. I liked to pass along all information in person so that I could view facial reactions. But then again, this was a small community. News traveled fast. And it wasn't a homicide.

"Thank you for coming," Mrs. Crawford said, taking my

hand in both of hers and squeezing. She held on a beat too long, those crystal blue eyes peering into mine as though she were reading my very soul. I saw pain—over a decade of it. The worst sort of heartbreak.

She eventually pulled away, and Mr. Crawford offered me a stiff nod. No handshake. They invited us to sit across from them on wicker chairs, and I felt sweat gluing the shirt to my back as I settled into the seat. It must be nearly a hundred degrees in the sunroom. It was like a sauna.

"We were just having lunch," Mrs. Crawford said, gesturing to a little table laden with sandwiches and a pitcher of iced tea. "Can I get you gentlemen anything?"

Rakow offered a polite smile and shook his head. I simply waited, knowing what was coming. Somehow not very eager to dive in.

It was Mr. Crawford who broke the ice. He sat stiff-backed on the couch across from us, his face taut. The deep lines around his eyes crinkled with years of stress as he addressed me directly.

"You saw my daughter?"

12

Mr. and Mrs. Crawford sat in perfect silence while I recounted the events on the highway, beginning with the crash and leading through my attempted rescue. I didn't glamorize any of my actions, sticking to a summary that focused on the moment I saw Delia. I didn't want them to think I was claiming to be a hero.

The point was Delia. And whether she was still alive.

Thomas Crawford sat perfectly still, his face set in stone-hard lines that reflected not a trace of emotion. His wife, meanwhile, shifted nervously in her seat, fingers fidgeting with the hem of her skirt while she hung on to my every word like a dog fixated on a fresh bone.

I concluded my account with Rakow's arrival on scene, and trailed off, opening myself up for questions.

But they didn't come. Thomas remained stone-faced and silent, and his wife simply closed her eyes and began to sob softly.

Rakow filled the gap, leaning forward with his hat still

cradled in his hands. "Thomas, have you heard anything? Any calls…an email? Has Delia reached out at all?"

Thomas moved for the first time in five minutes, smoothing his pants legs before placing a stiff hand on his wife's shoulders.

"Nothing," he said. "Not a word."

Rakow offered a sympathetic nod, and Mrs. Crawford spoke next.

"I'm so sorry, Mr. Sharpe. I'm…I'm not usually like this…"

She shook, and her words broke off. I didn't know what to say, so I remained quiet. Thomas turned hard eyes on me, a flicker of anger flashing behind them.

"How can you be sure you saw our daughter?"

I hesitated, caught a little off guard. Then I decided to go with the truth.

"I can't. I can only say the woman I saw matched your daughter's photo."

"It's been *ten years*," Thomas said. "No word from anyone. A completely cold case. We've had to make peace with that. Now you come in here and want to tell me she's alive…and you *let her go?*"

Rakow raised a hand. "I know you're upset, Thomas."

"*Mr. Crawford*," Thomas snapped.

Rakow stopped, hand still raised. One eyebrow lifted in just the hint of an "are you serious?" expression. But he kept his cool.

"Mr. Crawford, I know you're upset. But you can't take that out on Mr. Sharpe. He did everything possible to save your daughter."

"Like your father did?" Thomas spat.

"Thomas!" Mrs. Crawford placed a hand on her husband's arm. He yanked it away, ignoring her.

Rakow remained unfazed. "My father failed you. You're right. But Delia is not forgotten, and you have my word that my department will invest all available resources to follow this lead. I just wanted to keep you updated. You deserve that much."

Thomas didn't blink, but his wife nodded, eyes watering.

"Thank you," she whispered.

"I think you should leave now," Thomas said. "Call us when you actually have something."

Rakow stood slowly. I followed suit as he thanked them for their time, then stepped back into the house. A wash of welcome cool rolled over my face, and I noticed the maid standing halfway down the wooden staircase, her arms loaded with a meal tray full of dirty dishes. Pain drenched her face.

She looked struck by lightning, like the family she worked for. I could feel that pain in the very bones of the old house and welcomed the rush of Rakow's air-conditioning as he started the big truck.

"That was tough," I said.

Rakow adjusted his hat and slid his sunglasses on. Then simply shook his head.

"Grief hits everyone differently. Losing Delia broke her mother. Her father went hard...and very cold."

I watched the house fade as Rakow drove away, and thought I knew what he meant. The impossibility of longing to bring somebody back from the dead was so absolute, it could drive you mad. Leave you lost beyond all understanding. Broken, maybe. Or very hard.

Rakow pulled the Ford into a gas station, stopping alongside a diesel pump and leaving the motor running.

"Gotta fill up," he said. "Mind grabbing me a Coke? I think I need the caffeine."

He reached for his wallet, but I waved him off. "I got it."

I found his Coke in a stand-up cooler and grabbed a second for myself. On my way to the cash register, I recalled the pile of empty peanut sleeves riding in his console and grabbed us each a fresh pack.

Stepping back into the sweltering June heat, I cracked the Coke open and drained half of it before stopping for air. The rush of sugar felt good, assuaging some of the exhaustion I was battling from the night before. Lowering the bottle, my gaze fell across the street to the drugstore parking lot beyond, and I stopped.

The jet-black Raptor sat in the parking lot, facing me. Its bullish grille stood a yard off the ground, headlights tinted to almost black, the windshield reflecting noontime sunrays. Even through the glare, I could make out the figures seated inside. One very tall and skinny, one very bulky and thick. Bright blond hair, cold faces.

Both staring right at me.

I stood on the sidewalk, cradling the Cokes, and stared back. At fifty yards, it was difficult to make out facial expressions, but I knew they weren't inviting. There was some manner of hostility there. Something sinister.

"Hey! You coming?" Rakow shouted from the running board of his truck. I piled into the passenger seat and passed him the Coke and peanuts, still watching the Raptor. It was backing out of the parking space now. Turning for the exit.

"You know those kids?" I asked, gesturing.

Rakow swigged from the Coke, squinting through his windshield. He tore the peanut pack open with his teeth and immediately upended it into the Coke bottle, depositing the full sleeve inside.

"The Raptor?" he asked.

"Right."

"That's the Krol boys. Steve and Allen...or maybe Steve and Alick. Something like that. Why?"

I watched the Raptor roll into the street, turning past us and racing by with a howl of its big engine. Both boys caught my gaze as they flashed by.

Another cold stare.

"I caught them photographing my license plate this morning," I said. "They don't seem friendly."

Rakow shrugged, shifting into gear. "They're Polish. Or their family is, anyway. Kind of a weird lot, if you ask me. But I'm Southern, and they're not, so take that with a grain of salt."

"What are they doing here?"

"Bauxite." He turned onto the highway and leaned back in his seat, still crunching peanuts.

"I thought you said the industry was dead?"

"I said it was mostly dead. Just a few mines left. The Krol company bought them all up a couple of years ago. I think they do okay, all things considered."

"Why would they be photographing my license plate?"

Rakow hesitated, picking peanut from one of his back teeth. Then he shrugged. "Probably just want to know who the new guy is. Maybe you haven't noticed, but this is a close-knit community. People are suspicious of outsiders. Anyway, it isn't a crime to take a picture. It's a classic truck."

Fair enough.

We rumbled back toward Able, Rakow working his radio amid a mouthful of peanuts. I'd seen people eat Coke and peanuts before and never understood it. Sweet and salty was never my thing, but Rakow was clearly obsessed. While he communicated with his deputies about the crash scene and the missing girl, I watched the fields and pines roll by, and thought about the haunted look in Mrs. Crawford's eyes.

I'd seen it before, not long ago. Another woman in another town, her husband murdered by some thug protecting his criminal conspiracy. That look connected with me then because I saw it in the mirror.

I still saw it in the mirror, but I wasn't sure if I could play the hero this time. As badly as I wanted to find Delia for her parents, I really had no idea where to start, and there was nothing I could do about the girl with the barcode tattoo.

Rakow was a good cop. A better man, perhaps. The situation would be safe in his hands.

The Ford rumbled to a stop at the sheriff's station, and I broke the silence before Rakow reached for the door.

"I think I'm going to hit the road. Head on south to Florida. I'm not sure I can help you."

Rakow stopped, swirling the last drops of his Coke in the bottle. Then he nodded slowly.

"I appreciate you lending a hand."

"It's no problem. I wish I could do more."

He drained the bottle, and we both dropped into the growing heat. It was high noon, and Alabama felt like an absolute oven, my lungs heavy with dense, humid air. I wondered if Florida would be worse, and whether I should turn back north before I found out.

"You want a ride back to your truck?" Rakow asked.

"It's only a mile," I said. "I don't mind walking."

"I imagine your gear is still wet."

"Probably. I've got to spread it out someplace and let it dry."

"Why don't you bring it back here? You can spread it out in the parking lot where nobody will bother it. Let me finish up work, and we'll get a beer. I think I owe you one."

I hesitated, thinking about my truck and a bright afternoon spent behind the wheel. I could make Florida before sunset.

But the beer sounded good, and if my gear was still wet when I arrived, I'd need to find a hotel anyway. Another night wouldn't kill me.

"Sounds good," I said. "See you at five."

13

After retrieving my truck, I went to work rescuing my gear from the flooded plastic bins. My stove, cooking implements, hammock, and bedding were completely saturated, swimming in pools of rainwater and dust, but spread out in the sheriff's station parking lot, they dried quickly enough.

I spent the time kicked back under the shade of a pecan tree planted next to the station, diving into Hemingway's "Hills Like White Elephants", before indulging in an afternoon nap right there on the ground. The sweltering heat was suffocating at first, but after a while it became bearable with a light breeze and a little shade. It still wasn't as hot as Phoenix.

At seven thirty, the sun was starting to set, and Rakow finally appeared from the station. He looked harried and irritable, his collar unbuttoned and his shirt sweaty. My gear was repacked into my truck bed, and I sat on the tailgate, eating dried fruit from a plastic bag as he approached. I'd bought the fruit at a camping store outside Atlanta, and it wasn't very good, but at least it didn't spoil.

It was better than an MRE, anyway.

"Now I think I owe you the beer," I said. "Hell of a napping spot you've got there."

Rakow snorted. "Word to the wise. Don't ever run for sheriff. It's a thankless job."

I hopped to the ground and shut the tailgate. "I presume there's a watering hole around here?"

"Best spot in Delamar. Jukebox, greasy food, and ice-cold beer."

"Sold. I'm following you."

RAKOW LED me through Able before turning south, bumping along a pothole-infested county road that led deep into the sticks, two or three miles from downtown. The bar was a block building, painted brown, with a slouching front porch and a neon sign that read Bailey's.

A dozen pickups sat parked out front in the dusty lot. Even before I clambered out of the GMC, I heard the thumping beat and syrupy drawl of country music drifting through the open door amid a cloud of cigarette smoke. Rakow parked his Ford and dropped out, his duty belt and uniform shirt left behind, leaving only a simple white T-shirt with a backup-sized Glock barely concealed beneath it.

A good cop. And a wary soldier.

I followed him inside, ducking into the smoky haze of a classic bar scene. Tables lay scattered across a polished wooden floor, half of them occupied by dusty country folks in boots and jeans. A jukebox sat in the corner, blaring redneck country tunes, and beyond the tables a polished bar ran the entire length of the building, overhung by dim lights.

Three bartenders worked behind it—an older woman with red hair, a bald guy with a toothless smile, and one blonde in a black tank top, her smile bright enough to shame the morning sun as she polished a glass.

She was beautiful. No, she was gorgeous, but in a very casual way. The poster girl for all those songs about country girls. Tough, but not rough. Slender, but not skinny. All the right curves in all the right places.

Rakow caught me looking and cleared his throat. "*Off. Limits.*"

"Don't worry," I said. "I'm not in the market."

He sauntered directly for the blonde, taking a stool and shooting her a smile that said he wasn't in the market either. I could tell by the way her face lit up when she saw him that neither was she, but maybe neither of them were admitting it.

I selected a stool in the sheltered corner farthest from the blare of the jukebox, turning my back against the wall and resting one arm over the bar. The toothless guy approached, wiping his hands on a towel and regarding me with the semi-suspicion of a man who knew every face in the county and didn't recognize mine.

"Don't believe I've seen you before, sonny." He spoke with a slight lisp and a heavy accent, but there was no hostility in his voice. I lifted my chin in acknowledgment.

"I'm Mason."

"A pleasure, Mason. I'm Charlie, but folks call me Bob. What'll it be?"

I scanned the row of liquor bottles and tap handles lining the wall behind him. The selection was meager, focusing predominantly on whiskey and American lagers with *lite* tacked onto their names. After a long day of baking Alabama heat, I thought I understood why. I wasn't in the mood for anything heavy.

"I'll have the Miller," I said. "Cold as it comes."

"You bet. And food?"

I shrugged. "Surprise me."

Bob slid me beer in a glass, and I relaxed against the wall to watch the crowd. It wasn't yet eight p.m., but most of the occupants already had a good buzz going. Two women and a guy in a dirty trucker's hat danced near the jukebox, feeding it quarters and keeping Alan Jackson drawling through the speakers. Most of the others crowded around little tables, digging into bar food and swapping jokes, their torn jeans stained with dirt and their hair still glistening with sweat.

It was a working-class bar—maybe the only kind of bar this county possessed, and I liked it. It was very unpretentious. Very accepting. A community gathered at the end of a long week, ready to get a little sloshed before embracing the weekend. The stuff all those redneck country songs sang about, albeit with a lot less glamour.

I tipped the glass back and enjoyed the crisp burn of the Miller, already halfway to the bottom as the blonde slid up next to me and rested both forearms on the counter.

"So you're the new guy."

I lowered the glass, looking quickly down the bar for Rakow. He was gone—maybe to the restroom. The blonde grinned at me, slouching against the bar.

"I guess," I said, offering my hand. "Mason."

"Bailey. A pleasure!"

"Your place?" I asked.

Bailey laughed, jabbing a rounded chin toward the bar crowd. "Their place. I just put my name on the sign."

"Fair enough."

"Get you another?"

I slid her the glass, and she topped it off. I felt a dull buzz in the back of my skull from the flood of beer on an empty stomach, and the sensation felt good. It made me want to relax a little.

"Where you from, Mason?"

"Didn't Rakow tell you?"

She squinted. "Why would he have told me?"

Right. Because you're not together.

"I'm from Phoenix," I said. "Just passing through."

"I've been there! Hot as hell, man. Too hot for me."

I couldn't tell if she was joking, and decided not to investigate, rocking back the Miller instead. Rakow appeared out of the bathroom, returning to his stool, and Bailey shot me a wink. "Dinner'll be right up!"

She glided back down the bar as though she had someplace to be, but stopped halfway. Right in front of Rakow.

I indulged in a quiet smile, watching the swordplay of a fledgling relationship. Or maybe a very old one that, for whatever reason, had yet to blossom. The attraction was obvious. The familiarity mature. Old classmates, I thought. Maybe childhood friends. Exclusively nonexclusive, together but very far apart. Enjoying each other's company, but just not making the jump.

I'd seen it before, and I'd never understood it. The night I met Mia was like a hurricane, ripping right through my life and shoving aside everything I ever thought was important. Leaving only her.

I told her I was going to marry her at the end of our first

date. She laughed. She said I was crazy. But she showed up for the second. Fell asleep in my arms in the back of my truck on the third.

And she said yes by the end of the summer.

The memory brought a hot lump to my throat, and I turned away from Bailey and Rakow to find Bob waiting with a hamburger on a steel plate.

"Chef's special! Bomb appuhteet."

I offered him a smile and a nod, not bothering to correct his butchery of the French expression. The burger was expertly grilled, but it tasted a little stale in my mouth. I'd lost most of my appetite. I finished my second beer, and Bob brought me a third, giving me my space as I hunched over the plate and turned my mind off for a while. I was nearing the bottom of my fourth beer when a brunette slid onto the stool next to me, offering a cheery hello and a gentle jab to my ribs with her elbow.

"Well, howdy, stranger. Look what the dawg drug in!"

I looked up, more than a little buzzed now and temporarily disoriented. The woman was closer to a girl, early twenties probably, but I could see in her eyes that those two-point-something decades had been hard ones. She was slender, not unattractive, and dressed provocatively enough to earn her a street corner in South Phoenix. Deep, plunging neckline, and cutoff shorts that barely satisfied their most basic function.

"I'm Sadie!" she said, offering a hand. "What's your name?"

I accepted her hand dumbly, muttering my name and hoping my tone would communicate my desire to be left alone. It didn't. Sadie leaned against the bar, allowing that neckline to drop another inch under the weight of her assets as she grinned up at me like I was a rock star. I shifted uncomfortably on the stool, fixating on my burger.

"Where you from, Mason?"

I didn't answer, taking a bite and chewing slowly. Hoping I might bore her to death. Sadie persisted.

"Phoenix, right?"

I shot her a sideways glance. The grin remained, but it didn't meet her eyes. They were brown and tired, clouded with concealed thoughts. Or maybe she was simply inebriated.

Not like I could judge.

"Look, Sadie." I spoke softly, setting the burger down. "I'm really not—"

"What's that?" She leaned closer. "Damn, it's loud in here, ain't it? Wanna go someplace quiet and talk?"

Somebody had cranked up the jukebox, blaring the Zac Brown Band now. "Homegrown". One of Mia's favorites. The song snatched me back to that late night in the desert and sent a shard of glass punching through my chest.

"I'm not interested!" I called over the music. "Thanks anyway."

Sadie's grin faded, and she cast a glance over her shoulder. Then she leaned close, pressing her warm mouth near my ear.

"Look, buddy. I need to talk to you."

I shook my head, leaning away until my shoulder bumped into the wall. "I'm good, thank you."

Another glance over her shoulder. She leaned in again. "It ain't like that, dammit. It's about Delia. I know where she is."

14

Sadie's face turned earnestly serious, and the racket of the bar faded around me. I looked for Rakow and found him sitting at a corner table, enjoying a beer alongside Bailey. Oblivious to anything happening around him.

"Outside," Sadie mouthed. She took her purse and disappeared through the front doors.

I hesitated a moment longer, my mind moving a little slower than usual under the burden of the Miller. Then I dug out my wallet and dropped a twenty on the counter, nodding to Bob. Before the toothless barkeep could initiate a farewell interaction, I found my way to the gravel parking lot.

It was dusk, building rapidly into full dark, the bar illuminated only by a bright streetlamp mounted to a power pole. The cluster of pickups had doubled since my arrival, but it wasn't difficult to spot Sadie. She stood next to my truck, beckoning me over.

I hesitated, a soft voice deep in my mind raising a muted

alarm that I couldn't quite discern amid the beer fog. I wasn't drunk. I wasn't sober, either. I thought of the woman I'd seen huddling in the back of that overturned van alongside the highway. The panic in her face. The moment our gazes met, when I first noted those wild, different-colored eyes.

And then I thought of the agony in her parents' eyes. The way Mr. Crawford looked hard as granite, his wife as broken as shattered glass. And I walked to meet Sadie next to the truck.

"You know where Delia is?" I asked.

"Not here." Sadie shook her head, looking back to the bar. "They'll hear us."

"Who?" I looked back to Bailey's and saw no one.

"Come on," Sadie said. "You drive. I don't have a car."

She walked quickly around my truck and found her way to the passenger seat, helping herself to the unlocked door. I hesitated a moment longer, then piled in, digging my keys out. The truck rumbled to life, and I jiggled the shifter into reverse.

"Where?" I asked.

"Maybe a mile? Not far."

I followed her directions and made a left on the country road, my dim headlights spilling a yellow glow over the inky blackness. The lines looked a little blurry, and I blinked, second-guessing my decision to drive. How many drinks had I consumed? Just four, right?

I should be fine.

"Delia is here?" I questioned.

"Just down the road," Sadie said. "I'll explain everything."

She looked through the little glass window built into the back of the GMC's cab, then slid a little closer across the bench seat. I felt the outside of her thigh brush the outside of mine, and I stiffened just a little.

"Right up here." Sadie pointed through the dusty windshield to a dirt drive connecting with the county road, sheltered on either side by towering pines and covered in loose gravel.

"There," she said. "Just behind the trees."

I rolled to a gentle stop, back shifting into first and stopping a moment to peer down the drive. I could see almost nothing in the thick darkness. The drive led between the trees, and I thought it opened into a field not far beyond, but I didn't see any lights. No houses or vehicles.

"What is this?" I asked.

"It's just back there," Sadie urged. "Look, make up your mind, would ya? I can't stick around."

I glanced down at the girl. Noted those dark eyes darting toward the trees, one hand fidgeting with the hem of her shorts.

And then I understood. It was a setup, plain and simple. I should have guessed that from the start, and I might have, were I not four bottles in. Somebody was stringing me along. Somebody wanted me out in these sticks, where it was dark. Where the police wouldn't hear anything.

And that pissed me off. Badly. Because I'd done nothing to deserve the hostility, and I really hate bullies. I dropped my foot off the clutch and bumped down the gravel drive between the trees. My headlights illuminated a wide, grassy field beyond, leading down a rolling hill to another tree line. There was a deer stand built about twenty yards ahead, overlooking that green patch from thirty feet up.

But no buildings. No vehicles. Nothing.

"Right here," Sadie said, patting my dash.

I stopped the truck, leaving it in gear, still surveying the dark.

"I know what you're doing," I said flatly.

"Huh?" Sadie feigned innocence. I felt her hand on my thigh, starting just north of my knee, then sliding upward. I placed a cold hand on her wrist, clamping down and forcing her arm back. Surprise and anger flashed across her face, and then she screamed. Loud and shrill, so sudden I thought she might shatter my windows.

"Get off me, you perv!"

I released her, looking back through the windshield. Already knowing what I would see.

And then I did see it. Four guys stepping out of the woods like wraiths in the moonlight. Two I recognized almost immediately—the Krol boys. One tall and skinny, the other stocky and muscular. Their companions were unfamiliar to me. Thick, rough-looking country guys with dirty beards and muddy jeans. The four of them marched straight for the truck, and I cut the engine off, hot anger flooding my chest.

All right, you jerks. You wanna dance? Let's dance.

Sadie scrambled to the far end of the bench seat, curling into a ball, her voice dropping to a whimper now. "I'm sorry, man. They made me."

I ignored her, moving quickly out of the truck before I could be pinned in. The beer fog evaporated like mist in the morning, leaving only the rage. Not just at Sadie and the persistent nuisance of the Krol boys. At myself for being so gullible.

I know where Delia is.

Yeah, right. Well, it was my mistake, but I wouldn't be the

one to pay for it. Four unarmed bumpkins were almost an insult. They should have sent a battalion.

"You tryin' to rape her?" one of the country guys barked.

"I never touched her," I snapped. It wasn't strictly true, but it was true in any sexual capacity.

"That's my sister," the second country guy said. "Imma take this one outta your ass!"

I squinted. "What?"

He stopped mid-stride. Momentarily confused.

"Take what out of my ass?" I demanded. "Do you even hear the words you're saying?"

The two country boys exchanged a glance, contemplating a rebuttal. I hit the first one right in his exposed jaw, my right hook driving well beyond his face and sending him toppling backwards in a splash of blood. The second guy hurtled toward me and caught an elbow to the face before my right knee found his crotch. I kept driving, clobbering him over the left ear as he staggered back, hard enough to send his head snapping toward his shoulder.

He went down, and I whirled toward the Krol kids, ready to take either of them with my raw fists.

The first country bumpkin was back on his feet, fighting to claw a long hunting knife from his belt while the Krol kids stood back and egged him on—urging him to cut me.

The knife barely cleared the sheath before I struck it from his hand with a chop to his wrist, followed by a left jab to his nose hard and quick enough to shatter bone. His eyes rolled back, and he stumbled. I backhanded him across the face and slammed my knee into his gut.

He fell like a tree, and I turned for the Krols.

"You want some?" I demanded. "Come on. Show me what you got!"

Both kids took one long step back, into the shadows beneath the tree line. The tall and skinny one shot me a piercing stare, followed by a sadistic grin.

A split second later, I knew why. Powerful headlights broke through the gap in the trees, followed by the chirp of a siren. When I looked over my shoulder, I recognized Owen's Tahoe rolling into the clearing, its spotlight illuminating both myself and my truck.

I looked back toward the trees, but the Krol kids were gone, abandoning their wrecked buddies in the mud. The growl of their Ford Raptor rumbled through the forest from someplace beyond the pines, then the Tahoe's door groaned open, and Owen barked over the clearing.

"On your knees, Sharpe! Hands up."

15

I overnighted at the Delamar County jail, sitting alone in a holding cell equipped with multiple benches and a toilet, but no bed.

I didn't argue with Owen or bother to resist arrest when he handcuffed me and dragged me to the back of his Tahoe. The two country bumpkins I had pounded still lay moaning amid the pine needles, bleeding a lot and cursing me as I passed. Sadie huddled next to my truck, mumbling to Owen's partner and casting me apologetic glances as I was marched away.

I didn't blame her. She might be a stupid girl, but I was a lot stupider for falling into her trap. Owen's sudden arrival right in the middle of our confrontation could only mean one thing—the Krol kids had called in the crime long before it was even committed. They *wanted* me arrested, which was why they had fled instead of helping their idiot friends. I should have seen that coming. I should never have left the bar in the first place.

I should have known better, but all that was spilt milk now. More than anything, I just wished I had caught those two rats before they fled.

In the holding cell I caught a couple of hours' sleep, jammed on a bench and leaned against the wall, but the room was hot and the bench hard. The beer had worn off, and my knuckles burned like hell—something they don't show in the movies. The swelling would only worsen, turning gradually into bruising. Maybe I deserved that also.

Rakow himself appeared at a little after six a.m., according to the clock on the wall outside the holding cell. Owen had taken my watch, belt, pocketknife, phone, wallet, and even my shoelaces. I don't think he actually expected me to attempt a suicide, but Delamar County's chief deputy was *pissed*, that much was clear. He felt betrayed, probably. Trusting a stranger. Welcoming him into the community. And then turning up to find him wrecking a couple of local boys.

I didn't even bother to tell my half of the story. What was the point? Nobody would believe me.

Rakow stood outside the holding cell, fully dressed in his usual uniform, with a thermos of coffee in one hand. His eyes were cold as he regarded me in the back of the cell, not speaking for almost a minute. Then he tilted his head, and Willis appeared from around the corner, poking a key into the lock and twisting it. I got up and walked out with my hands in my pockets, stopping by Willis's desk to collect my personal effects before Rakow directed me outside, following just behind.

The Ford sat in the blazing morning sun, rumbling with a low diesel growl. I got into the passenger seat without comment as Rakow swung in behind the wheel. He slid his glasses on, still not speaking, and piloted us onto the highway. We turned toward downtown and then south toward the bar.

And my truck.

"I guess nobody's pressing charges," I said.

"Lucky you," Rakow growled. His voice was heavy with restrained anger. I couldn't blame him.

"It wasn't what it looked like," I said simply.

Rakow snorted. "I'm sure it wasn't. I've picked up Sadie Vincent half a dozen times for turning tricks in Muscogee. And those two mud brains you pounded are far from outstanding citizens. Records as long as my arm."

"So why are you about to kick me out?" I questioned.

Rakow gritted his teeth. "Because you screwed up, Sharpe. You should have known better. I mean, come on. Some skank walks up on you in a bar, and next thing you know, you're sending two guys to the hospital? What's wrong with you?"

"It wasn't like that," I repeated. "It was a setup. The Krol kids were there. I think they orchestrated the whole thing."

"Who?"

"The Krol boys. The two in the Raptor."

"Owen said there were only four of you."

"They left as he was rolling up. Check your dispatcher's call logs. They would have called the emergency line before I even left the bar."

"You can't prove what time you left the bar."

"I guess that's true. Seems my witness was lost in Bailey land."

Rakow stiffened. I didn't care. I was being given the shaft, and he knew it.

"I trusted you, Sharpe. I gave you the benefit of the doubt

and then some. I welcomed you into my home. I welcomed you into my county. And now I have to explain this mess to my voters."

The Ford ground to a stop at the gravel drive, and Rakow shoved the shifter into park. He didn't cut the engine, and he didn't unbuckle.

"You need to think about why somebody would want me out of this county," I said. "A long-lost woman turns up, then vanishes. A human trafficking victim appears out of nowhere. And now I'm being set up. Sound kosher to you?"

"Delia is still missing. You're the only one who saw her."

"Are you saying I made it up?"

"I'm *saying* she's still missing. Why would she run from you? Why would she hide?"

"I don't know. Sometimes police work is simple, and sometimes it's not. But there's always a reason."

Rakow shook his head, resting one arm over the steering wheel and looking away. The silence between us felt heavy, and I wondered if part of him believed me.

Part of him wasn't enough.

"I'll take it from here, Sharpe. Get back on the road. And don't come back."

I dropped out of the truck without further protest, watching as he made a slow, multipoint turn in the middle of the road. Then the oversized Ford howled by, and we made eye contact.

Rakow didn't wave.

Fifty yards up the dirt drive at the edge of the clearing, my GMC rested right where I'd left it, keys hanging from the ignition. All of the camping gear rested in the bed, unmolested by the Krol boys or any of their associates. That didn't surprise me. They didn't want to give me a reason to stick around and perpetuate our vendetta.

They wanted me gone. As quickly as possible.

But why?

I pocketed the keys and walked to ground zero of the one-sided beatdown from the night before. It wasn't hard to find the spot. Tangled and broken grass was stained in places by dry blood, the dirt torn and kicked up where boot heels had ground into it.

Tough guys. Or so they thought. Given the opportunity to find their footing and strike on their own terms, they might have got in a hit or two. But I don't believe in giving my enemy a chance to find his footing. I believe in violence of action—hit them with everything, all at once, right when they least expect it. Waste them.

The thought brought a weak smile to my lips, and I turned back toward my truck. As I did, something caught my eye in the grass beyond the fight ring. Something small and bright red—not a natural color amid the flowerless green and brown grass. It lay approximately where the Krol boys had stood, shaking their fists and urging their incompetent soldiers forward.

Leading from the rear. Like absolute cowards.

I stepped to the spot and reached into the grass. My fingers touched hard plastic, and I rolled the item over in my hand.

It was a memory stick—what I had always called a flash drive. A small storage device used to move files from one computer to the other. It was marked on the back side with a narrow white label. But not in English. The language was some manner of Slavic, I thought. Eastern European.

Like the Krols. Like the girl in the barn.

I looked into the trees in the direction of the Raptor, half expecting the Krol boys to be watching from the shadows, making sure I left town as instructed.

I saw only trees grown densely together, with another green field barely visible a hundred yards away.

Climbing back into the truck, I pocketed the flash drive and powered on my phone. It awoke slowly, requiring a moment to connect with whatever cell tower lay nearest to this place. I had barely any signal, but I didn't need much. I just needed my GPS. I had no clue how to find the highway on my own.

The map loaded slowly, a little broken circle spinning on the gray screen. As I waited, a banner appeared across the top of the screen, signaling the arrival of a new email.

It was from Eli Keen, the crime writer down in Dothan. I opened it and scanned the short paragraph of text. The message was brief, but enthusiastic. Keen was agreeable to meet—and soon. He wanted to discuss the case and ask about Delia's reappearance.

He believed me. He could make himself available at my convenience. He was thirsty for more of the story.

I looked over the dash of my GMC toward the trees and hesitated. But not for long. Thoughts of Florida and beach-side concerts were now long buried behind images of those sneering Krol kids setting me up. The panicked fear in the butterfly girl's eyes—a mirror of the terror I'd seen in Delia's face.

I wasn't leaving. Not even close. Rakow could kick me out of the sheriff's station, but he couldn't kick me out of the county. Not unless he was prepared to do so at gunpoint.

And I'd be damned before I let two kids in an oversized truck purchased with daddy's money push me out.

I replied to Keen's email, asking for a time and place. Then I hit *go* on the navigation app and routed south, for Dothan.

It was time to rattle some cages.

16

The drive to Dothan took about an hour and consisted mostly of rolling hills along Highway 431. I stopped for gas once and found an email waiting from Keen, every bit as enthusiastic as the first. He offered to meet me at a coffee shop downtown as soon as I was ready. I emailed back and said I was on my way, then rolled into town.

By national standards, Dothan wasn't a large city. But compared to Able or Muscogee, it felt like an absolute metropolis. Thick traffic gathered around me as I cruised straight into the heart of the city, passing banks and retail stores, mechanic shops and car dealers. The baking sun beat down on the vibrating green hood of the GMC, and I thought about the camping gear piled in the bed.

If I was going to keep visiting cities, I would need a way to secure my gear from theft, and ideally from the rain. I hadn't wanted to use a bed cover because I enjoyed inflating my mattress and sleeping under the stars. Maybe I should hunt for a little camper.

No sooner had the thought occurred to me than I stopped myself, a little surprised by the idea. Subconsciously or otherwise, I had always framed my wandering travels as a temporary thing. A strategy to work out my grief and find myself...whatever the hell *that* meant.

But the longer I spent camping beneath the stars and rolling in and out of towns at my leisure, the better I liked it. It felt deeply liberating and very natural. Maybe a little camper would add a further touch of home.

Not like I could afford one. I had been spending my wad of cash from Atlanta without regard for its finiteness. I didn't even know how much I had left, but it wasn't a question I was all that concerned about. For the moment, I just wanted to meet Keen. I wanted to know why Delia's possible reappearance could threaten somebody enough to have them sacrifice two mud-brained associates to run me out of town.

The coffee shop sat on a quiet downtown street, one block removed from the main drag, shaded by small trees planted along the sidewalk. All the buildings looked old—former factories or warehouses, I guessed, now converted to small restaurants and bars. It was all very quaint and tasteful. A good place to enjoy on a summer afternoon.

The coffee shop itself was built into a three-story building at the end of the block. All brick, with wide windows and a very tall black sign bolted into the brick and proudly displaying gold letters.

Mural City Coffee Co.

It was a good name. A nice-looking place.

I parked the truck on the street and stretched in the heat, looking for Keen. He'd said he would meet me on the sidewalk, but I didn't see him. Running a hand through my hair, I made a mental note that I was yet again due for a haircut, and found my way to a wide bench built in front of the coffee shop.

Keen arrived five minutes later, rolling up in a maroon Chevy Silverado with a small white sticker pasted onto the back glass. The sticker depicted a sausage dog, with the words "*I've got friends in low places*" written beneath it.

Cute.

The Silverado slid into a parking spot across from my GMC, and Keen spilled out. He was a lot younger than I expected—mid-twenties, maybe. Tall and heavyset, dressed in shorts and a collared shirt with rimless eyeglasses that seemed to blend into his face. As he stumbled out of the truck, a notebook and a cluster of pens spilled across the street, and he scrambled to collect them, waving toward me with a quick smile.

What the hell...?

The Silverado's door slammed, and Keen jogged across the street, narrowly avoiding a collision with a rushing sedan. He raised a hand in apology to the blast of an angry horn. By the time he reached my bench, I was questioning all rationale that drove me to arrange the meeting, but he took my hand with a confident grip and a nervous smile.

"Mason?"

"Yeah...I guess you're Keen."

"That's right. Thanks for meeting with me! You ever come here before?"

"No. First time."

"Great soda. One of my favorite places to write."

I double-checked the sign to confirm I was standing at a coffee shop, then followed him inside to the smell of fresh-ground coffee beans and a row of percolating brewing devices. The room was open and expansive, built with exposed brick walls and raw wooden floors. Mismatched seating was arranged along one side, with a brewing station encased in countertops sitting right in the middle. A dozen or so patrons sipped coffee and worked behind laptops while baristas hustled to fill new orders.

The place smelled amazing.

"What are you having?" Keen asked. "I'm buying."

I shrugged and ordered a large black coffee—no special flavors or garnishments. Keen ordered a strawberry Italian soda—whatever that was.

The drinks were served in short order, and Keen beckoned me to the back of the shop where a small table was surrounded by metal chairs. He spilled his notebook and pens next to the soda and almost knocked them across the floor as he found his seat.

The guy reminded me of a golden retriever. All enthusiasm. Zero coordination.

"I couldn't believe it when I saw your email," he said. "Thanks for agreeing to meet with me."

I settled into my chair, a little confused. I thought I was the one to request the meeting, not Keen. It didn't matter.

He clicked a pen open and flashed that nervous smile again. "So. What can you tell me?"

I squinted. "I'm sorry?"

"You saw Delia?"

Oh.

The reality of the situation I had just stepped into hit me like a brick in the face, and I couldn't help feeling a little stupid.

Of course.

This guy made his living writing stories. Based exclusively on his webpage and book reviews, he was a mid-grade author at best, probably not flush with retirement cash or enjoying a big house. But he was enthusiastic, and he was hungry. He wanted more material. He wanted more of Delia.

No wonder he had been so eager to meet with me. No wonder he'd bought my coffee.

"I think there's been a misunderstanding," I said. "I wasn't trying to be interviewed. I wanted to interview you."

Keen squinted. "But...you said you saw her."

"I did."

He stared at me like I was the slowest kid in math class, tilting his head and waiting for me to perform basic arithmetic. I said nothing, and he laughed awkwardly.

"Obviously I want to know about that!"

I shrugged. "It's a part of an ongoing police investigation. I can't comment."

Another incredulous laugh. "Are you kidding?"

"No..."

"So you're a cop?"

"No."

"A private investigator?"

"No."

"What are you, then?"

I hesitated. "Just a guy."

"A guy who saw Delia."

"Right."

"Why on earth would you want to sit on that?"

"Why would you want to know about it?"

"Are you serious?" He clicked his pen closed, disbelief flooding his face. "Dude, I've spent the last five years up to my neck in this case. It's the single greatest thing I've ever published—the great unsolved mystery of Delamar County. Don't you think I want to talk to the only man who's seen Delia in over eleven years?"

He stared wide-eyed at me, that awkward golden retriever smile plastered across his face. A dog fixated on a treat. Completely enraptured by it. Salivating over it.

I realized I should have seen this coming and kicked myself for walking in with eyes half open. I'd foolishly expected Keen would willingly discuss his book simply for the sake of it. Didn't all writers want to talk about their books?

But no. He was still drunk on this crime. He wanted another fix—the next scoop.

He wanted the *story*. And I wasn't sure I could give it to him. It felt wrong, somehow, to sensationalize the pain I'd seen in the Crawford couple's eyes. The pain I had so recently experienced myself. For Keen, it might be a book deal, but for a lot of people, it was real heartache.

I rose, cradling my coffee. "I'm sorry—it was a mistake to email you. Good luck with your writing."

I turned for the door. Keen was on his feet before I stepped away from the table, one hand on my arm.

"Wait!"

I stopped, shooting him a glare. His hand fell away, and he held up both palms.

"Look, I get it. You don't want the story sensationalized. Delia is a human. She deserves respect. That's how I write, okay? That's my whole ethos."

I said nothing. He adjusted those rimless glasses, looking serious for the first time since we met.

"What if we made a deal? You tell me what you saw. I tell

you whatever you want to know about the case. It can be off the record if you want."

I hesitated. Looked out at my truck and wondered what my next play would be if I walked out on Keen.

Then I returned to my chair.

"Okay, then. Off the record. Here's what happened."

17

I began at the car wreck, detailing the events that led the sedan to hurtle across the median and collide with the van. I described my efforts to gain access to the vehicle, skirting the more dramatic bits and focusing on the woman I saw in the back of the van.

How our gazes locked as the fire grew hot on my back. How she vanished before I got the door open.

Keen listened in raptured silence, fiddling with a pen in one hand but not taking notes. Respecting my request to keep this off the record. When I finished, he asked a few questions—who I was, what action the Delamar County Sheriff's Department was taking, why I wanted to know more about the case.

I told the truth, but selectively. I was an ex-cop from Phoenix, just passing through. The sheriff's department was investigating, but of course I wasn't privy to that investigation. My interest was entirely my own. I didn't mention the girl in the barn, the barcode tattoo, my encounters with the

Krol boys, or my falling-out with Rakow. That wasn't the kind of thing I wanted a guy like Keen digging into.

At the conclusion of my story, I began my own line of questioning. Open-ended but systematic, the way I had learned from the Phoenix PD.

"I understand you have a theory about Delia's disappearance. Something to do with human trafficking?"

Keen sat back with a dramatic exhale, eyes widening. "Where do you want me to start? I've investigated true crime my entire life—mostly as an amateur, of course. I've never seen a case like the Delia Crawford disappearance. Mishandled evidence, jurisdictional bickering, witness intimidation. It really was a perfect storm."

I held up a hand. "Whoa. Back up. Mishandled evidence? I thought they didn't find any evidence."

Keen laughed. "Is that what they told you?"

I didn't answer. He rolled his eyes.

"No evidence. Ha. Well, what about the shoe? They found Delia's shoe in the woods, a hundred yards from the girl's dormitory at the summer camp. All the girls put their shoes in their footlockers at the end of the day, and nobody remembers Delia missing hers. Obviously, she wasn't sleeping in them. So why was it out in the woods?"

"That lends itself to the wandering-off theory," I said. "The idea that she snuck out and got lost."

Keen hesitated, something quick and conflicted passing across his face. He looked away. "Sure. But why did she lose the shoe? That's not something you do by accident. It's indicative of a struggle."

His reasoning was solid, but I made a noncommittal shrug anyway, as if I weren't sold. That kept him rolling.

"Or what about the maintenance guy?" Keen said.

"What maintenance guy?"

"Several of the girls informed investigators that there was a maintenance guy on-site at the summer camp that year. They all described him the same way—tall and scary. Dark hair, dark eyes. He wore coveralls and a hat."

"Sounds like a standard maintenance uniform."

"Sure. Except they saw him *in the woods*. Multiple times. Not working, just watching the kids. You can't go there now —the property is a private hunting camp these days. But back then, when it was a summer camp, the tree line was, like, a hundred yards from all the facilities. What's a maintenance guy doing way out there?"

Any number of things, I thought. But instead of saying that, I went with a more productive challenge. "Didn't the sheriff's department investigate?"

Keen snorted. "If you want to call it that. They made an inquiry with the summer camp. The camp claimed to have three maintenance personnel on staff. All men, but none of them tall, and none of them matching the artist's sketch based on the girls' description. So when the FBI arrived, the tip was passed off to them, but no investigation was ever made. It's all in my book, man. Even the artist's sketch."

"You had a look at the police files?"

"Sure. The ones they would share. I had a look at every original document I could find. That's how true crime journalism works. I interviewed several of the kids who bunked with Delia, also. They're all adults now, of course. Many of their memories are fuzzy, and they don't really like talking about it. But they all remember a maintenance guy matching the artist sketch—a guy not employed by the summer camp. Like, four of them. How does a thing like that happen by coincidence?"

It was a rhetorical question, but I considered it anyway. Keen's enthusiasm was compelling, but as a professional, I knew there were plenty of rational reasons why investigators might have dismissed the "maintenance guy" testimony. The man could have been a random local wandering through the woods. Or some kind of specialty contractor called in for a single day to fix an HVAC unit. Something like that. Something the summer camp staff might have forgotten.

Children's minds are easily confused. But it still bothered me. And so did the shoe.

"What about the human trafficking? You thought you had a connection?"

Keen snapped his fingers. "Right! So that was another lead. Another rabbit hole, if you will. Turns out the FBI field office in Birmingham put out a memo around the time of Delia's disappearance, advising state and local police to be vigilant about unknown persons appearing in their communities. Particularly young women from overseas. People without proper identification or a reason to be present in the community. Apparently, the FBI was working leads at the time into a trafficking case involving gangs in Eastern Europe—organized operations facilitating the kidnap and transfer of vulnerable young women into the United States."

"An import scheme."

"Exactly. Straight into the United States. You might not believe it, but according to the US State Department, fifteen thousand or more people are trafficked into America every year, many of them as part of the sex trade. I mean, we're one of the largest countries in the world. Don't you think there's a demand for illicit sex?"

I had never reviewed the numbers myself, but Keen's claims didn't surprise me. I'd seen enough hell in the Army to permanently suspend any surprise I might feel at the depravity of mankind, and my tours of duty as a cop on the streets of Phoenix quickly taught me that such depravity was no stranger to the Land of the Free.

But Keen's story still didn't make sense.

"So the FBI put out a bulletin about a sex trafficking ring," I said.

"*Importing into the United States*," Keen clarified.

"Okay. What's that got to do with Delia?"

He slurped from his soda, nodding the whole time. "Right. So to understand that, you really have to understand why traffickers work so hard to move victims thousands of miles around the globe. At least where developed countries are concerned. Take these victims being imported to the States, for example. Children from Belarus, Romania, Ukraine, Hungary...what have you. Most of them won't speak English. They're lost in a foreign land, far from home, disoriented and helpless. The new environment deepens their dependency on their kidnappers."

"Okay..."

"And the thing is, it works just as well in reverse. You take a kid from the States, young and helpless. They only speak English. They don't know the first thing about fending for themselves. You take them back to Europe, using the same smuggling method you employed to bring victims into the States...and you sell them into slavery there." Keen snapped his fingers. "Double your profits."

I waited. Keen's eyes remained wide, fixated on me. When I said nothing, he blinked.

"Don't you see the connection?"

"You think Delia was kidnapped by sex traffickers," I said.

“Exactly! It makes perfect sense!”

“Except you have zero evidence to support that theory.”

“I have the shoe! The tall maintenance guy—a guy no local has ever seen. FBI memos warning police departments all over southern Georgia and southeast Alabama of traffickers working in the region. I mean, what more do you want?”

I swallowed coffee and tried not to let my frustration show. It was a good story. A solid idea, maybe. But Keen had clearly never been a cop. Any number of armchair investigators could kick back and craft wild theories, connecting dots without need for concrete substantiation. It made for a great podcast or, in Keen’s case, a great book.

But it wasn’t enough to build a case or propel an investigation. I’d seen this sort of thing before. A missing shoe. A ghost man no local recognized. A swirl of law enforcement agencies feuding over jurisdiction. It was a cocktail of theory and chaos, the kind of thing a true crime writer would feast on, but that didn’t make any of it important. People like to say that where there is smoke, there is fire.

Cops know better. Cops know that sometimes, nature be damned…smoke is just smoke.

I asked enough further questions to be polite, but I knew my conversation with Keen wasn’t leading anywhere. He was overflowing with passion and had certainly done his homework on the case, but if what he knew hadn’t interested the FBI, it probably wouldn’t help me, either. In the end, I flipped my coffee cup into the trash, thanked him for his time, and headed for the door.

“Here’s my card,” Keen said, pressing a small black business card into my hand as he hovered near my GMC. “If you learn something…call me. Please. Anything at all.”

There was something in his face—something a little more earnest than professional curiosity. More sincere. It caught my attention for a moment and made me wonder. But then I dismissed it because I really didn't have time to facilitate his career.

"I'm not here to sponsor another book," I said. "I was just curious about Delia."

Keen nodded slowly, surveying my truck and noting the camping gear. Then turning back to me.

"You were a cop, weren't you? An investigator?"

It was a bull's-eye guess, but I didn't show my cards.

"What makes you say that?"

"The way you questioned me in there. I've watched a lot of police interviews. You talk like an investigator."

I said nothing.

"Military beforehand?" he prompted. "You've got that stance. Army, I'd guess. There's a lot of Army guys around here, from Fort Rucker. But you're not a helicopter pilot. No. You picked a table in the back. Sat facing the door. Kept scanning the room even while we were talking. Special Ops? Ranger? Delta?"

"You've got a great imagination, Keen. I'll give you that."

I opened my door. He put a hand on the jamb, stopping me.

"Look. I don't really care what or who you are. I just want you to know I'm not done with her story. If she's back in Delamar County...I want to know. Her story deserves to be told."

And you deserve to be paid for writing it.

I thought it; I didn't say it. I simply nodded and got back into my truck. Keen drove away in the Silverado while I sat baking in the Alabama heat, thinking about the pieces.

Delia, disappearing at the wreck. Then that European girl turning up at the barn, the barcode on her neck. A definite indicator of human trafficking, which felt like a hell of a coincidence after listening to Keen and all his wild trafficking theories.

But what if those theories weren't so wild? What if they were right on the money?

I would need a place to start. Somewhere to dig, and not stop digging until I found bones or blood.

Reaching into my pocket, I fished for my keys, but touched plastic instead. Hard but smooth, I saw red when the item tumbled into my hand. It was the flash drive I'd found at the fight ring—the one with the little label marked in a foreign language.

An Eastern European language.

I thought again about the girl with the barcode tattoo, and I snatched up my phone. A quick Google search produced a public library only a few blocks away. I drove there and was granted access to a computer after only a few moments of discussion with the librarian at the front desk.

The building was quiet as I flicked the flash drive open and inserted it into the USB port. The computer read the drive without complaint, and I navigated to the file viewer to access the contents.

The drive was loaded with a dozen folders, titled by date, with no preview. I double-clicked the first, waited a split second for the contents to load, and then my heart stopped.

I snatched the drive from the computer, my hands feeling suddenly clammy and cold, my heart restarting with a thunderous rush of adrenaline. It pounded in my head, and my stomach convulsed.

It was kiddie porn. A *lot* of it. What I saw in the split

second before I yanked the drive was one photo displayed in landscape with dozens more listed as thumbnails beneath. That single image was seared into my mind long before I could tear that drive free of its socket—a child, wide-eyed and terrified.

My hand shook, and I squeezed the drive until I felt the plastic crack between my fingers.

I'd found my place to dig.

18

I saw red as I input keyboard commands to scrub the computer's memory, then stormed through the automatic doors of the library, back to my truck. The heavy door slammed, the inline six roared to life, and I smashed the gas.

Turning back toward Delamar County.

Blended together with those depraved images, I saw the Krol boys. Sneering and smug, barely old enough to be called adults, but still playing games with children. I imagined their necks snapping over the tailgate of my truck, faces blackened and blue by a thorough pre-mortem pounding, and I knew it wasn't enough.

Nothing would be enough. No death sufficiently violent to repay the evil they had visited upon youth and innocence. But by the time I reached the highway, and that sick feeling in my stomach began to subside, I started to think more clearly.

I didn't have proof the Krol boys had taken those pictures. I didn't even know for certain the flash drive had fallen from one of their pockets. In theory, it could have already been lying there before they even showed up, lost by another pathetic excuse for humanity who happened to be passing by. Or maybe one of the two men I pounded had dropped it.

I didn't really believe that, but I couldn't snap necks without knowing for sure. And even then, as my mind continued to calm, I realized I could be missing the forest for the trees.

Delia's reappearance, then encore disappearance. The girl with the butterfly pants. The Krol boys' dedication to running me out of town. The flash drive with the foreign language written on the label.

There was something going on here, and it was much bigger than two walking lumps of dog shit with a flash drive full of filth. Sure, I could run them over with my GMC, then tie their ankles to my bumper and drive them down one of Delamar County's pothole-infested roads.

But what good would that do? This situation didn't call for an ax; it called for a forest fire. And now that I was bereft of Rakow's good graces, I couldn't rely on the sheriff's department to light that match. They wouldn't believe me, anyway. They might even question how I came into possession of that drive in the first place.

No. If this thing was going to be dealt with, I was going to have to do it on my own. And I was just fine with that.

By the time I reached Delamar County, I had developed enough of a plan to get started. I bypassed the turnoff for Able and drove straight into Muscogee, finding the local Walmart and parking in back. I dug through my camping gear and quickly located my hiking boots, a fresh pair of jeans, and a plain black T-shirt. I changed in the Walmart bathroom, then located the sporting goods section and purchased a fresh can of camouflage face paint and a knife.

Not a folding knife, like the Victorinox Locksmith I kept in my front pocket. This was a fixed blade with a six-inch cutting edge and a rubberized plastic handle. Durable and discardable, complete with a cheap nylon sheath.

I grabbed beef jerky, trail mix, and bottled water on my way to the checkout, then piled everything into the bed of my truck. I tucked the knife into the small of my back, folding the belt loop portion of the nylon sheath over and affixing it to my belt to prevent the knife from falling down my pants leg.

The grip of the weapon rode against my skin, ready for quick access.

Taking the face paint, I returned to the cab and found my binoculars in the glove box. They were relatively new—a recent purchase during my escapades in Atlanta. I set them on the seat and returned to my phone, using the web browser to begin my search.

Krol family.
Krol company.
Krol mining.
Krol industries and bauxite.

It was the final search that produced the result I was looking for—a succinct webpage, complete with a Delamar County address. Apparently, Krol Industries was headquartered way out in the sticks, handy to the few remaining mines in the region. Bauxite, it seemed, was mined not by shaft like coal, but by simply scooping gigantic holes in the ground, creating lake-worthy craters. Like a massive swimming pool.

The website for Krol Industries bragged about the perpetuation of domestic industry. Keeping jobs in the good old US of A. They saw no irony in the fact that all the bauxite they mined was shipped immediately overseas, there to be processed into aluminum by cheap international labor.

I didn't care about that. I just wanted the address.

My phone's built-in GPS found the headquarters deep in the middle of nowhere, miles from Muscogee. Miles even from Able.

A quiet place, where nobody would get in the way.

I dropped the shifter into first gear and turned back onto the road.

19

Krol Industries' headquarters sat behind a ten-foot chain-link fence, topped not with barbed wire, but curled razor wire. Like a freaking prison. There was a guardhouse and an automatic gate sitting fifty yards off the same two-lane state highway the sheriff's office was located along—albeit fifteen miles apart.

I drove by with a quick glance, but I didn't stop. As much as I loved my old GMC, it wasn't much of a stealth vehicle, and I already knew the Krol boys had photographed my North Carolina antique license plate and were on the lookout against my return.

No. This would need to be a stealth mission, and I was just fine with that.

I found the entrance of a small field, planted tight with lush green peanut plants, and parked beneath a pine tree. It was a mile from the Krol place, but I didn't mind the walk. I loaded a robust backpack from one of my camping bins with my binoculars, a pair of bolt cutters I'd purchased in Atlanta, two bottles of water and a couple of packages of jerky. Then I dropped the tailgate, sat down, and went to work with the camouflage paint.

I've worn a lot of camouflage paint. I've always liked it. In Afghanistan, it was usually helpful to smear gray-green over my face prior to sneaking into a rural village for a little midnight door-kicking. Some of the guys complained about the sticky, smelling gunk, but I liked the idea of becoming invisible. It was one more unfair advantage in a conflict I always hoped would remain completely unfair. A platform for violence of action, in one of the most violent places on earth.

Back then, of course, I also wore full ACUs paired with combat gloves and a helmet. I wouldn't have worn all that gear in Delamar County for a million dollars. The baking wrath of the sun was worse than ever, the air so thick with humidity I thought I could cut it with a knife. Instead, I smeared paint over my face, down my neck, and from my short sleeves to my wrists—nice and thick. It beaded with sweat and smelled greasy, reminding me of days long gone by, and triggered a cold focus someplace deep in my mind.

Shutting the tailgate, I started into the trees with the pack on my back and my hands free—ready for anything. The hike through dense pines and thicker undergrowth was brutal. Barbed branches tore at my jeans and opened spider-thin cuts on my arms, while the canopy of pine needles overhead created a balloon to trap the humidity. It wasn't cooler in the shade—it was somehow hotter. Like walking through a greenhouse.

I found the fence for the Krol compound after fifteen minutes of aggressive hiking, streaking along the edge of the tree line. Still ten feet high, still topped with curled razor wire. Every fifty feet or so, a *Private Property, No Trespassing* sign was wire tied to the fence, facing outward—every bit as useless in preventing my intrusion as the fence itself.

I squatted behind a thicket and drew the binoculars from the pack. A quick survey of the open field beyond the fence revealed nothing. Tall green grass bent gently in a baking breeze, but the ground dropped off before reaching the core of the compound, sheltering it from my view. I listened intently and thought I heard the grind and pound of heavy machinery someplace beyond the fence, but I couldn't be sure. A mockingbird chortled in the pines overhead, obnoxiously hindering my ability to detect distant noises.

I checked both ways down the fence, then swapped the binos for the bolt cutters. This was as good a place as any. The high grass beyond the fence wasn't ideal concealment, but it was better than nothing.

The bolt cutters made short work of the fence, carving out a four-foot-by-four-foot panel in under a minute. I deliberately cut around one of the No Trespassing signs, discarding the sign and the chain-link in pine needles behind me before replacing the cutters in my pack and sliding through the fence.

Abandoning the canopy of the pines made me wish I had brought my sunglasses. It was just past noon, and the demon Alabama sun beat down on me like I owed it money. I jogged in a low crouch, moving quickly through the field with waist-high grass dragging at my legs. The closer I drew to the point where the ground began to drop off, the louder the distant machinery became. The heavy growl of diesel engines drifted toward me on a light breeze, joined by the occasional clank of hammers on metal and voices shouting.

I dropped to my stomach twenty yards out and army-crawled the rest of the way, sweat draining off my face in a waterfall. It was a little cooler near the ground, and I could hear small animals skittering around me amid the grass. A cricket chirped, and I felt the ground begin to drop off beneath me. Not a cliff—just the start of another rolling hill.

I parted the grass, and I saw the compound.

It was two hundred yards away, resting in a wide, dusty valley. A gravel drive wound in from my right, connecting the highway with a metal industrial building sitting fifty yards removed from a small vinyl-sided office building. Both structures were covered with dust, their metal roofs reflecting the blazing sun and causing me to squint. Half a dozen personal vehicles sat in front of the office, while two semitrucks were visible through the wide-open door of the larger sheet-metal clad building.

I retrieved the binoculars and swept the scene. Even with magnification, it was difficult to make out details so far away, but I caught the gist. This was a function-centric operational headquarters. The metal building appeared to be some kind of mechanic's shop, with the hood of one truck turned open, while the sparking flash of a cutting torch blazed from the shadows.

Everything around the compound looked very aged and worn. Even the personal vehicles gathered in front of the office building were several years old and heavily used—all but one, anyway. One of them was nearly brand new, a dark gray Nissan Titan set on beefy tires with all kinds of equipment poking from the extended bed.

I figured that to be the boss man's truck—whoever he was—and sipped water from my bottle as I continued my visual sweep of the property. I noted aged equipment, two or three people working inside the mechanic's shop, and a middle-aged woman headed for town with a bundle of mail under one arm.

Everything about the place said *business as usual.* Nothing to see here.

But I was patient. I had no place better to be. I tore my first package of beef jerky open and ripped into a large, tender strip. The flavor was teriyaki, which was a mistake. I don't like sweet things that should be salty, and jerky should always be salty. I must have grabbed teriyaki by accident.

I spit the strip out and was just turning to inspect the remainder of my supply when something caught my eye. I froze as a vehicle appeared on the gravel drive, hauling ass toward the office building.

It was a jet-black Ford pickup. The Raptor model. Barely a year or two old.

My old friends the Krol boys had arrived.

20

The Raptor ground to a halt in front of the office, and both boys piled out. The heavyset, muscular guy dropped out through the driver's door. The tall skinny kid through the passenger's door. They marched directly inside, as though they were on a mission. I watched the door slam and shimmering heat waves waft up from the hood of the truck; then I made a quick decision.

I would only get so far playing it safe. It was time to close in.

Stowing the water, jerky, and binoculars, I started down the slope in a low crouch, keeping near to the grass. It was an awkward position to move in, but it allowed me at least limited concealment for another hundred yards. Beyond that, the grass was cut short, not quite manicured, but at least semi-regularly mown to provide workable space around the complex.

I'd cross that bridge when I came to it.

I reached the terminus of the high grass at almost the same moment as the office door blew open, and the Krol kids emerged. The muscular one came first, stumbling and looking stupidly over his shoulder. His skinny brother followed shortly behind, walking half-turned and pointing toward the office. I raised the binoculars and found his face in the lens, his cheeks flushed a deep shade of crimson. He was shouting, but I couldn't hear him. The wind swept away from me, carrying his voice into the compound.

Then a third man appeared from the office building. He was a lot older than either kid—mid- to late fifties, maybe, with graying blond hair and a leathery, wrinkled face. But it wasn't difficult to guess who he was. This would be old man Krol, for sure. The resemblance between him and his sons was impossible to miss.

He gritted his teeth and snapped something at Skinny, then grabbed him roughly by the arm and hauled him toward the parked Raptor, snapping his fingers for Muscle to follow.

The trio turned their backs to me as they moved, and momentary hesitation froze my mind. If I sprinted now, it would be a mad eighty-yard dash to the lifted Titan pickup, my nearest form of cover. If one of the three of them glanced back, or if somebody inside the office building happened to look out a window, I would be toast.

But then again, lying here at the edge of the field would get me nowhere. There was some sort of argument underway. I wanted to hear it.

Rising quickly to my feet, I launched out of the grass and sprinted for the Titan. I didn't bother to bend over or zigzag or waste time thinking about my footfalls. The grass muted my steps, and the clang of machinery from the mechanic's shop helped also. I simply ran, gobbling up ground and reaching the parking lot. I watched the three of them out of the corner of my eye, their voices rising in volume as I neared. Still not quite audible.

I saw Muscle reach the Raptor and begin to turn.

I reached the Titan first and hit the deck. Heart pounding. Chest heaving. Before anyone could face me, I rolled beneath the truck and lay very still, listening.

The Raptor and the three men next to it were barely twenty yards away now. Close enough for me to hear so long as the wind carried their voices my way, or someone resumed shouting. I wriggled to the back of the Titan, passing beneath the rear axle with ease thanks to the elevated suspension. Fragments of the conversation drifted my way—an argument, with the whiny voice of a Krol boy reaching me just as I poked my faced around a rear tire.

Old man Krol stood with his back to me, the skinnier of his two sons sticking his chin up as his monologue concluded. No sooner had he closed his mouth than the old man decked him, right across the face, hard enough to send his head smacking against the Ford. I flinched despite myself. Skinny caught himself against the truck bed, almost falling, pure terror entering his eyes in a flood.

"I did not bleed to build this operation only to have half-witted idiots burn it down!"

The old man jabbed with his finger as he shouted, his voice heavy with a Polish accent. Both boys cowered, and I thought Skinny might be crying. I couldn't deny enjoying that.

The old man leaned in, speaking through his teeth now. His voice lowered a little, but I could still make out the words.

"We are at the half-yard line. See? This close!" He

pinched two fingers together right in Skinny's face. "This is no time for a Hail Mary play!"

"We didn't have a choice!" Now it was Muscle who spoke. His voice was less whiny than Skinny's, and more American than the old man's. "We had to run him off. He was asking questions. It was becoming an emergency!"

The old man struck again, not as hard this time, but just as sudden. He slammed Muscle against the Raptor, shaking him until his head bobbled.

"You do not decide what makes an emergency! *I* decide. It is no emergency for this idiot to ask questions. Now that you run him off, maybe the police will ask questions. Did you think of that?"

No answer from either boy. The old man cursed.

"Stupid fools. I came to this country, I built a future, and you will squander it."

"We ain't squandering nothing," Skinny said, wiping his nose. "The hobo is gone. The cops are clueless. And anyway, soon enough it won't matter. We'll be done."

"We still have to *live here*," the old man snarled. "And the police are not clueless. The police are asking *questions*."

Skinny shrugged. "So we deal with them, too."

"*You* will do nothing," the old man snapped. "I will deal with the police—the smart way. *You* will do what you are told, and nothing else."

Skinny didn't answer, and the old man cuffed him again, twice. One cheek, then a backhand across the other, so fast it took even me by surprise. Skinny dropped his face and held up both hands, proclaiming his submission. Old man Krol shoved him into the Raptor with a disgusted shake of his head, looking at his sons as though they were bad cuts of overcooked meat. A complete disappointment.

Taking a step back, he knocked a cigarette out of a pack and lit it up, smoking slowly. Both boys watched him in open, transparent fear, but he didn't move toward them. He finished half of the smoke, then ground it out with his boot and spoke calmly, still facing away. "If there is a problem—if you jeopardize our associates—I will bury you in a bauxite mine. I can make new sons faster than I can fix stupid ones."

I could tell by their blanched faces and unblinking eyes that the boys believed him. I believed him, too. His voice was cold as ice.

The old man spat into the dust. "Now get down to the mine! Take care of the train, and call me when it is done."

Old man Krol marched back to the office building. He crossed next to the Titan—his truck, I guessed—and marched up the wooden steps without pausing, his boots passing only a yard from my concealed body.

I remained focused on the Krol kids, watching as they did all the things shamed teenage males always do. Avoid each other's gaze. Spit and kick at the dirt. Curse and work themselves up. Convince themselves that the old man was the real fool.

"I told you not to tell him," Skinny snarled.

"Would have been worse if he heard it elsewhere!" Muscle protested. "That damn hobo nearly killed those fools. Word's gonna get around."

More kicking at the dirt, spitting, and angry cursing. Then Muscle looked to Skinny. "You...gonna tell him about the drive?"

Skinny spun on his brother, slamming him against the truck. Cuffing his face. "Don't you say a thing! I told you I lost it at the house. Ain't nobody gonna find it!"

The two of them tussled for a moment; then Muscle

shoved his brother off with a heave of his bulky arms. Skinny fell back, but continued to curse, ordering Muscle to get into the truck.

Muscle complied, starting the big engine while Skinny marched to the mechanic's shop and held a brief conference with one of the men inside. Then he returned to the passenger seat of the Raptor, Muscle turned the truck around, and the two of them sat waiting at the mouth of the gravel drive. I listened as one of the semitrucks grumbled to life, the voice of its throaty diesel magnified by the metal shell it sat in. I could see from my angle beneath the Titan that the truck was already hitched to a long silver trailer. A dump trailer, I thought, designed to haul loose dirt and minerals.

I contemplated for only a split second before making another quick decision. There was nothing to see here—maybe something in the office, buried on a computer or hidden in a secure drive. But I wouldn't be able to access that until after dark, if at all.

I was much more interested in what the old man had said—his parting order to his two idiot sons—*Get down to the mine. Take care of the train. Call me when it is done.*

It might be a simple business instruction. Some function of the bauxite industry that the two kids were responsible for performing. But the remainder of the conversation said otherwise, and so did my gut.

I crept to the edge of my cover beneath the Titan, only a quick roll away from being back on my feet. The Raptor's taillights were now facing me, fifty yards away. The semitruck was rumbling into place behind, both vehicles rumbling toward the gravel drive that led out of the compound.

The semitruck would pass within ten yards of my position in a matter of seconds. The dump trailer trundling behind it was fully loaded with something, bouncing heavily over heavier axles, its open top covered by an industrial tarpaulin.

An aluminum ladder hung from the back of that trailer, the bottom rung three feet off the ground. I waited until the back wheels crunched by, then rolled quickly from beneath the Titan and sprinted to the truck—not looking behind. Not checking to see if anyone was watching.

My hands closed around the ladder, and I yanked myself up as my boots scraped the rock. One shoe found the bottom rung, and then I was up. Climbing straight to the top. Lifting the edge of the tarp and wriggling atop a rough brown mound of crushed rock.

Pure bauxite. A brutally uncomfortable place to hide, but an effective one.

I was in.

21

The truck hit the highway and gained a little speed, but wasn't in a hurry. Peering out from beneath the edge of the tarp, I watched the rolling hills and pines pass, frequent potholes jarring the truck and shifting both the bauxite and my sprawled body.

I looked ahead, but I couldn't see the Raptor. It was long gone along the road, leaving the semi to catch up. We drove for half an hour or more, winding even deeper into Delamar County, the roads worsening by the mile. I saw no houses. No driveways or even fields, and after a while I realized that even power lines were missing.

We were truly in the middle of nowhere, and nowhere was growing wider by the minute.

It didn't concern me. So long as the Krol boys were waiting at the end of the line, I didn't really care where the line ended.

At last the truck slowed, then turned lazily off the road onto another gravel drive. This one was unprotected by any gate or guardhouse, the pine thickets parting to reveal wide-open spaces blazing with sunlight. I choked on dust and sheltered beneath the tarp as the jolting continued. The truck turned and squealed to a stop, and men shouted someplace outside.

Then the trailer shifted beneath me, and the loud, rhythmic beep of the semi's backup alarm began to blare. I lifted the edge of the tarp to see a mountain of rust red rock looming toward me—forty or fifty feet high and three times as wide, it was all bauxite, just like what I was lying across.

The truck accelerated, pushing the trailer all the way to the mound, then hissed to a stop again.

I didn't have to be told what came next. Lifting the tarpaulin, I rolled over the back edge of the trailer and took the ladder to the ground even as the dump trailer began to rise. Clouds of thick red dust exploded into the air as the trailer's gate lifted and the cargo poured out. I choked and stumbled to the side, temporarily blinded. Completely vulnerable to attack or identification as I circled the mountain of bauxite, still choking.

I reached the back side and pressed myself into a crevice between two identical heaps of mined mineral. Machinery ground nearby, and I cleared my eyes, peering around.

Directly to my left, barely two yards away, a sheer one-hundred-foot cliff plummeted into the earth. I recognized my own bootprint barely six inches from the drop-off, marking my blind progress from the trailer to my current position, and my stomach convulsed.

It was a bauxite mine—an old, exhausted one, carved like a gargantuan swimming pool out of the rock and clay, now collecting water far below. A few hundred yards beyond, I identified a second such mine and then a third, followed by a rolling hill covered in pines.

All the noise and chaos came from behind me—on the other side of the bauxite pile.

I dug water out of my pack and used it to clear my throat and eyes, then began to scramble up the mound, kicking down loose clumps of dirt and mineral before dropping to my stomach and peering over the top.

If my previous location had been a headquarters, this was the nitty-gritty heart of the industrial operation. On the far side of multiple truckloads of the rust red mineral, a heavy-duty front-end loader worked, its giant tires rumbling back and forth as it scooped massive helpings of bauxite and carried them fifty yards to where a row of rail cars sat—fully two dozen of them, open-topped and bulky. Like oversized versions of the dump trailer I'd ridden in on.

The open-topped rail cars were connected to a couple of boxcars, followed by a train engine resting under the blazing Alabama sun. Between the train and me, another office building sat—a mobile one, like you see on job sites. The Raptor was parked in front of it, and the two Krol kids were busy shouting orders at a steady row of trucks that rolled in and out of the staging field, each carrying another heavy load of bauxite.

I slumped down and breathed a disappointed sigh as the routine of dumping, scooping, and dumping ground on. It wasn't difficult to understand what was happening here. The mines behind me were long exhausted, but new mines had been developed somewhere else in the county. Somewhere inaccessible to the rail line.

So the bauxite was being loaded, moved, and dumped here, where it was loaded again and taken to...wherever bauxite is used.

Get down to the mine. Take care of the train. Call me when it is done.

Was this really all the old man had been talking about? A mundane logistics operation?

Maybe he wanted the kids out of the way. They'd caused enough damage with their apparently rogue action to run me out of town. Maybe this was busywork.

I watched the routine for the better part of an hour, my position atop a bauxite mountain invisible to the men on the ground and growing rapidly more fortified as the incoming truckloads of bauxite overwhelmed the progress of the loader, leaving additional rusty red heaps building toward the office trailer. At some point, Muscle took control of the loader himself, driving the machine like he drove the Ford—altogether too fast and reckless.

But I saw nothing of interest. Nothing that looked like it had anything to do with Delia or the girl in the butterfly pants.

Maybe this had been a waste of time. It was going to be a hell of a long walk back to my truck.

I decided to wait the Krol boys out anyway, figuring that if I did end up walking back to my truck, it would be more comfortable to do so after the sun went down. The afternoon wound closer to evening, and the train rolled out with a squeal of metal wheels on metal tracks. Muscle parked the loader next to a diesel tank and sucked down a soda while the beast slowly refueled, but neither kid seemed ready to leave. Even as the sun drifted steadily closer toward a summer sunset, and the other workers were dismissed and drove away, the Krol kids remained. They stood next to the tailgate of the Raptor and ate sausages from little metal cans, paired with saltine crackers and more soda.

I saw it all through the binoculars, repositioned on a new pile of bauxite, still invisible to the oblivious Krol boys. As the last of the other workers rolled away, I wanted to climb down and make a direct approach. Incapacitate Muscle with a quick wrenching of his skull into the rear fender of the Ford, followed by a more systematic interrogation of Skinny.

Skinny was the alpha dog, after all. The guy who should know things.

But as the two kids completed their meal, I noted Skinny routinely checking his watch and looking up the rail line to where it disappeared into the trees. Both boys remained standing, kicking at rocks and playing on their phones from time to time, but not moving from the truck.

They were waiting for something. Expecting it soon.

I decided to bide my time, but I didn't have to wait long. Just past six p.m., I heard the second train. It rumbled out of the trees in a rush, evening sunlight gleaming off the windshield and flashing in my eyes. More metal screamed as the engine braked, and another long line of open-topped dump cars raced into view. Thirty or more this time, winding back into the trees and out of sight as the engine stopped near the bauxite piles, all dust and growling diesel. I could smell it from a hundred yards out.

Sweeping the binoculars back to the Krol boys, I watched as they slammed the Raptor's tailgate closed, then hurried across the lot toward the train. The engineer met them as he swung to the ground, and a quick exchange commenced. Muscle was irritated. Skinny seemed all business, waving the guy away.

The engineer headed for the office building, wiping his sweaty face with a towel, and Skinny watched him go. Then he jerked his head to Muscle, and the two kids disappeared around the nose of the engine, circling to the other side.

Take care of the train.

I remembered the old man's words again, and suddenly wondered if I hadn't been wrong about their meaning. I was just looking at the wrong train.

I swept the binoculars down the length of tracks, noting each of the cars coupled together all the way back up the hill and into the forest. Most of them were dump cars, save for another pair of boxcars halfway down the line. All were faded and worn, and like most train cars, covered in graffiti. I recognized city names sprayed in artful curves—bright orange and green, yellow and crimson red.

Savannah. Baltimore. Newark. Boston.

It was an East Coast train, working the rail lines along the Atlantic.

Doing...what?

I lowered the binoculars slowly and thought back to three months prior, during my time in Atlanta. A lot of things had happened on those grimy streets. I wouldn't be in a hurry to return. My unfortunate collision with a hapless teenager had led to a much less fortunate and much bloodier collision with the drug gang that hounded him.

That drug gang had been up to their necks in Mexican fentanyl, and they had been preparing to distribute it via...trains.

The memory detonated in my mind at the same moment as Skinny and Muscle reappeared around from the front of the engine—but this time they weren't alone. Three men accompanied them. All short, all stout. Dressed in dark clothes with cold glares on their otherwise unremarkable faces.

They were all white, but a little darker than your average Caucasian. A little closer to olive-skinned, with black hair. I surveyed them through the binoculars and registered the immediate impression that they weren't American.

The five men disappeared inside the office building, and I clawed my way to my feet. Depositing the binoculars into my pack, I descended the sheltered side of the bauxite pile in a slip-sliding cloud of red dust.

That drug gang in Atlanta had wanted to use trains to move their product for a very simple reason. Rail lines in America touch every city. Every rural community. And unlike planes, buses, and American highways...rail lines are almost completely unhindered by inspection or law enforcement. They are ideal vehicles to smuggle fentanyl up the East Coast, and they would be just as ideal for human trafficking.

My feet hit the mud, and I sprinted for the train.

22

The train engine radiated waves of thick diesel heat as I danced across the tracks and landed in the gravel on the other side. Looking down the lengthy line of cars, I spotted the boxcars fifty yards away. Two of them, back-to-back, their doors rolled closed.

As I jogged toward them, I heard voices coming from the direction of the field office, but I knew they couldn't see me sheltered by the line of cars. Stopping at the first boxcar, I found the door held closed by a heavy padlock. The voices grew louder, and I ducked my head beneath the car to see Skinny, Muscle, and the engineer returning. The engineer carried a small black bag under one arm and chowed down on a sandwich, nodding irritably while Skinny lectured him about something. The Krol boy's face was twisted into hard lines, and he used his hands a lot, chopping one into the other like an ax.

I ran down the line to the next boxcar and tried the door. It was locked again, and I decided to take a risk, tapping on the door with my knuckles.

The sound boomed three or four times louder than I expected, and I froze.

"What's that?" It was Skinny. I recognized his whining voice from the confrontation with old man Krol. "You hear that?"

I ducked my head beneath the car again and made out three pairs of legs walking rapidly toward the train on the far side of the tracks. There was no time to try the lock or wrestle with my bolt cutters. I dashed for the end of the boxcar, swinging between it and the dump car hitched to its rear. The dump car was equipped with a metal ladder on the end, and I shimmied straight up, my nostrils confronted with an increasingly acrid odor the higher I climbed.

I reached the top of the ladder just as I heard boots crunching across the gravel, someplace near the engine. The voices were muted now, spoke in dull whispers, but the next sound I heard would be recognizable anywhere on the planet. Absolutely unmistakable to any cop, soldier, or even an action movie fan.

The sharp, metallic snap of a pistol being chambered.

I reached the top of the ladder and peered over the rim into the dump car. The stench I had detected before worsened by orders of magnitude, and I almost choked.

It was cow manure. A full load of it, packed to the brim, still a little wet from the rain two nights before.

I froze at the top of the ladder, unable to proceed. The gleam of an LED light flashed down the curving line of cars, and the first boxcar door rattled as it was tested. I looked over my shoulder, momentarily contemplating a leap onto the roof of the second boxcar.

It wasn't an option. The roof was constructed of sheet

metal. My boots would trigger a thunderclap loud enough to wake the dead.

The flashlight gleamed on the second car, driving back gathering evening shadows, and the boots crunched toward me. I looked back at the manure, momentarily contemplating the decision-making paradigm that was landing me in these...well. Shitty situations.

Then I gritted my teeth and flipped over the end of the car.

My legs sank up to my knees in thick, hot cow crap. My stomach convulsed, but I denied my desire to puke and lowered myself slowly into the muck, twisting my head to shield my nostrils from the bulk of the stench.

It was all I could do not to vomit. Flies swarmed up from the surface of the manure as I settled into it, swarming around my head and landing on my ears and face. I made a momentary attempt to wave them away, but it was a lost cause. There were too many of them.

I shut my eyes and embraced the suck, hearkening back to my days in Ranger School and combat training at Army bases around the country. I couldn't remember any part of those grueling experiences that matched this, but history is viewed through rose-tinted glasses.

The boxcar nearest me rattled, and the door rolled open. I heard voices, but couldn't make out words. A conference was held. I breathed slowly through my mouth, trying not to smell anything. Counting seconds that eased into ten minutes.

I smelled cigarette smoke, and for the first time in my life, the secondhand smoke felt like fresh air. Voices murmured in a language that wasn't English—some kind of

Eastern European dialect, I thought. Boots thumped around the inside of the nearest boxcar, and heavy items inside were shifted over slick metal.

I closed my eyes and swallowed, cursing cattle and swearing I'd shoot the next one I saw.

At long last, the boots crunched away, and the voices grew quieter. I waited two minutes to ensure my safety, then raised my head over the end of the dump car.

The sky was rapidly darkening. I couldn't see either of the Krol kids or any of the newcomers.

I started toward the ladder, and then I felt a deep groan, followed by a throaty growl. Very loud, and not very far away.

The train engine howled once, and the car beneath me shifted. Metal ground against metal, and the trees lurched sideways a few inches, all at once.

The train was on the move again.

I clawed my way over the dump car's rim and grabbed the ladder. My boots sucked and tugged against my legs as I fought to wrench myself free of the manure. The train jolted and gained speed. Railroad ties flashed by beneath the wheels, and I looked over my shoulder to see the heaping piles of bauxite now two hundred yards away, working on three.

I grabbed the ladder and pulled, hauling myself free. The manure shifted, and a gas bubble of pure hell exploded around me, choking off my oxygen. I hauled my feet free and swung them over the rim of the dump car, dropping straight toward the rails and dangling by my hands. My boots slipped off the jolting car coupling, and the backpack swung from my shoulders.

The train was rushing now—twenty miles per hour and still gaining speed. If I was going to jump, this would be my best chance.

But I wasn't going to jump. There was something in these boxcars, and I was going to see it.

Releasing the ladder with one hand, I finally planted one boot on the coupling and twisted to face the rear of the second boxcar. It gleamed red in the dying light, the ladder bolted to its back about a foot out of reach.

The train rattled, and I balanced on the coupling. Hot wind ripped around my face, bringing welcome fresh air, but not bringing the ladder any closer. One slip, one misstep... and it would all be over.

I'd be just another railroad safety statistic.

I gritted my teeth and lunged for the ladder. My right hand caught one rung of it just as my manure-soaked boots slipped from the top of the coupling. Both legs plummeted toward the flashing railroad ties as I swung from the ladder, muscles strained, heart thumping. The toe of my right boot skipped over gravel, and I yanked both legs up, finding the bottom of the ladder and quickly ascending well above the tracks.

Watch yourself, Mason.

The train squealed, and the boxcar leaned left as we swung into a turn. The bauxite mines were now long gone, lost amid darkening groves of mixed pines and hardwoods. The trees flashed by in a blackened blur, but I didn't focus on them. I used the curve in the tracks as an opportunity to lean around the back corner of the boxcar and look toward the engine.

The door was no longer padlocked, and it was no longer

closed. It lay fifteen feet away from me, riding half-open as hot wind whistled in. I couldn't see inside the car, but I knew I wanted to.

I briefly inspected the rails the sliding door ran along, momentarily contemplating an attempt at inching my way along them and swinging into the car from the side. But the rails were too far apart—I wasn't sure I could step along the bottom one with my toes while clinging to the top one with my fingers. Even if I could, the rails ended at the back side of the door, and the door was fully six feet wide. More problems.

No, better to climb onto the roof, then swing in from the top. Like a monkey. But I would have to move quietly, because there was a chance somebody might be inside. One of the dark-haired men hanging out with the Krol boys, perhaps. I didn't want to earn myself a bullet to the gut.

Starting up the ladder, I took my time to the top, where I found a roof constructed of thick, red metal. Much thicker than I had guessed before, meaning my body weight would be less likely to produce a thunderclap. Also, I now had the clack and rattle of the train to mask my movements.

I climbed until I could bend at the waist over the roof, then inched ahead on my hands and knees. It felt higher on top of the car than I anticipated, and I'm no fan of heights. The rushing gravel ditch to my right blurred into a strip of gray, and the train jolted rhythmically. Ahead, I marked the long string of cars leading to the yellow engine, each of them rattling and clacking along as though they were about to fly apart.

I ignored the stimulus overload and focused on the task at hand—crawling along the roof of this car, not putting my foot through a rusty spot, and not making any excess noise.

My stomach flipped a little every time we swung into a curve. There was a metal track running down the middle of the roof, about eighteen inches wide with roofing panels dropping off on either side. It served as a makeshift highway to the middle of the car.

By the time I reached that middle and twisted to inch my way to the top of the door, it was almost dark. The trees had turned to shadows, and I could no longer see the rushing gravel ditch.

Maybe that was a good thing.

I lay on my stomach and wormed my way to the edge of the roof, grabbing the rim and breathing deeply. Then I hung my head over the edge and peered inside.

I couldn't see anything. Only a dim patch of emptiness, right inside the door, with blackness on either side. I twisted my head and lay still, waiting for my eyes to adjust.

I still saw nothing. The car appeared empty, but from this vantage point, both ends of the car were almost invisible to me, and that was a problem.

I withdrew from the edge of the roof and lay still, calming my heart rate. Strategizing and contemplating. I could climb down the front end of the car and trying to inch my way to the door from that angle. That would remove the door as an obstacle, but without the door rails I would have nothing to cling to, and approaching from the front still wouldn't give me a view of the entire car prior to entering.

Alternatively, I could wait until we stopped. Drop to the ground and enter like a normal person—on my feet.

But how long would that be? We might not stop all night. We might be in Florida before we stopped, or head straight to Miami.

No, there was only one thing to do. Risky or otherwise, I

had to bite the bullet and simply barrel in. I only wished I had a gun.

Digging my LED flashlight from my pocket, I placed it between my teeth. Then I grabbed the thick rim of the roof and rose into a crouch. Balanced at the roof's edge, inching my boots ahead until my toes overhung the precipice. Breathed evenly, closed my eyes...and then leapt.

I slung my feet over the edge, propelled my body away from the train, and twisted. All while clinging to the edge of the roof. My weight descended on my arms, and my legs swung inward, through the open door. I released the roof and dropped, landing with a bang right in the middle of the car, the backpack snapping against my shoulders. I looked immediately left—because I had to pick a direction, and my odds were fifty-fifty.

The flashlight dropped out of my mouth, and I flicked it on, illuminating the back end of the car as bright as day.

And then my blood ran cold.

I saw piles of bottled water. Rolls of blankets. Two clear plastic containers packed with clothes. *Children's clothes*. I could tell by the patterns and styling. By how small the folded dresses and shirts were, and the reality disabled my mind for a split second.

It was a split second too long. I'd flipped a coin upon landing inside that car. Fifty-fifty. I'd turned left and found my gold mine.

And completely missed the man behind me.

I heard the creak first, a barely perceptible grunt of metal on metal, untriggered by a passing rail joint or a bend in the track. I twisted quickly around, bringing the light up to shield my face, already realizing my mistake. Already switching gears into combat mode as a long black baseball bat rocketed out of the darkness, piloted directly for my face.

23

There was no time to avoid the bat. The best I could do was shield myself. I swung my flashlight arm toward the incoming weapon, blazing light across the face of my attacker and catching the edge of the bat on the heel of my hand.

The flashlight flew from my fingers as the bat skipped off the indirect contact with my palm and raced down my arm, smashing into my chest instead of my face. The rapid change in direction killed a good portion of the bat's momentum, but not all of it. Concussive pain exploded across my ribs as I was sent stumbling backward, almost falling, grabbing the end of the bat with my free hand by sheer instinct.

My attacker grunted and fought to wrench the weapon free. I kicked out with my right boot, landing a strike on a shin or a knee—something solid enough to knock him off balance. We both toppled to the floor, the bat spinning free. As I struck the floor, the bolt cutters in my backpack slammed into my spine, knocking the wind out of me.

I gasped for air and reached for the knife tucked into the

small of my back. I couldn't find it, and I heard the guy scrambling to his feet somewhere nearby. My flashlight lay on the floor ten feet away, blazing uselessly at the wall. The glow was insufficient to illuminate my assailant.

I rolled to the right, and a boot landed on the backpack. My chest constricted, and I choked for air. My right hand found the knife, and I swept blindly toward where I thought his free leg was planted.

The blade bit something—pants, a boot, or flesh. A muted cry confirmed the last of the three, and the boot fell away from my pack.

I didn't waste time gasping for air. My head spun, and my vision turned black as I clawed my way to my knees, turning quickly to see the guy rocketing toward me again, a knife of his own outstretched in one hand.

I ducked the blade and went straight for his exposed thigh, slashing hard with the hunting knife. I cut through thick cargo pants and bit deep into taut muscle, earning a shriek and a stumble.

But he didn't retreat. He kept coming, falling over me, knocking me off balance and sending the knife spinning out of my hands. I landed on my shoulder blades, and he landed on top. His knees encased my chest, constricting airflow as he clutched blindly at the blood gushing from his leg. I made a fist and drove it into the wounded thigh with as much force as I could muster. The guy howled like an animal, and I shoved with both arms, fighting to displace him.

We both rolled, his legs wrapped around mine, my arms fighting to keep his flailing knife at bay. My head struck metal, and we tumbled toward the open boxcar door. Wind tore through the opening, accompanied by the dim light of a rising moon. I struggled to land on top, but he moved too quickly, forcing me back to the floor with a thud. My shoulder blades collided with the edge of the door frame, my head hanging outside the train as he landed on my stomach.

I saw his face and recognized the semi-olive complexion of one of the guys from the bauxite mines—black haired and brown eyed, his teeth clenched as he growled a curse in another language. The knife appeared in his right hand, point down, driving straight for my throat. I caught that arm with both hands and locked my elbows, forcing the hand back.

The knife dropped two inches, and I gasped for air as his knees squeezed. I wanted to strike his wounded thigh again, but I couldn't afford to release the knife hand. He doubled his grip, using both arms to bear down on me, his eyes blazing with maddened battle rage.

I'd seen it before. I'd felt it before.

I gritted my teeth and forced back. The train jolted hard, crashing over some imperfection in the track. The knife twitched and dropped three inches lower, dangling less than a foot from my face. My constrained lungs struggled for air, and every joint in my arms and shoulders throbbed. The dark boxcar turned steadily darker as my vision began to blur.

The knife fell another inch, and I knew I had lost. All the leverage was on his side. All the benefits of gravity and time were tilted in his favor. I could fight another two or three minutes, but eventually my muscles would give out.

A bloodthirsty grin spread across his face as his brain reached the same conclusion as mine, and he ran his tongue over dry lips.

"*Du-te dracu*," he snarled. The words reminded me of the little girl with the barcode tattoo. And butterfly pants.

The train rattled again, a noticeable shift in the clacking tempo of passing railroad irons ripping through the boxcar. I twisted my face to the right, peering ahead. In the light of the train's headlight, I could see a bridge racing toward us. An old one, built of an iron skeleton suspended over some invisible body of water far below.

I wrenched my head back toward my attacker, the knife dangling only inches above my face, and returned the grin.

"Hey, asshole. You like butterflies?"

Momentary confusion broke across his face. A split-second lapse in focus—just like I had experienced when I saw those clothes. A natural thing.

I detected that skip, and I executed, wrenching my body to the left at the same moment as I completely relinquished any resistance to the incoming knife. The weapon plummeted downward as the guy grunted in surprise, thrown off balance. Cold steel bit my shoulder, the blade narrowly missing my neck as my hands found his belt, and I yanked upward as hard and as fast as I could.

That force, coupled with the momentum of his own pressure on the knife, was too much. He tumbled over my shoulders with a panicked shriek, his arms flailing for purchase and finding nothing outside the boxcar. A split second later, a sickening explosion of flesh and blood blasted back across the boxcar door as his upper body collided with the skeleton structure of the bridge. His feet tore across my stomach and chest as he was ripped through the door—

And then he was gone.

I lay panting on the floor of the car, one hand wrapped around my bleeding shoulder, every part of me feeling like I had just been run over by a steamroller. The hot air blasting through the train door did little to restore oxygen to my deprived lungs, and one side of my face was coated in hot, sticky blood.

But at least I was the one still breathing.

Fighting into a sitting position, I found my flashlight and slouched against the wall, still holding my shoulder. For ten minutes I just sat there, catching my breath, the flashlight fixed on the piles of boxes sitting at the far end of the car.

Realizing that Keen had been right. There was some kind of operation at play here. A human trafficking scheme.

And I had fallen right into the middle of it.

24

I found medical and sewing kits buried in the boxes of clothes at the far end of the car. All the clothes were women's clothes, and they were all small.

Child-sized, just as I thought.

Sitting atop the stacks of water bottles, I held the light in my teeth and conducted the most jacked-up wound stitch of all time. My attacker's knife had sliced straight into the top of my shoulder, someplace between the joint and the base of my neck, leaving a nice gash that looked gnarly, but was mostly a flesh wound. Nothing I would die from, but it still hurt like hell, and it bled profusely. My stitching process was hampered by the frequent necessity to stop and pad the wound with a wadded-up sundress, mopping away the seeping blood until I could at least cover over the stitches with a full-sized bandage.

I would have a scar. A nasty one. But I'd experienced much worse in Afghanistan, and the mouth full of Tylenol tablets I'd swallowed would kick in soon.

After completing the stitching job, I used the flashlight

to search the boxcar. The piles of clothes, medical supplies, and blankets nestled in one end were an obvious indicator of the evil underway, but they told me nothing about the people perpetuating it. I turned to the front of the car instead, deep in the shadows from whence my attacker had lunged with his baseball bat. There was a bedroll there—just a cheap sleeping bag and an inflatable pillow stretched over a foam sleeping mat. I kicked through them both and found nothing, but on my second sweep of the darkness with the LED, I spotted a small sling bag propped up in the corner. It was black, almost invisible against the dark metal. I settled onto the bedroll with a restrained groan and dumped the contents onto the floor.

It was everything a person might carry in their pockets—especially a traveling person. A wad of American dollars, rolled and rubber-banded, a pair of nail clippers, a toothbrush, some coins, a cheap flashlight, a bottle of hand sanitizer...and stuck in the bottom, all by itself, a passport.

I ripped the document out and flipped it over beneath my flashlight. The LED light spilled across a maroon cover inlaid with the golden crest of a bird with two heads, splayed inside a shield. It looked a little medieval, and the script above it was printed in two different languages, the first of which I couldn't read. But the second was English, and that was enough.

Republic of Albania.

I flipped the passport to the ID page and scanned it, still holding the light with my mouth. The black-haired guy I'd just jettisoned out of the boxcar was pictured on the left-hand side of the page. Dark eyes and a cold glare. Alteo Gjoka, apparently. Born in Tirana, thirty-two years prior.

I thumbed through the back pages of the passport, noting Greek, French, and American stamps. Lots of them, in succession. A sort of repeat route, it seemed. Tirana to Athens, Athens to Paris...Paris to Atlanta.

I closed the passport and looked back to the pile of plastic boxes. I thought of the other pale-faced men I had seen alongside Gjoka. More Albanians, presumably. More criminals, apparently in league with the Krols.

But how?

I used Gjoka's bedroll to pad my position against the front of the train and took some time to collect my thoughts. By the time I even considered abandoning the train, it was after nine p.m., and according to my phone's GPS, we were someplace in rural southwest Georgia, a hundred or more miles from Delamar County. I drank water from the stack of bottles, helped myself to a box of crackers and three cans of sausages, then approached the door to look out over rolling wide peanut fields dimly lit by the moonlight. My phone displayed a town up ahead—Camilla, Georgia, barely a dot on the map, but I figured it was a better place to land than a peanut field on the backside of nowhere.

I waited until we were only a half mile out, the train slowing a little and blaring its horn as we approached a railroad crossing; then I took my backpack and Gjoka's passport and dropped into a grassy ditch.

More wrenching pain shot up my spine and through my body as I rolled, but the Tylenol muted most of it. By the time I reached a stop and slowly returned to my feet, groaning the whole way, the tail of the train was clacking by. Another dump car full of cow manure.

Every part of me ached as I reached the road and started to walk, head down, feeling like a complete idiot. Not just for allowing myself to be jumped in the boxcar, but for my moronic decision to investigate the boxcar in the first place. I should have gone straight for the Krol kids. Found myself alone with them someplace in the pines and had a long and productive conversation about that thumb drive.

There was a lot of emotional satisfaction in that fantasy, but I knew it was foolhardy. I could beat the truth out of them, and that would feel good, but it wouldn't lead anywhere. Nothing I discovered would be admissible in court. I'd wind up in jail.

And this depraved thing that was happening right in the middle of nowhere, Alabama, would grind on. I thought about the little girl in her butterfly pants, and red crept into the edges of my vision. It was enough to block out the remainder of my pain and carry me all the way into town.

25

Camilla was a nice enough place. A farming town, I judged. Bigger than Able, but smaller than Muscogee. According to my phone, there were four hotels and one Walmart, open until ten, which gave me just enough time to purchase an ill-fitting change of clothes and more painkillers before staggering to the nearest of the accommodations, a mile away.

The motel was old, worn, and featured a neon sign reading "Vacancy" that was only half illuminated. I paid forty bucks for the night before locking myself into a first-story room and climbing as quickly as possible out of my blood- and manure-soaked clothes. I'd caught plenty of crazy glances from both the Walmart employees and the hotel clerk, but nobody seemed interested in asking questions. They simply wanted to get rid of me as quickly as possible.

I couldn't blame them.

A hot shower and clean pants brought life back to my body, but when I lay down on the sagging bed, I couldn't sleep. Staring at a ceiling discolored by watermarks, I didn't think of the sickening explosion of flesh on steel at the railroad bridge, or of the moment the knife bit my skin, or of the burning driver in the van from two nights previously.

I only thought of the girl in the butterfly pants, and of Delia, and of how the hell the two of them fit together. Keen's theory about human trafficking now felt closer to a reality than a hypothesis, but I couldn't connect the maze of pieces in my mind in any logical way.

Assuming Delia had been the victim of a kidnapping, sucked into an underground world of sex traffickers from Eastern Europe...what the hell was she doing back here after all these years? And why had she run?

Then there was the matter of the boxcar, clearly prepped for human transportation, but empty save for Gjoka and his baseball bat. What was his part in all this? How were the Krol boys involved?

And finally, where did the girl with the butterfly pants fit in?

I knew only two things for certain. First, there *was* a link between Delia and whatever else was going on here. My investigation into Delia's disappearance had earned me an endless stream of aggression and misery. The Krols wanted me gone—permanently. Out of their hair.

I was *asking questions*, Muscle had said. It was *becoming an emergency*, which I construed to mean that my inquiries into Delia somehow threatened the bigger picture.

And the second thing I knew was that I was now working on a deadline. Skinny had claimed this would all be over "Thursday night". Today was Tuesday, and it would be Wednesday in just a couple of hours. That gave me just under two days remaining to make some progress and put my hands on something, or I might well miss the entire thing.

Whatever the *thing* was.

I closed my eyes and lay still until after midnight, but sleep never came. I ached from head to toe, and the mental clutter clogging up my mind kept me charged and agitated. Even when I drove back thoughts of the Krol kids and their victims, I thought of Mia.

The blood splashing across my face from the guy on the train reminded me of the blood draining across the elementary school floor the previous November. It was a gut-wrenching nightmare I very ironically lacked the energy to face.

I gave up any thoughts of sleep at two a.m. and left the hotel, shouldering my backpack and using my phone to chart a course back to Delamar County. It was a hundred miles, mostly rural, and completely desolate at this time of night. A hell of a long way, but I was on a deadline, so I might as well get started.

I walked for an hour before I saw the first car, just enjoying the calm of early morning. Crickets sang. A hot breeze wafted off the peanut fields, carrying the rich scent of dirt and growing things. I saw stars plastered across the inky black sky by the tens of thousands, almost as bright as the Arizona desert sky.

Maybe Rakow was right, I thought. Maybe I was jacked up. Eight months ago, I'd had a job, a mortgage, a retirement account. I'd watched football and drank beers with friends. I'd dreamed of a bigger house out in the desert. A new four-wheel drive, and maybe a dog.

Now I was walking alone in the middle of nowhere, a few bucks in my pocket, some spare water in the backpack.

Because none of those things really mattered without Mia. At least out here, alone in South Georgia, I felt a little peace.

At three thirty headlights blazed across my back, and I turned to see a semitruck chugging toward me, a lone light on the desolate state highway. I held out a thumb, and to my surprise, the guy slowed to a stop. It was a day cab hooked to a milk trailer, and I walked around to the driver's side to find a happy-looking old-timer with an Atlanta Braves baseball hat and a handlebar mustache smiling down at me.

"You lost, brother?"

"Is anyone found?" I asked.

He laughed at that and said he was headed to Montgomery for an early morning delivery. I asked if he would be passing near Muscogee. He said he'd be passing right through it, and jabbed a thumb at the passenger seat.

"I didn't know truckers were allowed to pick up hitchhikers," I said as I settled into a sagging leather seat, kicking aside Yoo-hoo bottles and empty cigarette packs.

The old-timer slapped his gear shift into first, and the truck lurched forward.

"Owner-operator," he said. "I'm allowed to do whatever I want."

We spent the next hour and a half swapping war stories. His name was Chuck, and he was an Army vet also, but didn't enjoy talking about it. He'd rather talk about baseball.

Lots and lots of baseball.

I relaxed in the seat and enjoyed his monologue punctuated by chain smoking and the thunder of wind through his half-open window. By the time we reached Muscogee, I knew more about the Atlanta Braves than their own general manager, and I couldn't help hoping they won it all that year.

Chuck dropped me off downtown, not far from the

Crawfords' residence, and I shot him a wave and a "Go Braves!" as he chugged out. Then I turned away from downtown and followed my phone's navigation toward the two-lane highway running twenty-two miles across desolate Delamar County into the little town of Able.

I made it maybe five miles before headlights broke across my back, and I turned toward a pale gray sky to see a gunmetal gray Dodge pickup bearing toward me. It was brand new, mounted on elevated suspension, the headlights blacked out, a brush guard equipped with additional lights. Also blacked out. Dual axles, one-ton chassis, diesel engine.

It was a gorgeous rig, but the sight of it somehow put me on edge. I stepped off the road and kept my hands down, ready to let it pass as thoughts of the Krol boys and their polished Raptor blinked through my mind. Maybe the Raptor belonged to Muscle.

Maybe Skinny liked a Dodge.

The truck slowed as it approached, then stopped twenty yards away. The high beams flashed on, even though the sky was rapidly brightening, and I shielded my face.

I didn't have the knife any longer. I'd lost it on the train. Maybe Gjoka had carried it with him onto the bridge.

Good riddance.

The high beams flicked off, and the diesel growled. I took another step off the road and braced myself, ready for whatever. The Dodge rolled up next to me, and the passenger window hissed down.

It was Owen. Rakow's chief deputy sat perched high above me behind the wheel, chewing slowly on a wad of tobacco as his gray eyes swept me head to toe. He didn't say anything, and neither did I.

"I thought the sheriff told you to move along," he

drawled finally.

I shrugged. "Free country."

"What are you doin'?"

"Walking."

He rolled his eyes. "Where *to*?"

"Able."

"Where's your old truck?"

"Able."

It wasn't strictly true. My truck was still parked outside the Krol compound—assuming it hadn't been discovered and towed. But the last person I wanted to explain that to was a local cop.

Owen regarded me for another long moment, chewing on his tobacco and spitting into an empty soda bottle. Then he jabbed his chin toward the passenger seat.

"Hop in. I'll give you a ride."

I glanced back down the highway toward Muscogee. There were no other cars topping the low hill. No other motors growling over the soft breeze. My feet hurt, and my shoulder ached like hell, and it was still thirty-plus miles back to my truck.

I reached for the door handle, kicking aside thick red clay on the running board as I hauled myself aboard the elevated truck. The cabin was spotlessly clean, fresh leather greeting my tired back as I slid the backpack off and rested it on the floorboard. Owen dropped his foot off the brake, and the diesel chugged. I shifted my feet self-consciously, hyper-aware of the bloodstains saturating my boots. At least the sticky red clay from Owen's running boards helped to mask them.

"Sheriff tells me you used to be a cop," Owen said, spitting into his bottle.

"That's right."

"But not no more."

"No."

Owen nodded slowly, rotating the bottle in his hands. When he next spoke, his voice had softened considerably.

"I lost my Rosie four years ago...breast cancer. Took her quick." He faced me. "I'm sorry."

Deep pain radiated in his eyes, and I wondered what news story he had read. The Phoenix school shooting was a publicized event, reported on by media outlets across the southwest region. Not a difficult thing to find if you knew how to Google.

"So am I," I said.

Owen faced the road again, leaned back with one hand riding the top of the wheel. He spat again.

"I feel obligated to warn you, Sharpe. Sheriff ain't gonna appreciate you turning up again. He was pretty clear when he told you to move along."

"He's welcome to arrest me," I said.

Owen snorted. "Apparently those retards you pounded ain't pressing charges. Not a lot he could arrest you for, short of vagrancy."

"It's a free country," I said again.

Owen nodded slowly, running a finger behind his teeth and prying out a chunk of tobacco. He sucked the finger clean, and we didn't speak again until rolling into downtown Able. I had him drop me at the General Store Restaurant, making up a story about my truck being parked nearby, and then I marched straight in and ordered the biscuits and gravy with eggs and bacon.

I gave Rakow ten minutes to turn up.

He showed in five.

26

Rakow stormed in just as I was cutting into my first bite of biscuit saturated in thick gravy with a chunk of sausage mixed in. He stopped by the end of my table and stood rigid and silent while I chewed slowly, completely ignoring him. The diner had been open for thirty minutes, and thus far, I was the only patron.

Rakow rested one hand on his service pistol, the other semi-clenched at his side, and when I moved for a second bite, he spoke in a low growl.

"I thought I told you to clear out."

I took my time in answering, chewing slowly. Savoring the rich flavor moderated by the flaky texture of the biscuit. They say the South boasts some of the nation's best cuisine, and so far, I couldn't disagree. Southern people liked a lot of rich flavors. A lot of oil, and a lot of grease.

And they absolutely knew what they were doing with both.

"Are you deaf, Sharpe?"

I looked up, still chewing. I swallowed and wiped my mouth.

"You don't own the county, Rakow."

Rakow's face twisted into a series of angry, exhausted lines. He looked like he hadn't slept in a couple of days—which I could identify with—and it left me wondering if he was simply venting frustration on me.

It hadn't been a great week.

"I don't have to own it," Rakow snapped. "I just have to keep the riffraff out. Now get up. You're going."

I cut off another forkful of biscuit, daring him to put his hands on me. Knowing he wouldn't. There still wasn't anybody else in the diner, but we were drawing the eyes of the cooks from behind the long counter. Cop or no cop, I don't respond well to being manhandled.

Rakow leaned down, speaking through gritted teeth. "I don't have time for your antics. There have been complaints. People don't want you here."

"Let me guess," I said. "The Krols?"

A hint of surprise flashed across Rakow's face, come and gone like a bolt of lightning. But it was there.

"It doesn't matter who," Rakow said. "I'm the sheriff. It's my job to keep the streets clean."

"I'm not pissing on your streets, Rakow. But somebody is. If you gave me five minutes, I could tell you all about it."

Another pause. Another flash of curiosity, or maybe indecision. Then Rakow's phone chimed from the belt holster mounted next to his gun, and he slid it out without breaking eye contact.

When he looked to the screen, the wrinkle of his brow shifted. Just before he flicked the answer button, he shot me a glare.

“We’re not done.”

He retreated across the room, lifting the phone to one ear. “Sheriff.”

Rakow stepped out of earshot, and I resumed my focus on my breakfast plate. Three cups of black coffee and the heavy recharge of protein and carbohydrates did their best to drive back my exhaustion, but it was the mental workout that really kept me awake.

I was thinking again about the Krol boys and where I could find them alone. I still didn’t have quite enough evidence to justify an interrogation—at least, not my style of interrogation—but I was getting close. The train proved my theory of distribution. The Krols’ association was clear.

But despite the girl in the butterfly pants, there really wasn’t anything to prove sex trafficking. Maybe there were images on the flash drive. Other girls with barcode tattoos, and perhaps an image with one of the Krol boys visible.

But at best, that would prove rape or child pornography. Serious charges, but not the heart of this problem. And anyway, I wasn’t about to review that flash drive. Just thinking about it made me sick.

Rakow’s boots thumped across the hardwood, and I braced myself for another confrontation. Two days ago, prior to the beatdown with those meatheads in the woods, I might have shared what I knew with him. Now I wasn’t sure if he would believe me.

“Come on,” Rakow said, dropping a twenty on the table. “We’re going.”

I looked up. Something in his tone had changed. The aggression was gone, and a dull undercurrent of strain had taken its place. He looked gray in the face, and he was fixated on his phone, typing a text message or maybe an email.

"Problems?" I asked.

"You could say that." He holstered the phone without comment and turned for the door. I hesitated over my empty plate, my mind racing through all the things that phone call could have meant.

Had they found my truck? The hole in the fence?

Or what about the dead guy at the railroad bridge? He probably looked like hamburger meat after exploding against the superstructure, but there was still a chance the engineer of the next train had stopped to inspect the body.

And then what? An arrest?

But no. Rakow was already outside, riding the running board of his massive Ford, beckoning me on. This wasn't an arrest.

So...

I left Rakow's twenty for the meal and found him outside, the Ford's diesel growling. He shot a thumb at the passenger seat, and I tossed my backpack onto the floorboard as I climbed in, still a little hesitant, but figuring I could deal with almost anything so long as I wasn't handcuffed.

"What's up?" I asked.

Rakow backed the truck into the street, then shifted into drive, punching the gas. The diesel surged, and we hurtled around the square with the soldier on the pedestal, quickly finding the road leading out of town.

Back toward Muscogee.

"Stewart County Sheriff called to report a body in Providence Canyon," Rakow said.

"Nearby?"

"It's in Georgia, about an hour away."

"Is he in the habit of advising you about dead bodies in his county?"

Rakow shot me a sideways look. "He is when they're young women...with different-colored eyes."

My stomach turned cold, and I felt a chill rush up my spine. Rakow pushed the truck to seventy and settled into the seat.

"I guess I'll have to run you off later, Sharpe. We may have use for you yet."

27

Rakow wasn't in a talkative mood on the way into Georgia, so I used my phone to look up Providence Canyon. It was actually a state park, and it sat just on the Georgia side of the state line, north and east of Muscogee. The park website proudly declared the site as "Georgia's Little Grand Canyon", and discussed how the deep, winding gullies were developed during the nineteenth century as the result of reckless agricultural practices—water runoff, I guessed. Rampant, unmanaged erosion.

Now the thousand-acre site had become a popular photography and tourist attraction, deeply wooded like most of the region, frequented by motorists and hikers. There was a parking lot with an overlook just off the two-lane state highway that fed the park, and when Rakow pulled his F-250 across the gravel, I noted two Stewart County Sheriff's Department Tahoes already parked there, with a third pickup truck towing a long, enclosed trailer nearby. The rear door of the trailer lay open, with a couple of large ATVs sitting in the dust just outside.

There were three cops—a woman working a radio, another deputy fueling an ATV from a gas can, and a short and stocky guy with bulging shoulders waiting near the trailer, smoking a cigarette. He had silver gray hair and a full beard. Maybe late fifties, in good shape, with a commanding air about him.

Rakow piled out without comment, and I joined him. The short guy met us at the nose of Rakow's truck, extending a hand.

"Hey, Don," Rakow said.

"Rakow." Don spoke with a gravelly smoker's growl, his voice toneless. The two men shook hands, Rakow towering over him like a skyscraper; then the sheriff turned to me.

"Who's he?"

"Sharpe," Rakow said, jabbing a finger. "He's here to identify the body."

I gathered that Rakow had already filled the sheriff in on the car wreck, and offered my hand. Don shook it once with a firm but somehow disinterested grip, then turned back to Rakow.

"Girl's in the bottom of the canyon, near the back. You'll want a ride."

He led the way toward the pair of ATVs, taking one himself while Rakow swung aboard the second, and I awkwardly clambered on behind him, gripping the rear cargo rack instead of his waist.

The engines fired up with rapid snarls, and Stewart County's sheriff led the way past a fence post entrance wrapped in crime tape, onto a packed clay trail that disappeared into the woods. As we passed the visitors' center, I noted the canyon stretching out to my left. I could only see part of it, but what I saw was breathtaking. Rolling miles of

Georgia foothills stretched to the horizon, all topped with deep green pines and leafy hardwoods, while the canyon itself lay just beyond a split-rail fence. I saw the top of sandy red ridges rising irregularly amid gullies and ripping wide trenches, but I couldn't see the floor of the canyon. The trail we rumbled down was quickly swallowed by trees, switchbacking on itself multiple times as the stocky sheriff led the way right to the bottom.

I relaxed into the ride, and for the first time since leaving Able, I considered whether Delia really lay on the sandy bottom of this park. After the incident with the girl in Palmer's barn, I felt skeptical by default of any reports of a girl with different-colored eyes. But Palmer was a crazy old coot, not law enforcement. If the local sheriff said the woman had eyes of two different colors, that report probably carried water.

Rakow certainly thought so. He'd driven all this way without even asking for photographs. But how many people could there be in a sixty-mile radius with heterochromatic eyes? I'd spent my entire life never encountering the phenomenon prior to the car wreck of two nights previously.

Something in my gut felt off. Like this situation was wrong, somehow.

We reached the floor of the canyon, and the sheriff accelerated through a shallow creek, splashing sand and water as he hurtled along. All around us, tall, skinny trees reached for the sky, hampered by the red clay of the canyon walls. Those walls soared a hundred feet or more, twisting like a maze as the trail wound deeper into the park. The soft soil kicked up by the aggressive tread of the ATVs made it easy for me to understand how erosion had so quickly crafted this geological masterpiece.

I had learned the hard way that life was like that. Big changes happened quickly.

And they always leave a mark.

The sheriff stopped at a yellow crime tape perimeter, where a third ATV and a two-seater utility vehicle were parked. The UTV was labeled with white letters: Property of Stewart County Coroner. It made me wonder how rural Stewart County was, and how often that UTV had been used to retrieve a body from deep in the Georgia sticks.

I piled off the ATV alongside Rakow, and the two of us followed the sheriff beneath the crime tape. The mucky slog of another creek bed left me grateful to still be wearing my hiking boots. They were getting a workout this summer.

A trio of small pines blocked our view of the crime scene, but I could see another deputy and the coroner crouched next to something on the ground. Don raised a hand for us to stop as he held a quick conference with the deputy. The coroner blocked my view of the body.

"Backwoods campers found her early this morning," the sheriff said. "Body was cold, but rigor mortis hadn't set in. Blunt force trauma to the skull. No ID yet."

He spoke with the clinical efficiency of a man who had conducted these sorts of investigations many times before, but there was an undercurrent of regret in his voice. As if it never got easier.

The coroner straightened, still blocking the body, and peeled his gloves off. He was middle aged and wore glasses and a protective white poncho. He looked very professional.

"The blunt force trauma killed her," he pronounced. "I'll conduct a more thorough inspection at the morgue, but based on my initial assessment, I'd say she was struck with a heavy metal object. Flecks of black paint in her hair. Definite skull fractures. A baseball bat, maybe."

"Baseball bat?" I said.

The coroner blinked at me. "Right. A metal one, likely."

"May we have a look?" Rakow said.

The coroner stepped aside. "Be my guest. Just don't touch."

Rakow moved in first, and I circled right. Then I saw her.

She was mid-twenties, with a cloud of dirty blonde hair. Five feet four, maybe five feet five. Not skinny, but not fat either. Small feet. Dirty jeans and a torn white blouse with a flower pattern embroidered on the hem.

A very nice face, were it not traumatized by fear. Her lips were parted, her eyes frozen open. Complete terror shining from one bright blue eye...and one deep brown.

But it wasn't the woman I'd seen at the wreck. It wasn't Delia.

"It's not her," I said simply.

Rakow met my gaze, his tired face twisted into a frown. "You sure?"

"Positive. The woman I saw was smaller than this. Very petite. Narrower features. And brighter hair."

Rakow's shoulders dipped, and he swept his hat off, running a hand across his sweaty forehead. I noticed streaks of gray near his temples and wondered if days like this had gifted them to him.

Rakow replaced the hat and spoke softly. "You were tired. It was a quick look. Are you *certain* this wasn't her?"

I moved carefully around the woman's feet, then crouched near her face. Studying closely, but not touching her.

"I know what I saw, Rakow. I'm not an idiot. This isn't her."

Rakow muttered an irritated curse and stepped away to consult with the sheriff. I focused on the body, looking into her wide and panicked eyes.

Something felt wrong. I couldn't put my finger on it, but something about her desperate stare didn't feel…real. The brown eye was misted, a little foggy with death. The blue remained brilliant and bright, reflecting the sunlight streaming into the canyon, even though it should have been dry by now.

I reached out and gently laid a finger just beneath her left eye socket. My fingertip touched cold flesh, and it sent a chill up my spine as I placed my thumb just above her eye and pinched softly.

"Hey!" the coroner shouted. "I told you not to touch!"

I ignored him, pinching a little harder. And then the contact lens popped into my hand, exposing a milky, deep brown eye beneath it. The lens hit my palm, and I rolled it over once, mind spinning. Then my gaze ratcheted up the canyon walls, beyond the pines, toward the ridge a hundred and fifty feet overhead. I saw the glint of gleaming glass in the noonday sun, just a flash, gone in an instant, and I lurched to my feet.

"On the ridge! *Go!*"

28

The glint on the ridge vanished almost as quickly as it appeared. But I knew what it was. There wasn't a doubt in my mind.

Without waiting for permission or assistance from the knot of cops and the very pissed-off coroner, I raced to the nearest ATV and hit the starter switch. All four tires spun, kicking up clay and sand before I spun the vehicle around and raced back up the trail—four times as fast as we'd come down it. Roaring along like Rakow on a back country road.

By the time I reached the switchback trail and was hurtling back to the top of the gulley, I had decided two things about the glint on the ridge. It was a spotting scope, not a rifle scope. And the man behind it had entered the park on foot, probably sneaking in across the fence from a remote point somewhere alongside the highway and stalking his way to the overwatch position above the crime scene. Stewart County deputies had already sealed off the park and blocked all entrances.

It was the only thing that made sense.

At the top of the trail I gunned the engine, vaguely conscious of another ATV roaring in behind me. Rakow, probably. Maybe he'd finally learned to trust my instincts.

I ballparked the distance from the bottom of the switchback to the crime scene and replicated that trek along the ridge line trail. Without any landmarks to guide my path, it was impossible to know when to stop the ATV, but I went with my gut and killed the engine. The vehicle slid to a stop in the damp mud, and I didn't move.

I just listened, blocking out the noise of Rakow's approach and focusing on the forest ahead. A field of quiet trees, damp with morning dew. Very still and bereft of wildlife. A perfect place to hide, so long as you didn't move.

But the guy did move. I detected the rhythmic crashing sound from eighty or a hundred yards ahead. Crunching footfalls pounding through leaves and pine needles at a mad-dash pace. I hit the starter switch and turned in the direction of the noise, instantaneously deafened again by the sound of my own engine.

Leaves and sticks exploded around me as I left the trail. The big tires caught the loamy floor of the forest and sent shockwaves up my spine as I hurtled over a small fallen log. I thought I saw a flash up ahead—an irregular splash of color that contradicted nature. Something man-made.

I focused on the spot and mashed the accelerator. I was now far beyond the crime scene. I was sure of it. I was driving my prey like a sheepdog driving sheep. Hurtling ahead all loud and aggressive, forcing them to flee.

But with only skinny trees to hide behind, a wall of Stewart County deputies on one side and a sheer, one-hundred-fifty-foot drop on the other, this particular sheep was running out of places to shelter. All I had to do was avoid passing him, and time would be on my side.

I slowed a little, then ground to a stop and hit the kill switch again. Behind me, Rakow's ATV had also fallen silent, and he shouted angry curses at my back.

I ignored him and focused on the forest ahead. The woods felt suddenly very calm, only the cooling tick of the overworked ATV and my own heartbeat to break the stillness.

But I knew I wasn't alone. I could feel it, the same way I used to feel a Taliban fighter on the loose, stalking me in those godforsaken Afghan mountains.

A stick snapped to my left, loud as a gunshot. My thumb slid directly from the starter switch to the accelerator, and the ATV rocketed forward. I saw a flash of orange from behind a skinny hardwood. A human body, just a little too wide for the tree. I hurtled through a low thicket, sticks and leaves exploding over the brush guard, and closed straight for the tree.

I saw the bent branch only a millisecond before my quarry released it. It was stretched backward around a tree —not very thick, and not very long.

But long enough.

I ducked my head and clamped on the handbrake. The limb snapped over my back, and the red flash moved to my right. The ATV's tires locked, and I felt the back end fishtail around.

Then I looked ahead and completely forgot about my prey. The canyon rim raced toward me, not ten feet away, shielded by only a thin line of brush. Even as the tires locked and the back end swung loose, I knew I'd never stop in time.

The brakes were shot. Almost useless. I released the handlebars instead and flung myself off the left side.

The hot body of the ATV vanished from beneath me, but the toe of my hiking boot caught on the rear cargo rack, tugging me another yard forward as the ATV hurtled over the edge and vanished into the canyon.

My foot broke free, but my body kept moving. Sliding over leaf and loam, my fingers thrashed frantically for the low brush as my legs cleared the edge. Loose clay crumbled beneath me, and my body began to drop. I caught the gnarled base of a twisted bush and sank my fingers in, my waist clearing the edge.

My left arm clawed at the forest floor as the bulk of my body weight descended on my right. I felt the roots of the bush begin to loosen, tearing free of the rain-softened soil.

And then I saw him. He stepped out of the trees just a few feet ahead, dressed in a camouflage hunting jacket with an orange interior. The jacket was unzipped, and the interior rippled as he moved. A short guy with pitch-black hair and dark eyes, tattoos rippling up his neck.

He fast-walked toward me with a heavy stick clenched in one hand like a club. I sank my fingers into the dirt and made one last, frantic attempt to haul myself back onto solid ground. To reach some sort of fighting stance before he closed on me.

It was useless. The roots tore free, and my body slipped another six inches. The dark-eyed guy closed another yard, raising the club. Ready to finish the job.

Then a gunshot cracked through the forest stillness, and the man dropped like a falling log. Rakow appeared behind him, jogging with his service pistol riding at his side, gun smoke wafting through the thick Georgian air.

He had the good sense to stop at the body first, although I wouldn't have credited him with it. After checking to ensure the man was down, he holstered the gun and raced to the ledge.

The last of the roots were just giving way when he reached me. One powerful hand wrapped around my free arm, and he tugged me upward. Clay and sand crumbled beneath my chest before my stomach crossed onto solid ground.

I lay in the loam, gasping for breath, muscles I didn't even know I had shooting into fresh spasms. Part of me wondered if I would have been better off simply letting go and hoping to ride the curving wall of the canyon to a semi-safe landing.

I rolled over, still breathing hard as I stared into a clear blue sky. Rakow stood over me, one hand on his gun, his face gray and cold.

"Damn you, Sharpe. Damn you."

29

I was invited to spend the remainder of Rakow's visit waiting in his truck. He didn't handcuff me, but I thought he wanted to. All the Stewart County deputies rushed to address the latest development at the top of the canyon, and with the window down, it wasn't difficult to hear Don dog-cussing Rakow before summarily directing him to leave Georgia—and not come back.

Rakow would come back, of course. There would be an investigation. All kinds of paperwork, and maybe a consultation with the district attorney, and probably some fuss by whatever local media served this part of the state. But Rakow wouldn't face any real consequences for two reasons. First, and most importantly, the shooting was about as justified as a shooting could be. Aside from me, there had been two Stewart County deputies on Rakow's heels who would testify as much.

And second, the dead man with the dark eyes wasn't a local resident. He wasn't even American. I knew that without needing to check his pockets for ID or refer his fingerprints to the FBI. There would be no local family to mourn his loss. No outraged relatives eager to see Rakow burned at the stake for doing his job. The dead man would be listed on the autopsy as "John Doe", and he'd likely be cremated as the same.

Rakow returned to the truck an hour later, slamming the door and firing up the engine but not saying anything for a full minute. Then he yanked the shift lever into reverse and shook his head.

"Damn you," he said again. "I've never wanted to murder somebody so bad in my life."

The monster Ford kicked up gravel on our way back to the highway, and I gave Rakow fifteen minutes to calm down. In my experience, that's about as long as it takes for a resting person to chill out. If they're still angry after fifteen minutes, they're probably going to stay angry for the foreseeable future.

"Did you check his pockets?" I asked.

Rakow snorted. "Are you seriously asking me that?"

"I am."

"Well, you know what? I'm not answering. Because your participation in this investigation has come to an end, Mr. Sharpe. The moment we get back to Able, I want your ass behind the wheel of that junker truck of yours, driving *out* of my county, or I swear to God, I will *bury* you under a pine tree. Am I clear?"

There was a lot of angst in Rakow's tone, but the rage had subsided. He was a rational man. Rational enough to know that, however infuriating my actions might have been, there was something much bigger at play here.

It was that knowledge that was really pushing him over the edge.

"There was nothing in his pockets," I said.

Rakow didn't answer, but his lip twitched.

I leaned back in my seat. "Maybe some chewing gum. But no ID. No wallet. And when you run his prints, you won't find anything, either."

I gave him a few seconds to ask, and he didn't.

"Want to know why?" I prompted.

His knuckles turned white around the steering wheel. He was driving like a bat out of hell again, but I was starting to become used to it.

"Why?" he growled at last.

"Because he's not an American. He came here under the radar, probably arriving within the past week. He could have carried a fake ID, but he didn't, because it's actually a lot easier to fly under the radar without one. I mean, what's a cop gonna do if you don't have an ID? He's going to believe whatever you tell him. Because he has no choice. It's not a crime to not carry an ID. So he left his passport with his luggage, wherever he was staying."

Rakow thought about that for a beat, then shook his head. "You're out of your depth, Sharpe. For all we know, I just shot the governor's illegitimate, coke-headed love child."

"You didn't. You shot an Eastern European. Probably an Albanian. And he wasn't a coke head. He was a child trafficker."

That got his attention. Rakow turned from the road and faced me longer than I was comfortable with at our current rate of speed. I knew he wanted to ask, and I decided to cut him a break and not draw it out any longer.

I began with the bar, telling the story he never wanted to hear about how Sadie had lured me into the woods, where the Krol boys had turned up. I didn't know if he believed me now, but I didn't care. I proceeded right down the line to my conversation with Keen, my eavesdropping at the Krol compound, my train ride from hell, and my return to Delamar County.

The only two points I left out were the flash drive—because I had already destroyed it—and Gjoka, the obliterated Albanian. Because telling Rakow about Gjoka wouldn't advance the investigation, but it might well take me out of it, and for that matter, it might land me in jail. I felt zero guilt or culpability in the Albanian's death. He'd come at me with a baseball bat. I'd thrown him into a bridge.

These things happen.

But even after trimming out the more colorful segments of my last forty-eight hours, the disbelief and outrage boiling beneath the surface of Rakow's tense demeanor intensified to nuclear levels. I noticed a particularly sharp spike when I mentioned my intrusion into the Krol compound, followed by my illegal ride on the train.

"I can't *believe* you," he snapped. "Do you have any idea the position this puts me in? The Krols are prominent citizens, Sharpe. Taxpayers. *Voters*. And they have very deep pockets."

"You ever wonder how they got those pockets?" I asked.

"From bauxite! Or from a pot of gold at the end of a rainbow. Who the hell cares? You can't assume just because a person is rich, they are capable of—"

"Trafficking children?" I cut him off. "Participating in an international slave trade? In pedophilia? Oh, but I *do* assume, Rakow. Not because they're rich. Because I followed the evidence. Did you not hear me about the boxcar? It was full of food, clothes, and medicine. Headed for the coast, I'm guessing. Which could mean it was headed to pick up a new load of children and bring them right back to Delamar."

"You can't be serious. There's zero evidence to support that theory."

"There's nothing *but* evidence to support that theory. Use your head, Rakow. Delia Crawford goes missing for over a decade. Let's say, just for conversation's sake, that she was kidnapped by child traffickers."

"That theory never held water."

I held up a hand. "Let's just *say*, Rakow. She was kidnapped by a trafficking ring. Young, pretty girl. Blonde hair and heterochromatic eyes. That's got to be some kind of commodity, right? So she's kidnapped, and now she's back."

"We don't know that."

"Maybe you don't know that. I saw her. She's back in Delamar County, and that's clearly set off some kind of ruckus. Everything that's happened since the car wreck proves that point beyond a doubt—these people *do not* want an investigation into Delia. They'll shut it down by any means necessary."

Rakow thought about that, lips pinched. "Explain," he said at last.

"Well, first thing they had to do is get rid of the lone witness. That's me. There must have been some kind of internal chatter about it, and at some point, the Krol kids took the initiative. They came up with an elaborate plan to use one local skank and two local mud brains to set me up and run me out. They didn't figure on me pounding their guys into near oblivion, but even when I did, those boys didn't press charges. Because charges would have kept me in town. They wanted me *gone*, and gone in a way that discredited me with the local sheriff. That being *you*."

Rakow said nothing. I continued.

"The problem, of course, is that I still told you what I told you about Delia and the van. You might not trust me anymore, after the deal with Sadie, but you still might wonder about what I said about her eyes. And you still might have Delia's parents on your back, pushing you for an investigation. The Krols had to derail that possibility, proactively. The old man said he was going to handle it *the smart way,* which leads us to the body in the canyon."

"What do you mean?"

"It's a shell game. They kill a blonde woman, put one blue contact in her eye, then dump her in that canyon. Someplace where the body was guaranteed to be discovered, but secluded enough to provide their man with an overwatch so he could confirm that the ploy was successful. You arrive, inspect the body, find the contact lens, and you assume this Jane Doe is the woman I saw at the wreck. Not Delia Crawford. Delia Crawford is still missing, probably dead. So Stewart County investigates this new victim and probably finds nothing. Either way, you're no longer looking into Delia, and I'm long gone. It's a pretty effective strategy, honestly. Except they didn't bet on me coming back, and they didn't bet on you shooting their lookout."

Rakow processed that for a mile. I could almost see the wheels turning in his mind. Computing. Calculating. Looking for obvious holes in my theory and finding none.

Yes, there were a few assumptions. But the logic was sound.

"You worked all this out in the bottom of the canyon?" he asked.

"Pretty much. It was the contact lens that brought everything into focus—no pun intended. It was a smart idea.

Stewart County will probably identify the woman as a prostitute. Maybe from Atlanta. They'll write off the lens as part of a pair. She probably lost the other one. Who knows why she wandered into the canyon? The case will hit a dead end and then turn cold. Because that's what happens with dead prostitutes, like it or not."

Rakow knew I was right. He moved directly to the next question in an obvious sequence.

"What about the girl with the barcode tattoo?"

I settled into my seat, tapping the armrest. And thinking.

"I'm not sure," I said at last. "Has anybody talked to her?"

He shook his head. "She's in Montgomery, but she's clammed up. Won't say a thing. The FBI attempted an interview and got nowhere."

"But they confirmed what I said about the tattoo?" I prompted.

Rakow sucked his teeth, looking irritable. Like I'd caught him in a corner, and he didn't want to admit it.

"They recognize the mark," he said at last.

"And?"

"And it belongs to an East European trafficking gang... headquartered in Albania."

30

We didn't speak again until we reached Delamar County, but I could feel Rakow calming as I directed him to my parked truck. It sat right where I'd left it, two hundred yards from the Krol compound fence, as yet unmolested.

Rakow stopped on the county road and peered up the short dirt drive to the GMC, his lips pursed. I reached for the door, and he held up a hand.

"Wait."

I stopped. Rakow took his time, surveying the trees. Looking pissed. But focused.

"Did they see you?" he said.

"Who?"

"*The Krols*. Who do you think?"

"No."

"You're sure?"

"One hundred percent."

Rakow nodded slowly, drumming his finger on his steering wheel, staring off into the pines as though the secret of the universe lay hidden somewhere amid the tangled thickets of briars and rotting needles. I relaxed in the seat, waiting patiently. Knowing that there was only one place his thought train could lead.

"I need time," he said at last.

"You haven't got time," I said. "There's something at play here. Something big, and something soon. It's the only rational explanation for all the reckless attempts to derail your investigations. If you don't move soon—"

"I hear you!" Rakow snapped like an overstretched rubber band finally reaching its limit. "You think I'm an idiot? I've got half a dozen state investigators crawling up my ass, the FBI on the phone, a mute foreign girl who won't talk to anyone, and some PTSD-ridden Army vet crashing around my county like a bull in a China shop. *I know* what my problems are!"

He finished the tirade red-faced, and our gazes met. I said nothing, and he looked quickly away, closing his eyes and drawing a long breath. I gave him time.

"I'm sorry," he said at last. "You didn't deserve that."

"You looked me up, didn't you?" I said evenly. I already knew he had. If Owen had read about Mia, it was certain that his boss had also.

Rakow looked out the window, still grinding his thumb into the leather-wrapped steering wheel.

"I'm sorry," he said simply.

He didn't need to apologize, but I appreciated it. I waited another couple of minutes for him to calm; then Rakow swept his hat off and ran his hand through dirty hair. He sighed.

"Look. We aren't gonna solve this thing today. I've got to get back to the station and get control of these state people before they burn the county down. And then I've got to deal with Don about that guy I shot. But we need to talk about this. I need to get a handle on what you know. Do you remember how to get to my place?"

I hesitated. Then shrugged. "I guess."

"There's a key under the flowerpot next to the door. Let yourself in and get some rest. I'll be back this evening, and we'll throw some steaks on the grill and start again...from the top."

Again, I hesitated. Part of me wanted to refuse his offer. To dive straight back into my investigation, drive over to the Krol place, and conduct a little interrogation.

But I was dog tired. The sleepless night in South Georgia was catching up with me, as were my injuries. My body felt run over by a bulldozer, and despite the surges of adrenaline that had kept me running, my brain was beginning to fog. A few hours of rest might be the only path forward.

"Okay," I said. "Meet at your place."

I let myself out, and he gave me another reserved nod. Then the Ford roared back up the road, hurtling toward Able.

My shoulders dropped as a wave of exhaustion toppled over my body like a tidal wave. I suddenly wondered if I could make it back to Rakow's place. Maybe I'd be better off inflating my air mattress and sleeping right here amid the pines.

Turning back up the drive, I navigated ten feet toward my truck. Then I stopped. I stared at the soft soil between my hiking boots.

A fresh pair of tire tracks lay pressed into the mud, just a little wider than the tires of my GMC. I crouched with a restrained grunt and examined the shallow tread marks.

Truck tires, certainly. Or a heavy SUV. I could tell by the smooth valley carved on one side of the track that at least one of the driver's side tires was balding—probably the front one. Probably out of alignment.

I stood and approached my truck cautiously. I peered around the clearing, noting the point where the tire marks disappeared over green grass, maybe twenty feet behind my rear bumper. I could see where the grass had been crushed and torn by a vehicle turning in place.

But no additional vehicle sat in the clearing. Only my rusty green GMC.

A quick inspection of the cargo bed and cab revealed nothing missing, and nothing tampered with. I had left the truck unlocked, but there was no indicator that anyone had entered it. All my bags piled up on the passenger side of the bench seat remained unmolested.

I frowned and looked back up the drive, toward the road. The Krol kids?

No. They would have sacked the truck. Maybe towed it. And anyway, their Raptor was far too new to have a balding tire.

Maybe it had been a cop. Or a local landowner. A lookie-loo, maybe?

I wasn't sure. But I did know that my brain was now far too tired to worry about it.

Climbing back into the GMC, I started it up and conducted my own U-turn back onto the county road before navigating for Rakow's place.

31

I slept like a corpse for the remainder of the day, only waking sometime after dark to the sound of metal clanging on metal in Rakow's kitchen. Rolling to put my feet on the floor, I gritted my teeth as sudden pain ripped down my body like a bolt of lightning.

I was beyond sore. I was almost rigid. It felt like every muscle in my body had been ripped and frayed, now only a slight tug away from snapping altogether and leaving me to dissolve into a puddle of goo.

My knife fight on the train, followed by my near-death experience at the canyon, was costing me. Or, more accurately, my relaxed lifestyle sleeping in the bed of my truck, exercising rarely and growing soft was costing me.

Another clang from the kitchen was followed by the soft, melodic voice of a woman singing. I stiffened, surprised by the tone, and twisted toward the bedroom door. The voice continued, right on tune, not the best I'd ever heard, but certainly one of the best. Some country song I recognized, but couldn't quite name.

I hauled myself out of bed and staggered to the door. I knew I would limber up in time, but I couldn't imagine running or jumping in the foreseeable future. Maybe I was getting old. Stuff like this didn't used to knock me out so badly. With thirty just around the corner, my body was slowing a little.

Down the hall, I walked softly toward the kitchen, padding on my socked feet, not really caring that I looked like the hobo Skinny had labeled me. Stopping at the end of the hall, I wasn't surprised to see Bailey from Bailey's bar standing in the kitchen, still singing softly as she arranged rib eyes in a tray full of marinade.

Three of them. Nice and thick. My stomach growled loud enough to wake the dead, and Bailey stopped singing abruptly, looking over one shoulder.

"Well, howdy, stranger. You sleep well?"

I looked for Rakow in the adjoining living room, then through the kitchen window to the front porch. I didn't see him.

"Luke will be along shortly," Bailey said. "State people are keeping him late. You like steak, right?"

I nodded dumbly. My mind was still working in slow motion, and even though I wasn't surprised to find Bailey in Rakow's kitchen, I hadn't really been expecting her either.

"Luke's helpless in the kitchen," Bailey said, kneading the steaks with her fingers and rolling them in the marinade. "But Lord have mercy, he can work a grill. I'll throw some taters in the oven, and we'll see what we can do about a salad. You want a beer?"

Another dumb nod. She popped the lid off a Miller Lite with the efficiency of a practiced bartender and slid it down the counter. The cold fizz tasted good on my dry throat.

"Luke tells me you're from Arizona."

"I get the feeling Luke tells you lots of things," I said coyly.

She looked up, hands frozen over the steaks. "What does that mean?"

My mind traveled back to the bar, recalling that song and dance Rakow and Bailey had performed while I watched from the corner. Together, but not together. Interested, but playing it cool.

What bullshit. I wasn't here to indulge bullshit.

"It means he likes you, and you like him, but for some dumb reason you're pretending otherwise. And you really shouldn't. Life is too short for that foolishness."

Bailey said nothing, hands still riding the air over the steaks. Then she looked away, but I saw a slow grin tugging at her lips.

"I think I like you, Mason Sharpe."

I finished the beer and started another, helping Bailey to wrap potatoes in aluminum foil for baking. Rakow turned up twenty minutes later, kicking off his boots on the front porch and giving Mossy some attention before stepping inside. Light returned to his tired eyes when he saw Bailey, even though he tried to hide it. I turned my back so they could exchange whatever sort of completely platonic, just-friends greeting they had agreed to.

What bullshit.

Bailey might be in denial about her relationship with Rakow, but she was in no way mistaken about his skills on a charcoal grill. The steaks sizzled over glowing embers while he and I stood on a sagging back deck and knocked back Millers like they were going out of style.

"Any progress with the girl?" I asked.

Rakow grunted. "A little. State people found a woman she would talk to, but they're still working on a translator. They think she may be Romanian."

Romania. That tracked. It wasn't all that far from Albania.

"What about the FBI? Have they got any leads? Maybe something from the tattoo?"

Rakow shook his head, probing the steaks with a pair of grilling tongs. He sipped beer, then let out a long, tired sigh.

"You know, Sharpe..." He stopped, tongs hovering over the grill. Lost in thought for a while. Then a subdued grin passed across his lips. "When I was a kid, we had this billy goat. Kept him right over there, in a pen next to the barn. His job was to drive back all the weeds around the pond. Every morning, I'd go to let him out, and without fail he'd ram his head against the gate, trying to break loose. But the gate swung inward, so I couldn't let him out until he stepped back. He never would. For two years I had to force that gate open, then nearly get run over as he burst out, all heels and horns, bucking like a damn bronco."

I sipped beer and joined the smile. I knew nothing about goats, but the mental image Rakow painted was a vibrant one. He was a good storyteller.

"Your point?" I asked.

"Sometimes you gotta take a step back if you want to break through," Rakow said. "I don't know about you, but I'm tired of ramming my head against a gate this week. Let's be off tonight."

I raised my bottle, and Bailey laid fresh baked potatoes and Caesar salad on a picnic table just in back of the house. More beer found its way across the table, and I tore into the best rib eye I'd ever tasted. No exaggeration. Marinated to perfection, grilled with the skill of a master. Five-star chefs could have taken a pointer from Rakow, and Bailey's potatoes and salad were no slouch either.

While she and I cleared the table, Rakow lit a fire in a little pit behind the house and arranged camping chairs. He produced a guitar from the living room and tuned it up as I carted fresh beer to the fireside.

"Didn't I see a violin case in your truck?" he prompted.

I hesitated. There was a case, all right. A beautiful, worn and loved instrument housed inside. A gift from a new friend in North Carolina.

But other than that new friend, I hadn't played for anyone since I played for Mia.

"Well, don't be shy," Bailey chirped. "Run and fetch it!"

So I did, and I tuned it up, and while Rakow plucked his way into John Denver, I found the strings and did my best to follow along. Bailey sang, and maybe it was the beer or the fire or the hellish few days that I had somehow managed to survive, but time seemed to stall out in Rakow's backyard. We worked slowly from song to song, sometimes together, sometimes playing solo. Sometimes Bailey sang. Sometimes she just rocked in her camping chair with a beer cradled in one hand, cheeks glowing, bright eyes fixed on Rakow.

Maybe it was an hour. Maybe it was three. I wasn't sure, and I didn't care. When Rakow finally rested his guitar on the grass and shifted his chair to sit alongside Bailey, I sat with the violin resting on my shoulder, eyes fixed on the crackling campfire, but not really seeing it.

My vision blurred, and I gently rubbed the worn wood of the violin bow. For the first time since witnessing the car accident two days prior, I wasn't thinking about the wreck or

Delia. Not about the Krols or the dead man at the train bridge or even about the girl in Palmer's barn.

I thought about Mia. I imagined her sitting next to me the way Bailey sat next to Rakow, my arm around her shoulders. Pulling her close. Her head resting on my chest the way Bailey's head now rested on Rakow's.

Alcohol had loosened their inhibitions a little. It brought a sad smile to my face.

I laid the bow across the strings one last time and closed my eyes. My mind traveled back to the little home in south Phoenix, and I pictured my beautiful fiancée curled up in a corner, a mug of something hot in one hand while I played her very favorite song.

"Hallelujah", by Leonard Cohen. A timeless classic, best performed by the gentle melody of a worn violin.

Bailey didn't sing this time. She and Rakow just listened. I dragged the sound out, pouring energy into every protracted note, only gaining speed as I reached the third chorus. With eyes closed, I tried to place myself back in that little house. I tried to imagine her so close I could feel her warmth as I leaned on the chair leg and played.

And played. And kept playing.

I might have played the song through four or five times before I finally wound down. When I opened my eyes, there were tears in both Rakow's and Bailey's. They sat across the fire, snuggled close, eyes fixed on me as though I were John Lennon.

I lowered the violin awkwardly, rubbing the smooth face and allowing the dream of the living room in Phoenix to fade.

It wasn't real. Not anymore.

"That was for Mia," I said softly. "She didn't believe in wasting a moment. And neither should you."

Then I got up and took my violin inside, leaving Rakow and Bailey to make their own decisions about life, while I closed my eyes and prayed for the dream to return.

32

I awoke early the next morning feeling a lot better than I deserved to. I was still sore enough to draw tears and sported a bitching headache from my overindulgence of Miller Lite the night prior, but despite that, my mind was surprisingly clear, and for once, I wasn't tired.

I felt vigor returning, and with it, thoughts of Delia. Thoughts of the girl with the butterfly pants.

And the Krols.

I dressed and eased my way out of the guest bedroom, unsure as to whether Bailey was still present, or if anyone was still sleeping.

I found answers to both questions when I reached the kitchen. A steaming pot of fresh coffee sat on the counter, and through a misted front window, I made out the shapes of Rakow's broad shoulder on the front porch, and Bailey's Dodge pickup in the front yard.

Not a moment wasted.

I poured coffee into the largest mug I could find and joined Rakow on the porch. A spare rocking chair offered a magnificent view of a dewy front yard and the pond beyond, both growing brighter with the gentle rise of the morning sun. Mossy lay at Rakow's feet, snoring softly while the sheriff sat quietly with a mug resting on one knee. I didn't see Bailey.

"Morning," Rakow said. "Sleep well?"

"Like a baby." It was true. I hadn't dreamed the night before of Mia, but maybe whatever spirits controlled the whims of dreams knew that I didn't need to. I just blacked out.

I relaxed into the chair with a gentle grunt, body still aching, and tasted the coffee. It was stronger than a mule kick, pure black. Just the way I liked it.

For ten minutes we just enjoyed the sunrise, crickets chirping someplace in the grass, Mossy rising abruptly now and then to woof indignantly at a passing chipmunk. Otherwise, all was still. The house lay quiet. Thoughts of the case and the Krols drifted through my mind, but I didn't try to control them. I just let them percolate. Mingle. Blend and morph.

"I wanted to thank you for...last night." Rakow spoke haltingly, staring at his mug. "I know...I mean, what I read..."

He trailed off.

"Don't mention it, Rakow."

He nodded, and we both drank coffee. Mossy wandered over to sniff my hand, making out like she was still suspicious of a stranger, but I had the feeling she was simply fishing for attention. I gave her a gentle scratch behind the ear, and the old collie slouched against my leg with a happy pant.

"The FBI sent some people down from Birmingham," Rakow said. "I'm meeting them later this morning."

"Are they here for the girl or Delia?"

"The girl. I don't think...well..."

"Nobody believes I saw Delia," I finished.

"Not quite nobody," he said. "It's just a back-burner issue. Until we get a handle on what happened with this girl."

"It's a tangled web, Rakow. These things always are. You can't liberate a single thread without unweaving them all."

"And how do you propose we go about unweaving them all?"

He turned an open, relaxed look on me, and I realized he meant it. Maybe it was an olive branch, or a simple extension of one Army veteran's hand to another. A sort of silent agreement to let the speed bumps of the past few days remain in the rearview.

I appreciated it.

"Something's bothering me about the Delia thing," I said. "I can't put my finger on it, but I know what I saw. I know she's alive, and I know she's back in Delamar County. Or she was, anyway. Three nights ago."

"Okay," Rakow said, still relaxed. "Let's assume that's true. Let's assume your theory about human traffickers is true, and Delia was kidnapped. Why is she back now?"

"I don't think that's the biggest question," I said.

"What's the biggest question?"

"Why is she *hiding*?"

I let that one linger, enjoying another long sip. I'd need a refill soon.

"She ran, Rakow," I said. "She saw me, and while I was going to get my tire iron, she squeezed through the window and ran."

"Maybe she was scared. She didn't know who you were."

"Maybe."

"She could also be brain-fried," Rakow said. "A lot of these victims are fed all kinds of drugs. Heavy stuff, to keep them compliant. She might not even know where she is."

"Did you ever identify the guy driving her van?"

Rakow shook his head. "No ID. No return on fingerprints. We're still working on it."

"What about the guy in the sedan?"

"College student at Columbus State. He was headed back to school after spending a couple of days with family in Pensacola. He was nineteen."

A random thing. Could have been anybody.

Another long sip of coffee.

"You think it's a coincidence?" I said. "The girl with the barcode tattoo and Delia. You think the two are unrelated?"

Rakow thought about that for a long moment. He chewed his bottom lip and studied the rugged front lawn. Then he shook his head. "No."

"Me neither. Something is going down around here. Something big, and something soon. You need to get a warrant and arrest those Krol kids."

"I can't. I've got nothing to go on."

"They set me up. They're working with these Albanians. I saw the stuff on the train."

"That evidence is circumstantial at best. No offense, but you aren't the most credible witness. Not when it comes to obtaining warrants from a judge who plays golf with old man Krol. If you want any action taken against them, we need something a lot stronger."

Something stronger.

I gave the percolating data in the back of my mind a stir, sifting through the key points in chronological order. The wreck. Delia. The girl in the butterfly pants. The Krol kids running me off. The industrial compound, and old man Krol's angry spiel. The train, and Gjoka, and then the dead girl at the bottom of Providence Canyon.

It was an alphabet soup that all seemed to point in one direction—a trafficking scheme. Yet I knew I was missing something obvious. A hidden subtext, blended beyond recognition. But still *there*. The pieces were in my hands.

"We're missing something," I said. "Something key."

"Usually." Rakow sighed. He still sounded tired. I remembered what he said about this being a thankless job, and was suddenly very glad I wasn't wearing a badge anymore.

We drank coffee in silence for another ten minutes; then Bailey appeared on the porch, all messy hair and big yawns. She wore sweatpants and a tan T-shirt with the Delamar County sheriff's logo printed on the chest. The T-shirt looked to be in Rakow's size.

Bailey shot me a wink on her way to Rakow's rocking chair, where she gave him a long kiss. I looked away and hid a sad smile while they debated a breakfast menu. Rakow said he had to get ready and head in. He'd stick with a bagel.

"What about you, Mason?" Bailey asked.

"I'm good, thank you. I think I'm gonna hit the road, actually. I need to clear my head."

Bailey made me a bagel anyway, and Rakow promised to give me a ring if he heard anything. I returned to my truck and spent a couple of long morning hours reorganizing my camping gear, then using Rakow's water hose to blast away dust from my windshield. Bailey packed up and rumbled away in her Dodge, and I continued to let my mind wander. Not focusing on anything in particular for too long. Asking myself the kinds of open-ended questions that always served me best as a homicide detective.

I had told Rakow we were missing something—something key. I put myself in the Krols' shoes, organized my assumptions about their illicit enterprise, and asked myself where the hole was. What integral piece had I missed?

I was repacking my gear into the bed of the GMC and struggling to find room for my ever-expanding collection of plastic bins when my mind finally clicked into gear. It was such a simple question it felt wrong at first. I dropped out of the bed of the truck and reviewed the tight stack of bins; everything fit together like the pieces of a puzzle.

A place to *put* everything. Where were the girls?

I thought back to what Keen had said about a dual trafficking operation—bad guys coming to America not only to kidnap girls, but also to sell them. An import/export operation. That theory was bolstered by the presence of the Albanians and all the paraphernalia on the train. Clearly, Delamar County itself was some kind of hub.

But *if* it was a hub, and *if* there was an operation trafficking children via the Krols, *where* were they? There should be a headquarters. A makeshift prison. A place to put them where they wouldn't be found. Someplace quiet and isolated.

Certainly, Delamar County itself was quiet and isolated. An ideal place for such an operation. But it was also a large county, full of particularly isolated corners. The classic needle-in-a-haystack problem.

I shut the tailgate and piled into the cab, still swirling that alphabet soup. Asking myself a question only very bad people or very good cops ever have cause to ask: if I was trafficking children, where would I hide them?

I fished for my keys, then remembered I had left them in the coin tray built into my dash. I scraped the little metal drawer open, dropped my fingers in…and touched busted plastic.

It was the flash drive. Skinny's stash of kiddie porn, now obliterated beyond use. Before I could put the brakes on my mind, that horrific image blinked across it. The terrified face of a child, eyes wide and desperate.

My throat turned dry, and I forced the picture away… then I stopped. My thoughts returned to the image, but this time I didn't focus on the child. I focused on what was *behind* the child.

A rough-hewn log wall.

My blood ran cold, and I slammed the drawer shut.

Could it really be that obvious?

Sweat trickled from my forehead, and I dug into my pocket again. Not for the keys this time. For my phone. I found Keen's business card and dialed, throat still dry. Heart racing.

Keen picked up on the third ring. "Hello?"

"Keen, it's Sharpe. What did you tell me about the summer camp?"

"The summer camp? What?"

"You said it was closed down now. That you couldn't go there."

"Right. It's a hunting club, I think. I don't know. There's a fence. Why?"

"Where is it?"

"Huh?"

"Where is it?"

"It's…down on County Road 12. A couple of miles past

Carter's Crossroads, on your right. Kind of in the middle of nowhere. Why?"

I didn't answer. I just hung up, found the keys, and started the engine. The GMC coughed and rumbled, then lurched as I punched the gas, not giving it time to warm.

I found the driveway; then I found the long dirt road. I followed the blue line on my phone's GPS and pointed my truck deep into Delamar County—toward the quietest, most isolated, most desolate corner.

33

Keen wasn't kidding about the summer camp lying in the middle of nowhere. Carter's Crossroads itself was nothing more than the intersection of two county roads, with a boarded-up and rotting service station sitting on one corner, a boarded-up and rotting diner facing it from across the street.

A used-to-be place. Maybe a lunch spot for local farmers and bauxite miners, or a hub for kids on bicycles to meet up and buy sodas. Now vacant, with vintage fuel signs rattling in a light breeze, displaying even more vintage fuel prices.

No people.

I turned onto County Road 12 and decreased my speed to barely over thirty miles per hour, puttering along with both windows open as I inspected either side of the road. The grass was high and uncut, climbing up the sides of power poles and growing in the busted cracks of potholes. White and yellow paint, once bright on the asphalt, was now so faded as to leave the road almost gray.

I drove five miles without seeing a thing, then turned

back and retraced my path, looking a little closer this time. Keen had said two miles, hadn't he?

I retreated all the way to the crossroads and was beginning my third pass when I finally noticed the transmission line breaking away from the main power grid and leading down a narrow alley between the pines. Just beyond it, a gravel drive led across the ditch, dropping quickly into shadows. Easy to miss unless you were staring directly at it.

It wasn't what I expected when I pictured the entrance of a summer camp. I had imagined a wide, possibly paved drive, with one of those big, suspended signs that hung from a cowboy-style arch over the middle of the road.

Maybe that was true of a big camp someplace on the East Coast. This looked little wider than a regular driveway, but the soft clay and gravel were in good repair. I checked both ways again, then turned onto the drive and rumbled between the trees. Rocks popped beneath my tires, and I noticed the underbrush was cleared on either side; the ditches were clean and maintained. There was a fence, also. Ten feet high, constructed of four-by-four wire, racing along the tree line just outside the ditch...with curled razor wire running along its top. The same kind that I'd seen outside the Krols' industrial compound.

The fence looked relatively new, and as I rounded a curve, the fence pinched in from either side to meet a heavy steel gate that completely blocked my path. I noted a security camera pointed down at the nose of my truck, and a little keypad mounted beneath a rain shield on a post.

But no people. No signs. No indicator of what sort of place I had found.

I hesitated twenty yards out, then released the clutch and rolled right up to the keypad.

There was a call button. I pushed it.

The little speaker mounted next to the button remained silent, but a red light flashed beneath the keypad. I waited patiently, and then a female voice crackled through the speaker.

"This is private property. Please return to the road."

I squinted at the camera. It hadn't moved, but even from an imperfect angle, I was confident it could see into my cab. I thought back to my discussion with Keen and how he had called this place a hunting camp. The logic that led me here was solid, but to some degree I was still shooting in the dark. Without knowing for sure whom I was speaking with, or whether they were even associated with the Krols, it seemed unwise to disclose my actual interest in the property. I went for a safer approach instead.

"I'm looking for the hunting camp," I said. "I'd like to make a reservation."

Long pause. I waited patiently.

"The camp is already booked. Please return to the road."

The speaker crackled into silence, and the red light disappeared. I spent a long minute tapping my steering wheel, watching the gate. Looking into the desolate woods beyond. Something about the voice on the other end of the call box was vaguely familiar, but I couldn't place it. I searched the trees beyond the gate for a while, but there was nothing else to see.

All quiet.

I shifted into reverse and slowly turned my truck around, taking care not to drop the rear wheels into the ditch. Then I bounced back to the road, still questioning the interaction at the keypad.

The camp is already booked.

It was an odd thing to say. I hadn't mentioned dates, or even how I knew that the camp was available for reservation. The woman had simply stated that the facility was unavailable. A very unilateral claim for a property that, presumably, made its money off of renting out space to hunters.

Why not say the camp wasn't available for rent at all? That it was a private club?

For that matter, why was there anybody on-site to answer the gate buzzer in the first place? I don't know a lot about hunting, especially in the Southeast. But I was pretty certain that white-tail deer season was regulated to winter months. Had I just happened to approach the gate while a summer custodian was on-site?

None of it felt right. Every question in my focused mind served as gasoline on the fire of my own suspicions. There was something here. I could feel it.

I braked at the road and looked both ways, even though I hadn't seen another vehicle of any sort since leaving Able. I was still preoccupied with the interaction at the gate when I happened to glance down into the soft dirt at the mouth of the drive, right where the gravel met the pavement.

And then I stopped again. There were tire tracks. Fresh ones. Wider than my GMC, and only lasting for a moment before the gravel erased them. But I didn't need to step out of the truck and kneel in the mud to notice that washed-out left tire. Going bald on one side, losing traction.

It was the same print I had noticed outside the Krol compound. I was certain of it.

Looking back up to the road, I glanced quickly both ways as my heart rate began to quicken. There was no one there. No truck parked along the roadside. No gentle rumble of a nearby engine carrying on the hot morning breeze.

I was completely alone. Yet I couldn't be, because I was one hundred percent certain I hadn't noticed those tracks on my way in. I sat another five seconds, calculating quickly. Realizing that whoever it was, they couldn't have followed me very far down the gravel drive. I would have seen them.

But the fact that they had turned in at all said something. They weren't familiar with this place. They had to see it for themselves. But they weren't trying to trap me, either. If they were, why not block the drive, just out of sight of the camera? Be waiting for me on my way out.

They were trailing me, yes. But not to confront me.

They wanted to watch me.

I shifted into first and turned right down the road, taking my time. Making a lot of noise. I monitored my rearview mirror as I bumped deeper into the county, topping hills and slipping into valleys.

But I didn't see anyone following.

Two miles from the entrance of the hunting camp, I reached the mouth of another dirt road. I had noticed it during my search for the summer camp. It was another hunting plot entrance, maybe. Or the path to a cattle farm or a bauxite mine. I didn't know or care. All that mattered was that this road was constructed entirely of loose Alabama clay, torn and rutted, still wet from the deluge of two days previously, and dropping sharply down a hill on its way into the pines. A death trap for anything short of a four-wheel drive.

I had already run through a list of possible suspects—people who could be following me. I had seen a lot of trucks during my time in Delamar County. A lot of people who might want to trail me. But only one person made sense—

only one person whose truck was old, not new. Tires worn, not fresh.

And that truck wasn't a four-wheel drive.

Turning off the road, I rolled a few feet down the mouth of the dirt drive before hitting the brakes, then reversing out. My front tires left deep, mushy tracks in the clay. Easily visible on even a passing inspection. Impossible to miss for anybody on the lookout for them.

Back on the road, I punched the gas, driving quickly over the next hill and stopping just beyond it. I checked my watch and decided to give my tail four minutes to catch up.

It seemed like the right number.

Then I hauled the truck around again and piloted to the mouth of the dirt road. Fresh tracks had joined the ones I had left. Wider than my GMC, with one balding tire on the left side. I parked on the shoulder and jogged quickly through the ditch and into the trees. The dirt drive made a hard right turn shortly after reaching the bottom of the slope, but I could already hear a big engine straining someplace not far away.

Tires spinning. RPMs racing. But not moving—because the vehicle was hopelessly stuck.

My hand dropped into my pocket, closing around the Victorinox Locksmith, my thumb ready to deploy the locking three-inch blade. But I didn't expect to need it. As I neared the rush of the motor, muddy maroon paint became visible, followed by the outline of a four-door Silverado.

Two-wheel drive. A sausage dog sticker in the back glass.

I've got friends in low places.

It was Keen—the writer.

34

I gritted my teeth and circled around the nose of the truck as a shower of mud exploded from the rear tires. Keen sat behind the wheel, looking over one shoulder as he attempted to reverse out of his own stupidity. When I rapped on his window with the butt of the Victorinox, he nearly jumped out of his collared shirt, rimless glasses flying across the cab as his face snapped toward me.

I stood back from the glass and shot him a long glare, then ran my finger across my throat. To his credit, Keen was smart enough not to argue. He shifted into park and cut the engine off, his face still a little pale as he wound the window down.

"H-hey, Sharpe. What are you doing here?"

Coy. I wasn't in the mood for it.

"Why are you following me?" I demanded.

"F-following you? Me? No, no." He shook his head and grinned. "I just came out for a drive. I didn't even know you were here."

"Bullshit. Try again."

I left the knife clenched in my right hand, eyes cold. Keen's gaze dropped to the weapon, and a trickle of sweat ran off his lip. He chuckled nervously.

"Okay, okay. You got me. But look, it's a free country, right? You can't fault a guy for wanting to research."

"Research *what*?"

Keen looked away. Swallowed hard. "You know."

I thought I did know, and I pocketed the knife in disgust. I had tipped my hand by calling him about the summer camp. I should have called Rakow, instead. I pictured Keen on his computer back at whatever cluttered apartment he called home, piles of notebooks everywhere, already typing out an email to his publisher.

She's back. Let's do another book.

Turning for the hill, I marched straight through the mud. Leaving him right where I found him.

The Silverado's door groaned open, and Keen dropped out. I imagined his nice tennis shoes sinking up to the ankles, and figured he deserved it.

"Hey, wait! I want to talk."

"We've got nothing to talk about, Keen."

"I want to talk about Delia!"

He slogged up the hill after me. I kept walking.

"Look, man," Keen said. "I believe you! You saw her. Don't you want to talk to somebody who believes you? There's a story here!"

I gritted my teeth, whirling in the mud. He'd almost caught up, now only a couple of feet behind, startled by my sudden movement.

"Is that what this is to you?" I barked. "A *story*?"

Keen hesitated, mouth half-open. I closed the distance between us and gave him a hearty shove—sudden enough to send him tumbling to his ass in the clay.

"She was kidnapped, Keen. You were right. Kidnapped and *trafficked*. This isn't a damn book deal. This is a *life*. I'm not here to facilitate your research!"

He lay back in the mud, his shorts and shirt all slick with red dirt, a sort of shell-shocked look on his face. As though he was still confused. Still taken off guard.

I turned back up the hill, boots squishing. I made it five feet before Keen called back to me.

"You think I have a book deal?" He coughed on an incredulous laugh. "Does that look like a Lamborghini to you?"

I kept walking. Keen scrambled to his feet behind me, slipping and grunting.

"*Wait, dammit!*"

His voice turned suddenly cold, a tone I hadn't heard before. All the goofy insecurity and bumbling uncertainty was gone. I paused despite myself and looked over one shoulder.

Keen stood coated in mud, one finger jabbed at me, shaking a little. His eyes rimmed red, and his voice choked.

"I paid for that book, Sharpe. I worked doubles at the nuclear plant to get it printed. Do you know why?"

I didn't answer. He took a faltering step forward.

"Because *nobody* cared about Delia. She was a flash in the pan, and then everybody moved on. I kept her story alive when nobody else would. I ran down the truth when nobody else cared!"

A lone tear slipped down his face, and he scrubbed a muddy hand across his cheek. "Don't you stand leering over me like some kind of self-righteous white knight. You have no *idea* why I do what I do."

I still didn't answer. Keen's shoulders dropped, and he exhaled slowly. Then he looked at the mud.

"Everybody deserves to have their story told, Sharpe. Everybody."

He turned back for the truck, fighting through the mud, suddenly looking a lot less bumbling and foolish, and more sad and alone. I noted the absence of a wedding band on his finger, and glanced again at the sausage dog sticker.

I've got friends in low places.

I closed my eyes and exhaled slowly, rolling the knife in my hand. Then I thought of Delia. The girl with the butterfly pants. The dead Albanian on the railroad bridge. The Krol boys.

And the summer camp in the woods, now converted to a hunting camp. Unreasonably secure, with curled razor wire atop a ten-foot fence.

Just to keep deer in? No.

Keen reached his truck and kicked his shoes against the step rail to scrape away the mud. I pocketed the knife and approached the tailgate. He shot me a glare as I reached it, looking a little flushed now. His eyes still red and puffy.

Maybe embarrassed by his outburst. But somehow his reaction felt too emotional to be triggered by simple indignation.

"You care about Delia's story?" I said.

He looked away. Gaze dropping. Voice turning soft. "More than my own."

"Why?"

Keen was very quiet. He fixated on the mud, and I narrowed my eyes. I thought back to what I knew about Delia. How she disappeared. How they found her shoe in the woods. How none of the other girls heard any disturbance.

How the window was found unlocked. As though she had snuck out by her own free will.

And then it all made sense.

"You were there that night, weren't you?" I asked.

No answer. I saw the red return to his eyes.

"You're mid-twenties," I continued. "Say, twenty-five. So you'd be about Delia's age. Fourteen...summer camp. Puppy love and first kisses."

Keen turned his head away, but he couldn't hide the well of tears now bubbling up. He sniffed hard, and when he turned back, both eyes were red. His muddy cheeks lined by fresh tear trails.

"Everybody's story deserves to be told."

I nodded slowly. Thought about what long, festering pain could do to a person. Then I tugged the latch on his tailgate and dropped it open.

"Sit here." I smacked the tailgate with one open palm.

"Huh?" He looked confused. I circled toward the cab.

"Your tires are worn, and you've got no weight on the axle. Also, you don't know how to drive. So you sit, and I'll drive."

I slid into the driver's seat, for once not having to adjust it to compensate for my height. Keen looked at the tailgate, still hesitating. Then back to me.

"What about Delia?" he said.

I shut the door. Started the engine and looked through the open window.

"We're going to find her," I said. "*You* are going to find her. Now sit your happy ass on that tailgate and hold on."

35

Getting Keen's truck out of the mud was easier said than done. The tires were several thousand miles overdue for a change, and even brand new, they were hardly mud tires. But with his bulk concentrated on the tailgate, adding nearly three hundred pounds of pressure to the rear axle, I found a little traction. I reversed, then rolled forward, slowly rotating until I had the Silverado's nose pointed out of the forest. I made good progress until I reached the base of the muddy hill that led up to the county road, and then the Silverado slid to a stop again, tires spinning.

I bailed out and returned to my own truck, digging out a thick coil of military-grade 550 cord from the bottom of a bin—so named because a single strand of the narrow rope could support as much as five hundred fifty pounds of weight. I'd bought the cord at a surplus store in Georgia and had been using it at my campsites to support a tarpaulin.

Backing my truck up to the mouth of the road, there was just enough line to loop around my rear bumper and connect to the built-in tow hooks of Keen's Silverado four times—a combined strength of twenty-two hundred pounds. Hardly recommended towing strength, but I only needed enough force to keep the Silverado from backsliding.

Then I directed Keen on how to manage his accelerator, got behind the wheel of my GMC, and locked into first gear. We spent ten minutes easing forward, gaining a few yards before Keen clamped on the brakes long enough for me to reverse and choke up the line. 550 cord stretches a lot. It's designed to. But it didn't break before Keen rumbled back onto the asphalt, a euphoric grin on his muddy face.

I returned the line to my truck and had him follow me down the busted road another mile to a level spot overgrown with three-foot grass and a thicket of barbed undergrowth. I parked the GMC behind the undergrowth, then dug through my camping gear for my backpack. It was still loaded with the bolt cutters, binoculars, and face paint. Gear I was growing a little too accustomed to using.

Keen's passenger seat was coated with a thick layer of red and gray dog hair, and the leather was scratched by tiny toenails. I pictured the little dogs bouncing and barking on the seat, and the image brought a subdued smile to my face.

I like dogs.

"Dachshunds?" I asked, slamming the door.

"Chiweenies," Keen corrected.

"What the hell is that?"

"Dachshund and Chihuahua mix. Best dogs."

"How many?"

He shifted uncomfortably, voice dropping to a mumble. "Six."

"*Six?*"

He shrugged. "I've got friends in low places."

"Yeah. I read that someplace."

I pointed up the road, and he shifted into drive. "Where to?"

"The summer camp."

He stopped, the discomfort returning. Not fear, I thought. Probably bad memories. A lot of them.

"It's closed," he said. "It's a hunting camp now."

"Yep. With a lot of high-tech security. In my experience, deer aren't that adept at evading execution. I have the feeling there's something else at play."

"You're gonna ask for a tour?"

I snorted. "You've got a lot to learn, Keen. Now drive."

I directed him back up the busted county road, rolling right past the entrance of the hunting camp to a spot about half a mile closer to Carter's Crossroads. There was another grass drive leading across the ditch to the edge of the pines, with a double cattle gate chained closed to block it. A barbed-wire fence connected to the gate, and beyond it a winding road led between the trees to a row of power lines cutting toward the summer camp.

It was a service road, probably. For the landowner or the county.

"Is this part of the old camp?" I asked, jabbing my thumb.

Keen shook his head. "No. The camp is all south and west. They've got the whole place fenced in now."

"Okay. Hang tight."

I drew my bolt cutters and dispatched the chain, wrestling it free before pulling the gates open. Then I beckoned Keen into the trees. The muddy Silverado rumbled through, and I shut the gates and wrapped the chain around them again, leaving the broken ends on the inside of the gate. It would pass casual inspection by a quick passer-by.

"Another hundred yards," I said. "Stay on the road."

We bumped along tight-packed earth held together by shallow pine roots and blanketed by needles. The tires slipped a little, but I felt we were in no danger of getting stuck this time. It was all level, and no clay.

Just short of the power lines, well inside the trees, I motioned for him to cut the engine. Then I climbed out and slung the backpack on.

"What now?" Keen questioned.

"Now you stay here while I have a look. Keep the engine off and don't make any noise."

"Wait...I thought I was helping?"

"You are helping. You're my getaway driver." I started into the pines.

"But wait! I'm...not really a fast driver."

I looked over one shoulder. A long, piercing stare.

"It's a joke, Keen. Try laughing."

He didn't laugh. He looked stressed and uncertain, like a spastic dog tensing at the approach of the mailman.

I remembered his six Chiweenies and wondered who was training who.

Turning back into the trees, I broke into a jog, the thump of my hiking boots muted by the bed of damp pine needles beneath them. I figured it was maybe five hundred to a thousand yards back to the fence line. If the property beyond was nothing more than a private hunting camp, booked for the summer to some self-indulgent lawyer from Montgomery, then I expected to take a quick look and return to Able in time for lunch.

But nothing about the security at the gate spoke to self-indulgent lawyers and summer relaxation. Neither did the coiled razor wire. The whole thing reminded me of the Krol compound, and that was more than enough justification for a second look.

I found the fence racing between the trees along a clear-cut lane. Thirty seconds with the bolt cutters was sufficient to open a panel in the wire wide enough to squeeze through before entering yet another grove of planted pines. Unlike the grove I had just left, these pines were thick with undergrowth and dense bushes.

Odd, for a fancy hunting camp. Unless you were trying to conceal something.

I saw the road fifty yards ahead, winding west from the gate, and I crouched lower to the ground. Briars and nettles tore at my arms, opening fresh cuts while my body continued to throb with the aches and pains of the last few days. I tuned it all out, falling into the stalking rhythm of a trained soldier slipping up on a village.

Maybe looking for somebody. Maybe ready to kick a few doors down. The only thing I lacked was my M4 rifle equipped with a holographic sight and enough ammunition to subdue a dozen Taliban fighters.

I followed the road on my left, weaving between the trees and wading through a four-foot creek. The drive crossed the creek via a worn wooden bridge, and I noted the rotting tail of a rope swing dangling from its bottom. It made me wonder if the bridge dated back to the summer camp days. Maybe Delia had swung off that rope, shrieking with fear and delight as she plummeted into the cool water below. Maybe she and Keen had sat on the creek bank later, giggling like kids do. Telling bad jokes and pretending they didn't like each other.

Maybe it had been the summer of first kisses and a lot of blushing and avoiding each other in the dining hall. Puppy love, forever shattered by unthinkable tragedy.

I clawed my way onto the far creek bank and wriggled beneath the brush. I heard noises now. Dull engines and the groan of heavy suspension. Somebody shouting an order.

That order wasn't in English.

I army-crawled forward, ignoring the aching pain of my battered body. Zeroed in now, like I'd been a hundred times before. I pictured eleven other men in the shadows around me, moving in practiced unison. Narrowing on the target with the efficiency of trained killers.

Those men were shadows in the back of my mind, but the focus I felt wasn't. And neither was the deep anger burning in the bottom of my stomach at the thought of the girl who loved butterflies.

The edge of the tree line approached as the voices grew louder. I wriggled beneath a line of bushes and stopped, scooping my hand into the backpack for the binoculars. The lenses focused with a gentle manipulation of the adjustment dial.

Then I saw it. And it was far worse than I ever imagined.

36

The lodge was built like a cabin, constructed of heavy logs, sixty feet wide and half as much deep. Two floors, a metal roof, and a wraparound porch. It sat in a wide clearing now heavily overgrown by high grass and more of those damn Alabama brambles. Behind the cabin, a wide field dropped gently down to a lake, both the field and the lakeshore overgrown and unmanaged save for paths cut by bush hog that led to a series of long, low cabins. They were imitations of the main lodge, but much smaller.

Dormitories, obviously. Bunkhouses. But bunkhouses no more. The windows of each building were now boarded over, the doors replaced with full-metal variants.

Locked on the outside.

A cold chill ran down my spine as I swept the binoculars slowly over the property, hovering over the dormitories and noting one of the Albanians sitting on the front porch of each one. Jet-black hair, dark features. Kicked back on folding chairs with shotguns and rifles leaned against the railings next to them. Like prison guards.

Once more, I recalled the horrific image on the flash drive. Blocking out the child's face, I focused on the wall behind. Rough-hewn logs, aged and dark.

They matched the log walls of the dormitories perfectly.

Pivoting back to the main lodge, I saw more Albanians scattered along the wraparound porch. Dirty, grungy-looking guys with long guns and sidearms. Not hunters. Not of the white-tail deer variety, anyway. There were a dozen or more in total, and they weren't doing much of anything. Just standing guard, smoking cigarettes and drinking from water bottles, weapons close to hand.

A row of vehicles sat parked in the lot. Two Jeep Wranglers on beefy, all-terrain tires. A couple of white panel vans caked in orange clay. And one elevated Nissan Titan—a beefy monster loaded down in the bed with equipment and tools.

I'd seen it before, back at the Krol compound. It was old man Krol's personal vehicle.

My jaw clenched, and I pivoted back to the dormitories. It was so obvious it was almost blatant. A prison compound, built with the orchestrated care of an organized operation. And not a new one, either. How the *hell* had this passed beneath Rakow's nose? Isolation and security aside, how could you not know? How could this many foreigners operate with impunity and never be noticed?

The rumble of an approaching engine resounded from the driveway. I turned in that direction, adjusting the binoculars again to see another large panel van, this one decorated with the bright and happy logo of a gourmet catering business. The address printed on the passenger side door read *Columbus, Georgia*. Two women rode inside, dressed in branded hats and shirts, chattering and laughing as they parked next to Krol's pickup.

They had made it past the gate. They had been admitted into the compound. They were *expected*.

Old man Krol himself appeared on the porch, waving to the Albanians. They made casual attempts to conceal their weapons, and Krol greeted the caterers. The hardened, ugly shell of a man I'd noted at the compound melted entirely, replaced by a jovial grin and what must have been another joke—both women laughed. He was dressed differently than I'd seen him before. Gone were the dirty jeans and the stained work shirt. Now he wore fresh jeans, fancy cowboy boots and an open-collared white button-down. Like this was some kind of special occasion.

Krol guided the caterers up the stairs and inside the lodge. They were gone for two minutes, then returned to unload the van. Steaming metal containers appeared on metal trays. A *lot* of it. I watched for half an hour as they unloaded and were paid in cash; then they returned to the van, slowly rumbling back up the drive.

Just two happy caterers, filling an order for a hunting camp in the middle of nowhere Alabama. Tipped well for their long drive, but not so well as they'd remember it a week from now.

I remained motionless behind concealment, mind spinning, heart thudding. A large part of me wanted to leave the trees and go straight to work. I could jump one of the Albanians without much trouble—my Victorinox would make short work of his windpipe. I could take his firearm and go to work on the others. Outnumbered or otherwise, I liked my odds. I could take my time. Move like a ghost amid the trees and slaughter them all before storming the lodge.

But no. It was still too soon. There was still too much that I didn't know. I had to be *sure* of a killing strike. Sure that when I made my move, nobody escaped. All innocent lives were recovered.

So I waited. I nestled down in the bed of pine needles, and I let the clock grind deep into the afternoon, studying the compound and memorizing every face until I was certain I had an accurate body count of the gunmen securing the property. Thirteen in total, plus whatever men were inside the lodge.

At just past three p.m., the Krol boys arrived. I recognized the growl of their Raptor even before it emerged from the trees. Doors slammed, and they sauntered out. Old man Krol appeared on the wraparound porch, and a conference was held. They were too far away for me to hear anything, but the rising tension of their interaction was obvious. The old man grabbed Skinny by the ear before it was over with. He marched them both back to the Raptor, and now I could hear voices. Still muted. Still coming in short bursts, but audible if I listened closely.

"Get back to the house...quiet...no more bullshit!"

That was the old man. Skinny jerked away, face scarlet with indignation. Even Muscle looked ready to fight.

"You heard what Sadie said!" Skinny whined. "Sharpe was *here*. At the gate!"

Sadie. I knew I recognized the voice at the gate. Distorted by the crackling speaker, and no doubt intentionally masked by the woman on the other end. But still familiar. That sad girl from the bar had found herself a new job working for the Krols and their "hunting camp".

"And she *ran him off*," the old man snarled, voice still heavy with his Polish accent. "He left! I have enough men here to subdue an army of nosy outsiders, but not if I have fools running around drawing attention."

His voice rose to a shout. Both boys cowered. Krol shook his head in restrained disgust, then spat on the ground. "You are both as stupid as your mother. I should have drowned you in the lake like mutt puppies."

Skinny's eyes bulged. His lips trembled. I could see that he was struggling not to cry. The old man jabbed a finger at the truck.

"Go home! And stay there. I'd better not hear from either of you."

"But you said we could be here when—"

It was Muscle who spoke. The old man cut him off with a brutal blow to his face.

"We are this close!" he shouted, pinching his fingers together just like he had back at the Krol compound two days prior. That same irate, infuriated gesture. "Two million dollars on the line. Cops all over the county. One false move and tonight *does not happen.* Do you understand? They will scatter!"

Both boys cowered against the truck. Krol hit them again, both of them. Kicking and shouting until they scrambled into the Raptor. The engine fired up, and from the porch the Albanians watched and laughed, not even trying to conceal their disgust.

Tires spun. The Ford slid back and turned. Then it was lost down the drive while the old man shook his head and cursed at his men. The smiles faded. They all hurried back into line.

"Get yourselves together!" Krol shouted. "Any man screws this up, I'll kill you myself!"

He disappeared inside. The Albanians went back to their

patrols, muttering darkly to each other as the sun dropped lower toward the trees.

I clenched my jaw and backed slowly into the pines, remaining on my belly for twenty yards before I returned to a crouch and headed back for Keen's truck. I'd seen all I needed to see. Heard all I needed to hear. The heat in my stomach had warmed into a sizable fire, not the least bit cooled by another plunge through the creek. By the time I ducked through the fence, I had enough pieces organized in my mind to draw reasonable conclusions.

Delia was mixed up in this somehow. So was the girl in the butterfly pants. But how and why no longer really mattered. The catering van and the old man's outbursts told the more immediate story. The story of what this lodge was now used for, and what would be happening in just a few short hours.

It was a story I would terminate, by any means necessary.

37

Keen's truck loomed up in the midday sun, parked right where I'd left him on the service drive. But I didn't see Keen. The writer was gone from the driver's seat, the driver's door hanging open.

I stopped at the tree line, hands loose at my sides.

"Keen?" I called softly across the road. A snapping crunch answered my voice, and then Keen appeared from the far side of the Silverado, stumbling out of the brush…at gunpoint.

The Krol boys followed him, triumphant grins plastered across their ugly pale faces.

"Enjoy your tour, Mr. Sharpe?" Skinny said. He was the one with the pistol—a midsized Glock, maybe a 19 or a 23, jammed into Keen's spine like a stun gun. Muscle walked beside him, shoulders all tensed, glowering at me like I'd slapped his mother.

They approached the rear of the truck, Keen still stumbling ahead, more embarrassment on his face than fear. Ashamed of himself for being caught.

Maybe he should have been. I wondered how the Krol boys had detected his presence just outside the hunting compound, then decided it didn't matter. These two blobs of flesh and blood weren't even human. They were cockroaches —creeping creatures of the grimiest sort. The kind of scum that survives nuclear blasts and remains to feast on the roasted carcasses of the dead and slowly dying.

Living off the heartache of others. Thriving on instinct, not wit, because these cockroaches were hopelessly stupid, just as the old man had said. Stupid enough to lose that flash drive, and now stupid enough to confront me without calling for an army of backup.

It would be their final mistake.

I walked straight toward the truck, ignoring the two boys. Ignoring the gun.

"Hey! Tough guy. Stop right there!" It was Skinny, his voice dripping with triumph and glee. I paid him no attention. Wrenching the back door open, I found the rear seat clouded with more gray and red dog hair, along with a mess of chew toys and pet owner paraphernalia. Grabbing the seat by its outer edge, I wrenched it up, exposing a storage compartment beneath. Books, notebooks, more dog stuff, and a tire-changing kit.

"Hey, asshole! I'm talking to you. I'll kill this jerk!"

It was Skinny again. But I knew he wasn't about to shoot Keen. Neither of these devolving piles of excrement knew what Keen knew—and they needed to. They needed to know what he might have told Rakow or the FBI.

Daddy wouldn't approve of two dead bodies. He'd want prisoners.

My fingers touched a tire iron as the trio rounded the rear of the truck. I yanked it free and slammed the door, the heavy implement riding in my hand with the crooked tire lug portion swinging near my knee. Nice and heavy. Solid steel.

I fast-walked toward the back of the truck. Skinny's face flushed with rage. He spoke through gritted teeth. "You think you're tough, Army man?"

My pace quickened. Uncertainty flashed across Skinny's eyes. He snapped an order at Muscle in a language that wasn't English, and Muscle took the lead, reaching for the grip of his Glock.

Too little, much too late. Stupid fools. I closed the distance between us and brought the tire iron down like a broad sword, aimed right for Muscle's face. He ducked and leaned out, just as I knew he would, and I effortlessly redirected my blow right for the shoulder of his shooting arm.

Metal met skin and bone with a crunch, followed by a shriek of pain. I backhanded the tire iron like a fly swatter, nearly ripping the nose right off his face. He clutched his right shoulder with his left hand, raising his right in a helpless plea for mercy. The gun abandoned.

I didn't even break stride. The iron obliterated the fingers of his right hand, smacked him in the jaw sharp enough to shatter teeth and bone, then slammed into the back of his skull.

Muscle went down like an opossum clipped by a truck tire, and I turned for Skinny. He stood behind Keen, both of them wide-eyed, frozen in some state of shock. It had been maybe four seconds since Muscle had fumbled for his gun.

Skinny was just as slow, like the biological refuse he was. But as I turned toward him with the bloody tire iron, his mind finally clicked into gear. He shoved Keen left, away from the truck, and raised the Glock. It was a .45, not a 9mm or a .40. I knew that by the gaping mouth of the muzzle. A heavy, overkill round just like the heavy, overkill truck Skinny rode around in.

And once more—too little. Too late.

The tire iron smashed into the side of the Glock a split second before Skinny pressed the trigger. Fire and gun smoke erupted into the air as the redirected weapon hurled a slug through the rear window of Keen's Silverado. Cubes of glass rained across the bed, and I lunged forward. A quick blow to Skinny's extended forearm, hard and fast enough to break both the ulna and radius while sending the Glock toppling. He fell back against the corner of the truck and fought to regain his footing. I followed him up, raining blows like lightning strikes, ignoring his desperate screams.

A shattered shoulder. Two broken ribs and another obliterated hand. He twisted and almost fell. His knee hit Keen's bumper and left his lower leg pinned awkwardly over the ground. I raised my boot and stomped down, full force, shattering the leg and sending him crumpling into the mud. He bit dirt, and I circled slowly behind him.

Breathing easily. Not even sweating.

I pivoted the tire iron to align the back side of the curve with my striking motion. Skinny lay writhing on the ground, sobbing and choking on his own screams.

I silenced him with a strike to his left temple. Quick and decisive. Lights out. Unconscious, but not dead.

Better than he deserved.

The forest fell suddenly silent, two piles of broken bones and brainless skulls lying motionless on the pine needles. I flicked the bloody tire iron into the truck bed and turned to see Keen staring wide-eyed, ten feet away. Pale as a ghost.

"Welcome to the story, Keen."

38

"Wh...what...what did you do?" Keen could barely get the words out, choking on his own tongue as he fixated on the broken bodies. For a true crime writer, he seemed oddly shocked by the sight of actual carnage.

I dropped the tailgate on his truck. "Help me. Quick!"

I grabbed Muscle by his ankles while Keen continued to sputter. I was still thinking about Skinny's gunshot and the thirteen or more gunmen lounging half a mile away who would have heard it.

"*Move!*" I said.

Keen snapped out of his stupor and grabbed Muscle by the shoulders. Together we heaved his body into the bed of the Silverado, followed by Skinny. They both shifted and twisted in ways the human body wasn't designed to shift or twist, their eighteen- or twenty-year-old bodies a mass of broken bones and shattered cartilage. It was a brutal sight, but one thought of Skinny's flash drive full of filth was enough to erase any remorse I might have felt.

I took the driver's seat and piloted the Silverado out of the pine grove, passing the jet-black Ford Raptor halfway out. It was parked amid the pines, concealed from the road, the front doors still open.

"What the hell happened, Keen?"

Keen sat next to me, still pale. He shook his head. "I...I heard a noise, and I went to the road and..."

"They saw you," I snapped. "Stupid."

That shut Keen up long enough for us to reach the busted county road. I turned away from the hunting camp, back toward Carter's Crossroads. It was the nearest place I could think of to hide, and I pulled the Silverado behind the abandoned service station where it was invisible to the intersection.

"You got any tape?" I asked.

"T-tape?"

"Duct tape. Rope. Zip ties. Something like that."

He hesitated. "I...have dog leashes."

"That'll work. Let's go."

I flipped into the truck bed, and he brought me a fist full of tangled leashes, most of them the small, retractable kind. I pulled the cords out and cut them free of their automatic winders with my Victorinox. Then I went to work hogtying the two Krols, wrists to ankles, using multiple layers to ensure they wouldn't budge when they came to.

"Are they...are they dead?" Keen whispered.

"Would I be tying them up if they were?"

He didn't answer. I flung the remaining leash paraphernalia through the shattered back window and returned to the ground. Retreating ten feet to the far edge of the lot behind the service station, I positioned myself where I could see the passing road while remaining concealed, and I folded my arms.

Now that I had secured my prisoners and retreated to a secure location, automation and instinct took a back seat to calculated thought. My mind began to spin. Not with stress or fear or any particular concern about wrecking two kids to within an inch of their lives.

It was something they had said. A throwaway comment Skinny made right before I went to work on Muscle.

"You think you're tough, Army man?"

It bothered me, but I couldn't determine why. At the time I just thought it was a snotty comment, and it fueled my desire to reduce them both to puddles of slobbering goo.

But now...

A Jeep rolled up to the stop sign—one of the Wranglers I had seen at the lodge. The top was up, and the windows tinted well beyond the legal limit, rendering the occupants invisible. But I knew who was inside. Three or four of the Albanian gunmen, on the lookout for the source of that lone gunshot.

It was a certain indicator that Skinny and Muscle had failed to report their detainment of Keen. Otherwise, there should have been more—and more competent—personnel on hand to deal with me. I figured it was an ego thing. The old man had roughed them up. Talked down to them. Humiliated them in front of the Albanians.

Skinny and Muscle were probably eager to prove themselves. To silence their old man's disrespect by bringing Keen and me in on their own.

Another idiot move. They should have called for backup.

"What now?" Keen hissed, stepping in behind me. The Jeep was gone, but I knew it would be back. I wanted to wait for it to pass before I left the shelter of the service station. Even if the Krol boys hadn't called in Keen's appearance, the Albanians would be on the lookout for an unfamiliar truck. The busted rear window would only make the Silverado more suspicious.

"Sharpe?"

Keen sounded like a shell-shocked private just subjected to his first burst of combat. Maybe just having witnessed one of his buddies from boot camp blown in half by an IED.

What now? An odd, yet predictable question. An immediate search for meaning. Something I had experienced a lot in the Army.

The Army. The thought unlocked a sudden reinterpretation of the challenge Skinny had thrown at me. It wasn't the challenge itself that had bothered me. It was the nickname —*Army man*.

"They're running a trafficking operation, just like you thought," I said. "The old summer camp is their headquarters. I think it's some kind of distribution hub. They ordered catering—for a lot of people."

"What...what does that mean?"

I folded my arms, watching as the Jeep reappeared at the intersection, and turned back for the hunting camp. Probably resolved that the random gunshot had been a kid in the woods with a new shotgun. Or maybe a hunter poaching a summer buck.

I thought again of the conversations I had overheard between Krol and his boys. First at the compound and then at the lodge. All the little remarks about things being over soon, and Skinny and Muscle wanting to be present for whatever big event was about to take place.

"One false move," Krol had said, *"and tonight does not happen."*

I remembered his words, and then I thought of something else he had said. A prophecy of what would happen if any drama were to erupt. "They will scatter."

Who? Who will scatter?

I chewed on it for only a moment before deciding that the most obvious answer was probably the right one. *Buyers.* People from out of town, coming in to view the product and make their selections. To participate in an auction, maybe. Like a cattle sale. Not online, but in person. Where the FBI couldn't monitor any websites or trace any IP addresses. Keeping it old school, right here in the middle of nowhere.

That would explain the catering. It would explain the old man's fancy clothes, too, and his agitation about everyone remaining on point. There was going to be a party—tonight.

"It means we're running out of time," I said at last. "The girls are here. Krol and the Albanians are preparing for a sale. Tonight."

"You can't be serious..."

"You don't order sex slaves online, Keen. What did you expect?"

I turned for the Silverado. Keen rushed to follow me. The keys still hung in the ignition. I fired up the engine while using my phone to calculate a route back to my GMC that didn't lead me directly past the entrance of the hunting camp. If I was right about the auction, they would have somebody on lookout.

"We've got to call the cops!" Keen said. "Call the sheriff. Have him bust them."

I shook my head. "Not an option."

"Why not?"

I didn't answer as I mashed the gas, turning left out of the parking lot. It was a ten-mile circle to reach my GMC from behind. I pushed the Silverado up to seventy, driving like Rakow down the narrow, bumpy roads. A quick glance at the clock confirmed what I already suspected. It was after four p.m. The sale would take place at night, I thought. Or early evening. That left me with very little time to calculate.

"I need you to find someplace quiet to lie low and work a phone," I said. "Someplace they won't find you."

Keen hesitated. "My buddy has a lake house. Just south of Muscogee."

"Great. Use it. Get on the phone and call the FBI. Try to get in touch with the Montgomery field office. Tell them you've got a sex trafficking case in Delamar County, and they should send HRT, ASAP."

"HRT?"

"Hostage Rescue Team. They'll know what you mean."

"Will they...take me seriously?"

"Probably not, so keep selling. If you hit a wall, call the Alabama state police. Call the FBI field offices in Atlanta and Birmingham. Keep ringing until somebody listens."

"What about them?"

Keen looked toward the bed of the truck. I had already forgotten about the two Krol boys. I had half a mind to pull off the side of the road and dump them in the woods, letting the coyotes finish the job later that night.

But Keen could never stomach that, and I needed him focused.

"Does your buddy's lake house have a garage?"

"It's got a boat shed."

"Good enough. Drag them in there. Put some tape on their mouths. We'll deal with them later."

"Okay..."

He still wasn't sold. Still a little shell-shocked by my ruthless beatdown.

"You remember those dormitories?" I said. "You remember how big they were?"

Keen's gaze dropped. He nodded slowly.

"They're prisons now. Boarded up, guarded by men with guns. Probably full of trafficking victims. Can you picture that?"

He could—I saw it playing over his face. First disbelief, followed by horror. Then came a storm cloud of rage that darkened into a hurricane by the time I pulled off next to my GMC and piled out. Keen circled around to take the wheel, stopping as I fired up my old engine.

"What are you going to do?" he asked.

"Work things from the other end," I said simply. "Don't stop calling. I'll update you when I can."

He nodded and stepped back as I punched the gas. The old GMC rumbled like a bucket of nails as it hit the pavement, and I turned south and east.

Not toward Able. Not even toward Muscogee. Toward a lone patch of dirt deep in the county, with a little house and a rugged yard and a scruffy collie who liked to be scratched behind one ear.

Because there was only one person I ever told about my Army career. Somebody who shared that heritage. Somebody the whole county trusted, who would also have the power to shield a complex trafficking operation in broad daylight.

It was so obvious I wanted to hit myself. I remembered how old man Krol had told his boys that he would handle the police “the smart way”. What smarter way could there be than to buy them off?

Or better yet, save a little money. Buy just one of them off —the guy at the top of the pile.

Rakow.

39

I reached Rakow's aging country home an hour before sunset and parked my GMC behind the barn. Mossy woofed loudly at my approach, but she calmed as soon as she recognized me. I gave her a good scratch behind the ears until her tongue dropped from the side of her mouth and her whole body relaxed. Then I approached the back door and tried the handle.

It was unlocked, which didn't surprise me. Who would be dumb enough to rob a sheriff's house?

I left Mossy outside as I entered. Skinny's Glock 36 rode in my waistband, still loaded with five rounds of .45 ACP hollow points. Respectable firepower, but I had a feeling there was heavier firepower to be found somewhere in Rakow's house. He was ex-Army and a country boy.

Country boys are addicted to firepower.

I found the master bedroom in the rear corner of the house, but it was obviously not the room Rakow used. It was furnished with tired hardwood furniture, thick with dust, and a queen size bed with a patch-quilt bedspread.

A wedding photograph sat on the nightstand. It was old and faded. The man and woman standing in it both sported decidedly 1980s hairstyles, all big and puffy. She was pretty, and he was serious.

He also looked a little like Rakow. But older.

I checked the nightstand drawers and found no handgun. There were dusty clothes in the closet, and shoes lined up on the floor, but no rifle or shotgun. It was Rakow's parents' room, I decided. His father had left his mother's clothes in the closet when she died, and Rakow had left his father's clothes when he died.

Like some kind of shrine. The thought of it twisted my stomach, reminding me of the little house in South Phoenix. The one I had abandoned.

Clothes in the closet. Dishes in the sink. Not touching a thing. Walking away as if leaving that house could somehow erase the pain.

I could tell by the dust on the hardwood that Rakow hadn't opened that door for a long time. But he had opened other doors. He had entangled himself in other pits of hell. And he was going to answer for that.

I briefly scanned the spare bedroom I had slept in during my two overnights at Rakow's house, but I didn't expect to find anything. Down the hallway, I located Rakow's room behind another battered wooden door. There was a double bed and a desk, with a shelf full of baseball trophies over the window. A chest of drawers sat next to the bed, a handful of coins and two photos of Rakow in military dress resting atop it. In the first, he stood alongside a buddy, both smiling and shooting up peace signs, both wearing dark sunglasses, the glare of the Iraq desert blasting over their shoulders.

In the second photo, he stood in full dress uniform at

some kind of military function. Army Class As—a deep black coat with gold braid, his rank on his shoulder...and a medal on his chest.

It was a Silver Star. I scooped the picture up and squinted at the glass, adjusting the angle to double-check my interpretation. But my first glance had been accurate. The U.S. Army's third-highest decoration for valor in combat —only two levels beneath the Medal of Honor—was pinned to Rakow's chest like it belonged there.

The crossed pistols insignia of the U.S. Army Military Police was affixed to his lapels, but you didn't earn a Silver Star by working guardhouse duty—not like Rakow claimed. He must have done something heroic. Something above the call of duty.

Something that involved running to the sound of the guns.

My jaw clenched as I set the photo down, thinking again about the lodge in the woods. The girl at Palmer's place.

Being a hero only matters if you remain a hero. Switching teams at halftime erases everything that happened in the first two quarters.

I moved to the closet, but found nothing save boots and rows of sheriff's department uniforms. The drawers of the dresser were stocked with socks and underwear, and there was a hook on the wall where he might have hung his duty belt. I found a pair of earrings in a desk drawer—probably Bailey's. But no weapons.

Then I dropped to my knees and looked beneath the bed. A hard plastic rifle case rested on the hardwood, gathering dust and scraping as I dragged it out. The buckles snapped under the tension of compressed foam, and I flipped the lid open.

An AR-15 lay inside—full black, with an A2-style front-sight post, a six-position adjustable stock, a vertical foregrip and a stainless steel trigger. It was laid out a little like a GI-issue M4, but with obvious upgrades. The red dot optic mounted to the upper was an Aimpoint Comp M4, and a Surefire light was linked by an M-Lock clamp near the end of a free-floating handguard.

There was even a bundled two-point sling wrapped around the adjustable stock, and four magazines loaded with green-tipped, semi-steel core ammunition were pressed into narrow foam slots beneath the rifle.

It was a warrior's load-out—ready at a moment's notice to respond to any manner of threats, foreign or domestic. Lifting the rifle from the foam, I completed a quick break-down to find carefully cleaned and oiled internal components, which only served to reinforce what I already thought about Rakow.

He might have worked guardhouse duty, but that was far from the only service he'd rendered his country.

I smacked one of the metal GI mags twice against my knee to ensure the top round was properly seated against the feed lips, then drove it home into the rifle's magazine well and pulled the charging handle. The top round stripped free and slammed into the receiver.

Then I flicked the Aimpoint on and found my way to the kitchen. A fresh pot of coffee brewed in under five minutes as the sun disappeared behind a row of hardwoods. Mossy chased a squirrel outside, and I turned all the lights out.

Then I set a dining room chair in the corner of the living room, my back to the wall, my face to the door. I rested the muzzle of the AR across the back of the couch, pointed at the driveway.

Then I sipped coffee. And waited.

40

Rakow's growling Ford pulled in at a quarter past seven—but to my surprise, it wasn't alone. I heard another truck rumbling in behind it, and a nervous chill ran down my arms. Was it Bailey?

But no. I could see the pair of heavy vehicles through a front window. The second truck was a Dodge, but it wasn't Bailey's. It was deep black, not crimson. It was Chief Deputy Owen's rig.

Momentary indecision raced through my mind. I briefly considered whether Rakow had somehow discovered my presence at his house and had brought backup to flush me out. Then I decided that was unlikely. The vehicles were parked too near to the house. If they knew I was inside, they would have parked the trucks up the road and approached on foot. Tried to get the jump on me.

Owen was here for some other reason. Whatever it was, it didn't matter. I could deal with them both.

Boots hit the front porch. Rakow stopped to scratch Mossy behind the ears, and the old collie gave no audible warning of my presence. Owen belched and muttered something unintelligible. Then the doorknob twisted, and hinges groaned. Rakow's arm appeared, and he flicked the light switch, but the lights didn't come on. I'd already unscrewed the bulbs.

Rakow grunted in confusion and passed through the door. His gaze was drawn upward, toward the light fixture. Owen appeared behind him, holding a clenched fist against his mouth to suppress another belch as he crossed the threshold.

Owen saw me first, but not soon enough. Using my thumb, I flicked the rifle's selector switch from *SAFE* to *FIRE*. The switch made a little *snap* in the stillness, and both men froze.

"Sharpe?" Rakow said, gaze dropping to my shadowy position behind the couch.

"Hands up, Rakow," I said. "You too, Owen."

Neither man moved from the door. I kept the muzzle of the AR centered on Rakow's chest, already knowing he wasn't wearing body armor. I hadn't seen him wear any since we met at the crash scene. Owen didn't look to be wearing any, either. With a quick flick of my finger and a twitch of the muzzle, I could take them both out.

"*Hands. Up*," I repeated.

Rakow and Owen slowly raised their hands, Owen stepping inside and kicking the door closed. Rakow faced me, looking battered and exhausted. Much as he always had. Maybe a little worse today.

Lying to the feds must be draining work.

"I don't know what you're thinking," Rakow said. "But you're wrong."

"Drop the belts," I said. "Very slowly."

Rakow sighed and unclasped his duty belt. Owen's jaw locked, and his face turned scarlet, but he followed suit. The heavy police gear dragged the belts to the floor with a thumping clatter.

"Sit," I snapped, gesturing with my empty coffee cup to the second dining room chair I had arranged to face me. Right in the middle of the room, where I could ventilate Rakow's ass if he tried anything. I hadn't arranged a chair for Owen, but the chief deputy took his place standing behind Rakow without comment, thick arms crossed.

"Is that my gun?" Rakow said.

I didn't answer.

"It is, isn't it? You should have checked the bolt carrier, Sharpe. I always remove the firing pin when I store a gun."

That earned him a derisive snort. "Nice try, Bob Lee. But I did check. I've got a green tip ready to usher you into the afterlife."

Rakow leaned back in the chair, resting both palms on his thighs with an irritated smack. He didn't look scared. He didn't even look concerned. He just looked extremely irritated, and tired. And maybe a little fed up.

"I told you he weren't no good to have around," Owen said softly. His lips twitched, his stocky bulk quivering with suppressed rage. I wondered how much angrier he would be when he learned what a scumbag his boss was.

Rakow ignored Owen's comment and kept his gaze fixed on me.

"All right then, jackass," he said. "What the hell is this about?"

"I think you know," I said.

"No, I really don't. But I've got to tell you, Sharpe. I've extended more than your share of grace since you crashed into my county, and the well is going dry. So get to the point."

"The hunting lodge." I spoke through gritted teeth.

Rakow swept his hat off, running a hand through sweaty hair. He vented a long, irritated sigh, as if he were indulging a bratty six-year-old. "The what?"

"The *lodge*," I repeated. "The old summer camp where Delia went missing."

Neither man seemed to register what I was saying.

"I went for a stroll in the woods, Rakow," I said.

"You found something?" He raised both eyebrows.

"I found everything," I said. "Still not entirely sure what to do with it. Which is why you're gonna start talking, or I'm gonna make whatever you did to earn that Silver Star feel like a trip to Disneyland."

A shadow passed across Rakow's face. Maybe a memory. Maybe deeper anger at my intrusion. Either way, it was gone in a split second. Owen opened his mouth, but Rakow cut him off.

"I have no idea what you're talking about," Rakow said.

"They all say that."

"I really don't."

"Let's start with something easy, then. How about the human trafficking ring operating at that old summer camp? Run by the Albanians, facilitated by the Krol Company...and sheltered by *you*."

"*What?*" Rakow spat the word like bad chewing gum. I didn't so much as flinch.

"I'll deal with them as soon as I'm finished dealing with you. Right now, I need intel. How many people are inside the lodge? What's the security like? How many people are coming for the sale?"

"What sale?" Rakow demanded. "Cut the bullshit. I'm not playing around. What did you find?"

An earnestness crept into his voice. A semi-desperation. For a split second, I questioned myself. Had I miscalculated? Had I jumped to a conclusion?

But no. Only Rakow knew.

"It's a large operation, Rakow. And not a new one. Even in a county this rural, they had to have help. Somebody sheltering them. Somebody keeping good cops away from better questions. And you were the only one I told."

"Told *what*? *What* are you talking about?"

"I'm talking about the Army, dammit. I disassembled those Krol kids. They're broken in about a dozen ways, crying like babies in the back of a truck right now. But you know what they said right before I went to work on them? They called me *Army man*. Because they knew I was a veteran...and you were the only person I told."

Confusion clouded Rakow's eyes. Then sudden understanding. I had seen it before, during my days as a homicide detective, interviewing suspects. It wasn't like the movies. People rarely broke down and spilled everything out of sheer guilt alone. But there was something to be said for cornering a person. If you could place a suspect between a rock and a hard place, then drop some damning evidence on them, you could usually see them break. Usually see the moment where reality struck them in the face like a sledgehammer, and they went all cold and silent. The moment they demanded a lawyer or refused to speak at all.

I didn't see that moment on Rakow's face. The sudden understanding wasn't replaced by cold calculation or the strike of reality. Instead, he simply looked confused. Conflicted.

"Sharpe, I didn't tell anyone—"

"You didn't have to," Owen snarled. He sidestepped quickly behind Rakow, his folded arms unfolding to reveal a subcompact Glock clenched in one hand. It was one of the baby models—a G26 or G27. A backup gun.

In a split second the muzzle of that gun was pressed against Rakow's temple, Owen's finger on the trigger. The rage in his face had hardened now, a hint of desperation joining it.

"I pulled your records when I booked you for the bar fight, you stupid SOB," Owen snarled.

"Owen, what the hell are you doing?" Rakow's voice dropped to a growl, but he didn't move. My blood ran cold, and I swung the rifle's muzzle above Rakow's head to zero on Owen's bulging chest.

"*Drop it*," I snarled.

"I ain't droppin' nothing!" Owen snapped. "You been a thorn in my side since you stumbled into this county. Shoulda rammed your ass into the ditch the day I gave you a ride."

Gave me a ride.

I remembered again the gleaming Dodge 3500 that Owen had picked me up in on my way back to Able after the train incident. All modified and tricked out like a show car. A sixty-thousand-dollar vehicle, maybe an eighty-thousand one. Could Owen afford that on a cop's salary? I'd been so tired and preoccupied, I hadn't even thought about it at the time.

Then I thought of Sadie. The bar fight. How Owen had turned up so quickly. How he had turned up at Palmer's house, also.

And how the girl had fled when she saw him.

Shit.

I felt like an idiot, but the problem was easy enough to rectify. I placed a finger on the stainless-steel trigger as Rakow's eyes blazed with unbridled rage. Maybe at me, maybe at his traitor of a chief deputy. Maybe at all of the above. I still wasn't convinced that Rakow wasn't in on this thing—that Owen wasn't simply placing a gun to his head to knock me off my guard. They could both be dirty.

"I'm gonna rip this thing out by the roots," I said, addressing Owen. "I can do that with or without you. The only way you walk out of here alive is if you start talking."

"Is that so?" Owen smirked, a dribble of sweat dropping off his nose.

"You can take it to the bank," I said.

"Owen..." Rakow growled.

Owen responded by ramming the muzzle of his gun deeper into Rakow's temple, forcing his neck to bend. Rakow gritted his teeth, and Owen's gaze darted sideways. Toward the window.

My gaze did, too. Through the darkened glass, I saw a darker shadow flash by. The silhouette of a man. Then the gaping muzzle of a shotgun swung to face the living room.

"Oops." Owen laughed.

I hit the floor, and the glass exploded. Hot buckshot ripped over my head and peppered the dining room table. Rakow shouted, and boots smacked the floor from his position. Owen's gun went off.

I rolled onto my back and opened fire against the shattered window. I couldn't see my target, but the hail of green-tipped ammunition exploding from Rakow's AR-15 blasted through thin sheetrock and even thinner siding, and I was rewarded by a muted cry. The shotgun chambered a new round with a harsh *shlick-shlick* of metal on metal.

I scrambled for cover at the end of the couch just as the front door burst open.

There was nowhere left to hide. The shotgun had me on one side, the door on the other. I pivoted the rifle toward the front door as another Albanian barreled through, another shotgun raised. Next to him, Rakow lay on the floor, bleeding from his temple while Owen rained kicks on his chest like a madman.

I dropped my finger over the trigger. Then I heard footsteps behind me, approaching from the back door. The door I'd left unlocked so that Rakow wouldn't know somebody was in his house.

I fired twice at the guy crashing through the front door. He took one round to his chest and another to his throat; then something heavy hit me in the back of my skull. My brain spun, and I saw stars. I rolled over and dragged the AR with me. Another blow blurred my vision into a haze of cloudy shapes. I clamped down on the trigger and fired blindly toward the ceiling.

The rifle was wrenched away. A boot landed on my chest and rammed down. The breath left me.

Just as I gasped to recover it, a sticky wet cloth was pressed over my face. I inhaled deeply.

Then everything went black.

41

I saw her on the floor. Ten feet away, maybe less. A wide lake of pure crimson stretched out between us like an impassable surging river.

My heart pounded, and my vision blurred. I looked at my hands, and they were both red. I felt the blood streaming from my back and over my shoulders, dripping onto the floor. Killing all traction as I fought to inch my way forward.

And Mia. Propped against the wall, a massive hole in her chest. Her sad eyes facing me, one hand outstretched as the life slowly left her eyes.

"Mia!" I rasped. My voice felt thick and heavy. I clawed my way forward, slipping in the crimson lake. My feet felt very cold—an icy touch that crept slowly toward my knees.

It was death, coming for me. I knew it. I kicked my legs, and my vision continued to blur. I clawed my way toward her, the current of blood catching me. My body began to spin, and the hallway around me faded.

Yet somehow, I still saw her. Seated just a few feet away,

leaned against the wall. Still smiling sadly. One hand lying open on the floor, reaching for me.

"Mia!" I screamed.

That cold feeling reached my waist. I gasped, panic flooding my system. The falling, spinning sensation worsened as I plummeted deep into the unknown. I couldn't see the school at all now. I couldn't see the hallway.

I only saw Mia. I only felt the fingers of death clawing ever higher.

"Go," she whispered.

"No! Wait!"

The cold reached my stomach. I gasped. Mia vanished. Everything turned black.

MY EYES SNAPPED OPEN, but all I saw was darkness. The cold I felt creeping up my stomach now lapped against the bottom of my ribcage. I moved my hands and found them free.

Then I heard a sloshing sound, and I looked down. Water. Lots of black water, rising quickly up my chest. I was seated in a vehicle, the cabin around me drenched in darkness save for the dim lights of the dashboard, glowing in pale blues and greens.

It was Rakow's Ford, and the moment I realized it, the lights flickered out, and everything went black.

The panic I felt in my dream multiplied by an order of magnitude. My mind shut down, a primitive desperation for survival commanding me to fight like mad. I launched myself forward and felt a seatbelt lock around my chest. The water was up to my elbows now, headed for my shoulders. I couldn't see anything. My heart pounded like a snare drum, faster and faster. Even in the darkness, I could feel my vision fading. Tunneling. My mind shutting down.

I clamped my eyes closed and held my breath. Commanded my heart to calm. I reached down deep in my gut, someplace beyond the fear and desperation, and touched an invisible concrete floor. Something solid. A firm foundation that wouldn't break.

It was something I'd learned to do in Ranger School when I first confronted my fear of leaping from a perfectly good airplane. It served me now as my heart began to slow. My breaths came steady and strong.

I opened my eyes. The darkness was perfect, but I still felt more in control with my eyes open. I unbuckled my seatbelt, then swatted to the left with one arm. Water sloshed, and my fingers collided with floating glass. Not a piece of the windshield—this was a bottle. I threw it aside and felt another bottle. Then my fingers touched a damp shirt and slick skin. A motionless, slumping body in the driver's seat.

"Rakow!" I called.

No answer. I swatted again, smacking him in the face and knocking his hat off. His head rolled, but I still couldn't see him.

Turning for the glove box, I reached underwater to pry it open. Empty peanut wrappers glided past my hands on their way to the surface, and I felt leather gloves and a road flare.

Then a flashlight. Small and plastic, clicking on under the pressure of a tail switch.

LED light flooded the cabin, illuminating a lake of black water rising past my body and into the back seat. The nose of the Ford was pointed downward, and all the windows were inky black.

But we weren't falling. Not anymore. As I shifted in the truck, it didn't sway or roll. The tires were planted deep in the mud of...something. A lake? A flooded bauxite mine? Who the hell cared?

I turned back to Rakow. He lay buckled into the driver seat, empty whiskey bottles bobbing around him. The water had almost climbed to his chin. His face appeared ghostly white.

I smacked him hard. Yanking his face around, I shook it and splashed water into his eyes.

"Rakow! Wake up!"

His eyes blinked once, and his neck stiffened a little. He was doped, hard. Chloroform, probably. An old-school trick from an old-school thug.

More water to his eyes and another smack across his face. Rakow blinked and grunted; then consciousness seemed to return in a flood. He sat up, gasping and thrashing in the water. The same panic that I had felt, now redoubled by a much higher water level.

"Stay calm!" I shouted. I grabbed his shoulder and clamped down with one hand, forcing him to relax into the seat. He continued to thrash and gasp.

I hit him again, right across the cheekbone.

"Snap out of it, soldier!"

Clarity returned. Rakow breathed a little slower, then peered toward me across the cabin.

"What—"

"We're in your truck. We're underwater," I said. "Listen carefully, I won't be able to repeat this. When the water level reaches the ceiling, we'll run out of air. The only way out of here is to wait for the cabin to flood to equalize pressure and allow us to get the door open. Then we kick for the surface. Do you understand?"

A confused pause. Then he reached for his buckle and tore the belt off. "Break a window!"

"No!" I caught his hand on the way to his driver's side window. "We can't do that. They'll be waiting to make sure we don't surface. We have to ride this out as long as we can."

Rakow stopped, and I released his arm. His quick eyes scanned the flooded cabin, and he noted the empty whiskey bottles. Realized he wasn't tied up.

And neither was I.

This wasn't an execution, this was a staged accident. Two drunk fools flying off the road and crashing into a lake, there to drown. The autopsy wouldn't support that, of course. But with Owen in charge of the investigation, that was a simple problem to solve.

"Breathe normally," I said. "Stay calm. We're gonna get out of this."

I was less sure, but if Rakow panicked, we were both dead men. He nodded twice, and I lifted my wrist from the water, checking my watch. The digital numerals glowed dully in the dimness. I couldn't be sure how long we'd been under, or how deep we were. But by calculating the flow of water into the cabin, and thinking in reverse, I knew it couldn't have been long. Five minutes, tops.

How long would Owen's goons wait? How long would *I* wait if I were standing on the shore with a stolen AR-15, watching to see if my victims made a last-ditch effort to survive?

I'd wait twenty minutes, at least. Because I know how long it takes a car cabin to flood. Alternatively, I would have knocked a hole in the windshield prior to driving the truck into the lake, and sped up the process.

But they hadn't thought to do that, and I was willing to bet they were more impatient than smart.

Another five minutes, then we'd roll the dice. Our oxygen would be gone by then, anyway.

"We'll use a back door," I said. "It'll be less likely to be buried in the mud. We wait for the pressure to equalize, then force it open and kick straight for the surface. Okay?"

Rakow nodded slowly, still looking rattled but coming around. He'd done something to earn that Silver Star. He'd been under pressure before.

I glanced to the back glass, looking for Rakow's shotgun. It was gone. Empty Coke bottles, whiskey bottles, and assorted paperwork were the only things I could see in the rear compartment.

"You keep a handgun in here?"

"Console," Rakow rasped. I dropped my hand to the massive center console and flipped it open. A large bubble of precious oxygen erupted to the surface, and the sharp beam of the flashlight cut into the compartment.

Chewing gum, a screwdriver, and more peanut wrappers. No handgun.

"They took it," I said. "Stay loose. Stay calm."

Water touched my chin, and I pushed myself out of the seat, pressing my head against the ceiling. There was barely six inches of air left. Maybe twelve near the rear glass, where the angle of the roof allowed for a larger space.

"Into the back," I hissed.

Rakow went first, unlocking his seat back and rocking it toward the rear to allow himself room to slosh through. I followed him into the back seat, finding the interior door lock and disengaging it. Then we sat with our backs pressed against the rear glass, heads held inside that precious pocket of air.

Waiting.

"You're a real asshole," Rakow muttered.

"Stop wasting oxygen," I retorted. "You can punch me after we survive."

I checked my watch. Four minutes had passed like lightning since I last looked, but I knew those four minutes had crawled for anybody waiting on the bank. Whoever these guys were, they were three guys short after my dispatch of the Krol kids and the one Albanian at Rakow's place. Short on manpower, with a big operation underway back at the lodge, they had better things to do than watch a lake.

I hoped.

"Three more minutes," I whispered. The water had filled the front of the cabin now, leaving only four inches in the back of the cab. I had to rock my head back and press my mouth near the ceiling to draw air. Water filled my ears, and I heard my own heart thumping in my chest. Still straining. Consuming oxygen faster than it should.

I thought about PPI—pounds per square inch. The amount of water pressure forced against the outside of the door, bearing down on the truck. That pressure grew exponentially stronger the deeper you dove, and I had no way of knowing whether we were ten feet or a hundred feet from the surface.

If we were a hundred, there would be other things to worry about. Decompression sickness—the bends. A potentially lethal condition obtained by rising from the bottom of a deep body of water too quickly. A real problem for scuba divers, but also a hazard for free divers, or fools caught in a truck with chloroform headaches.

But none of that really mattered, because our only shot of survival was forcing that door open, rising to the surface without running out of air, and finding dry ground without being shot through the head.

A lot of ifs and maybes. I switched my watch to the stopwatch function and closed my eyes. Thought about Mia. Saw her again propped up against that wall, reaching for me. A sad smile and sad eyes. Saw her lips part, and her soft voice call to me, one final word.

Go.

42

I smashed the start button on the stopwatch and reached for the door handle. The cabin was flooded now, murky water reflecting the glare of the flashlight. I heard Rakow sloshing behind me and felt his arm on my shoulder.

One quick, confident pat. The soldier's signal that he was in place and ready to go.

I yanked the handle and shoved on the door. Even with equalized pressure, gallons of water stood in the way of the heavy steel panel. My lungs were already burning as I threw my shoulder against the glass and shoved. Cold, rushing water passed across my face, and I dug my foot into Rakow's back seat. The door swung open slowly, as though I were forcing it through a mound of sand. I measured the opening with a quick pass of my hand and felt a two-foot gap.

Good enough.

Kicking free of the back seat, I rotated instinctually upward, the flashlight still gripped in one hand. Then I reached out with both arms and surged for the surface. Deep shadows and more cold water closed around me on all sides. My head thumped, and my chest began to constrict.

I was out of air to exhale. My lungs were now frozen in place, my heart pounding.

But there were still yards to go. Dozens of them, maybe. I had no idea whether Rakow was on my heels or whether he had become tangled in a seatbelt and was still trapped in the Ford. There was no time to worry about that now. I had to get to the surface.

I kicked harder and reached out with both arms. My head felt light, and I wanted to inhale so badly I almost sucked down water. I clenched my teeth and kicked one more time.

Then I broke the surface like a submarine conducting an emergency blow. My head and shoulders erupted out of the lake, and I gasped, thrashing and fighting to obtain my balance. I went under again, just briefly. Then my legs found a rhythm to tread water, and I began to bob.

I flipped the flashlight off and immediately stopped my watch. A sound like a Mack truck breaking across a mud puddle erupted to my right, and Rakow broke the surface also. He kicked near me as I continued to gasp for air and check my surroundings.

It was a flooded bauxite mine. I could tell by the relatively straight and rectangular boundaries of the lake, illuminated by a moon that now shone as bright as day. No trees overhung the banks, with the nearest stretch of dry ground lying forty or so yards away.

I looked quickly for people and didn't see any. The night was still, broken only by our desperate heaving and the lap of water against rocky shale walls on either side of the lake.

I motioned to the shore, and we both put our faces back

beneath the surface, kicking out strong. I dug in with both hands, instantly remembering why I was a better combat Ranger than I ever would have been a rescue swimmer. I can keep myself alive in the water, but I'm no Michael Phelps.

When I reached the dry, dusty bank twenty feet ahead of Rakow, my breathing came in ragged gasps. I pulled myself quickly back to my feet, inspecting the shore for signs of the enemy. There were plenty of tire tracks, including a wide and obvious set of tread marks that led down a dirt drive and straight into the water.

Rakow's Ford. I figured the mine was scooped like a swimming pool, much like the bauxite mines I had seen two days prior near the rail yard. Shallow on one end and sloping deeper and deeper toward the far end. In theory, the heavy Ford would keep on rolling once it was underwater, dragging us helplessly along with it.

What a clever little murder method.

I checked my watch. It read only fifteen seconds, and I reversed the math in my mind. Maybe five seconds to force the door open. Ten to kick for the surface. I knew a standard, safe ascent speed was generally accepted to be sixty feet per minute, but we were kicking our way back to fresh oxygen a lot faster than that.

So maybe...twenty feet from truck to surface. Twenty-five, max. No risk of decompression sickness at that depth.

I mopped water out of my hair and reset my watch, shivering in the cold. It had felt so much longer than fifteen seconds. So much deeper.

Rakow pulled himself to his feet next to me, dripping and looking mad as a hornet. He spat water over the rocks and stared at the black surface of the lake a long time. Then he gritted his teeth.

"That was my father's truck."

I said nothing, giving him time to clear his strained head. Then I dug through my pockets, fishing out wet and sopping gear. My wallet, Victorinox, and phone were all present. They hadn't wanted to take anything, I figured. Easier to convince people of a tragic accident if I still had my stuff in my pockets.

"Why was Owen with you at the house?" I asked.

Rakow snorted. Shook his head. Spat lake water on the ground.

"He said he wanted to talk to you. He had questions about something you were discussing when he picked you up the other day."

I thought back to my conversation with Owen during our ride between Muscogee and Able. I hadn't said much—certainly nothing worth following up on. But Owen's pretext for joining Rakow at his house was a smart one. It wasn't something Rakow was likely to question. I figured old man Krol had been more concerned by my visit to the lodge than he let on to his two idiot boys. He'd probably called Owen and advised him to be present whenever I next talked to Rakow. To run interference, in case I should draw police attention to the hunting lodge.

Owen had deployed the two Albanians into the woods around Rakow's place as backup, just in case things turned violent. And they had.

"Still think I'm dirty?" Rakow snapped.

I held his gaze, and he didn't blink. The rage in his face had turned white hot, but it wasn't directed at me.

No. I didn't think he was dirty. Not only because Owen had tried to drown him, but because I recognized that fury. I'd felt it every day for months.

I dug through my sopping pocket to retrieve my phone. The screen was waterlogged and a little blurry, but still powered on under gentle pressure of the power switch. I found Keen's business card in my wallet and dialed his number as I started toward the road.

"Where are you going?" Rakow called after me.

I paused, the phone rising to my ear, and looked over my shoulder.

"To finish this."

43

Keen arrived forty minutes later, rolling up in his maroon Chevy and piling out all wide-eyed and pale. It was becoming a trademark look. He inspected our saturated clothes, the lake still visible in the backdrop, and ran both hands through his hair.

"Oh man. Oh man. Oh man."

"Get back in the truck, Keen." I helped myself to the passenger seat, and Rakow piled in back. Keen buckled himself in and gave the sheriff a wide-eyed look through the rearview mirror.

"What...I mean where now?"

"Just drive," I said.

He nodded several times and shifted into gear; then we ground back onto the rough county road, headed north. Generally toward Able.

I dropped Keen's glove box open, looking for a handgun. I found dog treats and poop bags.

"You got a gun?" I asked.

Keen hesitated. "Not with me."

I slammed the glove box shut. *Then what good is it?*

"Get me back to the station," Rakow said. "And hand me your phone."

Keen reached for his phone, but I put a hand on his arm. "No. You don't want to do that."

"Why not?" Rakow snapped.

"Because your chief deputy is bought and paid for. You don't know who you can trust. We need to think about this."

"This is still my county, dammit!"

"Which is why you're going to make this right. But we're gonna do it the smart way. All right? *Think*, Rakow."

He gritted his teeth and looked away, using a rag in Keen's back seat to wipe his face. The rag was coated in dog hair, and Rakow spit and threw it onto the floorboard.

"Where are they, Sharpe? What did you find?"

I ignored him, turning back to Keen. "Any luck with the FBI?"

Keen's shoulders fell. "They don't believe me."

"Did you call Atlanta? Birmingham?"

"I called eight different field offices. Three state departments."

"And you got *nothing*?" I couldn't conceal my disbelief.

Keen shifted uncomfortably, gaze dropping. "I...um, I've...called them before. A few times. About this. I guess they must have put my name on some kind of list. I'm sorry..."

"Dammit, Keen. You should have *told me that*."

"You can call them! The sheriff could call them!"

"It won't matter now. We're out of time. It'll be hours before they get here."

I scrubbed my hand over my face, mind spinning. Calculating. Thinking about the dozen men with fully automatic weapons. Maybe more in the house. No, *probably* more in the house. An unmapped interior with endless numbers of rooms and hallways. The FBI's HRT would take hours to plan the mission. In fact, they might not move in at all. They might build a barrier and trigger a standoff. Try to negotiate the hostages out alive.

Somebody always died when doors were kicked in, which was what I had done with the Rangers. In villages across Afghanistan, looking for the men responsible for prolonged terrorist activity. We barged into plenty of homes whose interiors were unfamiliar to us, but only when there was no other option. Only when we were out of time.

I was out of time now. I recalled old man Krol's outbursts. The incoming buyers. The piles of catering food.

The sale was going down *tonight*. Probably, it was going down right then. Long before the FBI or even state police could arrive, those buyers would be back on the road, dispersing Krol's load of innocent lives across the region.

I couldn't allow that.

"Pull over," I said.

"Huh?"

"Pull over, Keen!"

He pulled the truck to the side of the road and shifted into park, but he kept the motor running. I ran my hand across the back of my neck and came up with dog hair plastered to my palm. I scrubbed it off on my knee and looked out the window.

Thinking. And knowing.

There was only one option.

"*What* did you *find*?" Rakow demanded, angry now. A bulldog in a corner, being challenged for his territory. Probably feeling embarrassed and humiliated. Eager to know where his enemy lay hiding.

So I told him. I told him about the lodge and the guys with automatic rifles. The dormitories converted into prison cells. The vehicles out front, including old man Krol's truck. And the catering van. The oversized aluminum dishes of food.

The impending auction.

Rakow's face turned a dark shade of crimson as I finished my account, teeth clenched. To his credit, he didn't launch into an angry outburst. He only faced the window and shook his head slowly. Grinding through the same options I had already reviewed and reaching the same conclusion.

If the sale was now—*tonight*—we couldn't wait for morning. It might take a full day for the FBI to deploy an HRT unit out of Birmingham or Atlanta. State police would be just as slow. And by then, this would all be over. The children in those dormitories would be long gone.

The FBI would find a few. But they'd never find them all.

"You got any more guns at your place?" I asked.

"Just a shotgun," Rakow said.

"We need rifles and a lot of ammo. What about the sheriff's station?"

Rakow thought for a moment. "We keep a small arms locker in the back. Glock 17s, Mossberg 590s, and Ruger Mini 14s. No AR-15s."

"Ammo?"

"Yeah. Few thousand rounds for each. But it doesn't matter. If there's even a chance that somebody else in my department is bought, there's no way for me to retrieve anything without tipping Owen off. We almost never access that locker."

"You don't need to retrieve them," I said. "You just need a single person you can trust. Any name come to mind?"

Rakow snorted. Didn't answer. Then he shook his head.

"I trusted Owen more than any of them. Chief deputy is assigned at my discretion."

"Spilt milk," I said. "We need somebody else."

I reviewed my memories of my time at the station. It had been brief, and I had been relatively preoccupied, but I had noticed half a dozen deputies. Mostly men, maybe one woman. All busy and preoccupied. I didn't recall any interactions.

Except...

"What about the old guy?"

Rakow frowned. "Willis?"

"Right. The desk sergeant."

"He's...been there forever. I think he was a deputy before my father was sheriff."

"What does he drive?"

"Drive?"

"His POV."

"Oh...some old beater. Mazda, maybe. A pickup."

"He's your man. Give him a call."

"How can you be sure?"

"I talked to him the day I was at your office. He said he kept retiring, but his wife drove him nuts, so he kept coming back. I've worked with old guys before. The ones who keep working do it because they love the work, and they almost always blame it on their wives. If he's driving an old beater, he's probably not making money under the table. One of the first things people spend dirty money on is vehicles. Just look at Owen."

Rakow's face turned dark again. "He told me a rich aunt died."

"More spilt milk. Call Willis. I need a rifle and at least a dozen fully loaded magazines. Body armor and a sidearm. I'll take a shotgun, too."

Rakow shook his head. "No. I can't let you go full Rambo on this. We have laws."

"What you have is an unknown number of *children* about to be sold at auction like cattle. You're the sheriff. Are you going to do something or not?"

A short pause. Rakow snapped his fingers, and Keen reached for his phone.

"Call the station and ask for Willis," Rakow said. "Don't hand me the phone until you're sure it's him."

Keen complied, and Willis picked up the phone. I recognized his old, scratchy voice. It put a little warmth in my chest. I've always liked old guy cops. The good ones, anyway. They know more about good police work than most of the people they work with combined, and somehow, they usually still have a sense of humor.

"Willis, it's Rakow...right. No, don't tell anyone. Are you alone? Go someplace where you can talk."

Long pause. Willis returned.

"Listen, I don't have time to repeat this. I need you to access the small arms locker and retrieve two rifles, two shotguns, and three pistols. Get plenty of ammo, and body armor. Handcuffs, too. A lot of them. Bring it all to my place, ASAP. Don't let anyone see you, and if they do, make something up. Under no circumstances do you mention me or Sharpe...that's right...the bum."

Rakow shot me an apologetic look. I ignored him and

motioned for Keen to drive, guiding him back onto the road. As we hit the pavement, Rakow put in one final request.

"Willis, one other thing. Bring me a couple of badges."

Rakow hung up, and Keen and I met his gaze in the mirror. His eyes were still ice cold, his face that ugly shade of red.

"If we're going to do this, we've got to do it right. I'm going to deputize both of you."

Keen swallowed, a little too visibly. "Both of us?"

I faced the wide-open highway ahead of us, pierced by Keen's headlights. "Time to tell your own story, Keen."

44

Rakow's place seemed like a bad option at first consideration, but the more I thought about it, the better I liked it. Nobody would look for him there. Rakow said Bailey was working the bar tonight, and nobody else ever came by. The Albanians thought he was slowly rotting at the bottom of a bauxite mine.

And it gave me a chance to change clothes and find my camouflage paint.

Keen parked in front of the house, and Willis turned up twenty minutes later, bumping along in a twenty-year-old Mazda B3000. Rusting and dented, with fishing poles sticking out of the back and cigarette smoke drifting from an open window. The truck stopped next to Keen's Silverado, and the little engine quit. Then Willis appeared with a lot of grunting, fully dressed in his sheriff's department uniform with a Glock 17 on his hip. Rakow and I met him at the door, and Willis gave a little nod.

"Sheriff, I got the stuff in back."

He dropped the tailgate, and I flicked on the flashlight

from Rakow's Ford. The bed of the Mazda was loaded down like the bed of a Taliban Toyota—everything Rakow had requested and then some. Half a dozen Glock 17s riding in a bin on top of loaded, seventeen-round magazines. Four Mossberg 590 pump-action shotguns, complete with side saddles, and another bin loaded with buckshot and breaching rounds. A bucket full of handcuffs, a stack of body armor plates with *SHERIFF'S DEPT.* embroidered over their nylon carriers.

And four Ruger Mini 14, semiautomatic rifles. They were Ruger's Ranch model, equipped with solid wood stocks and uncompensated muzzles. A rotating, Garand-style bolt, ghost ring sights, and no optics.

A weapon that was, by modern combat standards, sorely outdated. Yet it fired the same ammunition as an AR-15, at the same velocity and roughly the same rate of fire, and police departments around the world still preferred them for their appearance. A traditional-style rifle with a wooden stock was a lot less scary to the average, uneducated citizen than a black rifle with a pistol grip. The Phoenix Police Department owned a couple of hundred of them.

"I got what I could, Sheriff. You wanna tell me what this is about?"

Rakow leaned over the truck bed and spent a moment considering. Then he told Willis what I had told him. All about the summer camp and the armed Albanians. The barricaded dormitories and what they were thought to contain.

Willis's puffy old face wrinkled into rage as Rakow spoke, his handlebar mustache twitching with irritated tension. I left Rakow to finish the spiel and selected one of the Rugers from the stack. It appeared the cleanest and the least battered by lengthy service. The heavy steel magazines Willis had brought were all loaded with full-metal-jacket, .223 Remington rounds. Twenty-round capacity, which was a disappointment. But again. Shorter magazines appeared less threatening to uneducated citizens.

The magazine rocked in like an AK mag, rolling and snapping. I chambered the first round, stepped twenty feet away, and opened fire on a tree forty yards across Rakow's property. Bark and shreds of wood erupted into the air, empty brass casings showering the ground. I dumped the full magazine, the rifle thundering almost twice as loud as an average AR-15, blasting fire at every shot. The bolt locked back on empty, and I lowered the weapon.

The sights were dead on. The action buttery smooth.

It would do.

I turned back and found the three men transferring the gear into the back of Keen's pickup. There was a lot of dried blood in his bed, and I knew Rakow noticed. He didn't question it. I pulled a duty belt out of the pile and strapped it on, equipping myself with one pair of handcuffs, a Glock 17 with two spare mags, and a lot of other junk that I jettisoned into the pickup truck bed. I didn't need a Taser, pepper spray, or a night stick. Nonlethal options would be useless as soon as the fireworks started, and I didn't want the additional weight.

I pulled a bulletproof vest over my chest and locked it in place. Rakow did the same while Keen stood near the tailgate and fumbled with a duty belt. His face was still pale, his fingers slick with sweat. I put a hand on his arm. When he faced me, I saw nervous tears in his eyes.

"I...I can't do this, Sharpe. I'm not like you guys."

"Says who?" I asked.

He swallowed hard. "I'm not military. I'm not a killer. I don't think—"

"Keen." I cut him off, squeezing his arm. "I need you to listen to me. This isn't about training, and it isn't about being a killer. It's about black and white—good and bad. Very simple. Delia may be in that lodge. I can't get her out by myself. Neither can Rakow. We only need you for support, but I need to know that you'll have our backs."

Another protracted pause. "Support?"

"I'm working on a plan."

"What if I...I mean, I don't know if I could...kill anybody."

"You ever hunt deer?" I asked.

"Sure."

"You ever kill a deer?"

"Yeah."

"It's just like that. Except the deer was innocent."

"Right."

I patted him on the shoulder, then handed him a Kevlar vest. "Find your grit, Keen. Delia is depending on it."

I went to my truck for the camouflage paint, and when I returned, I found Willis tugging on a bulletproof vest, huffing and puffing and sucking in his old-man gut to get it down over his shoulders. Rakow appeared from his house carrying spare flashlights and bottled water. He confronted his desk sergeant near the tailgate.

"Willis, what the hell are you doing?"

Willis shifted the vest, wriggling it down until it covered the majority of his vital organs. Then he reached for a shotgun.

"What's it look like I'm doing?"

"Put the gun down, Willis. Margie needs you home alive."

"Marge needs a vodka tonic and a sense of humor," Willis snorted.

He proceeded to mash twelve-gauge buckshot into the 590's magazine tube. Rakow put a hand on the old guy's arm.

"Willis, listen to me. I can't have you—"

"Sheriff, shut the hell up."

Rakow blinked. He glanced at me. I shrugged, not about to insert myself into the drama. Rakow sighed and held out his hand. Willis dropped two gold stars into it, about the diameter of coffee mugs. Gleaming in the moonlight.

"All right, you old goat. Stand witness."

Rakow called Keen from the truck's cab and positioned us both in a line. He extended his right hand, propping a worn black book in his palm. It was a Bible, heavily used and battered by age. A silver script inscribed the name *Mary Rakow* across the cover.

"Raise your right hands and place your left on the Bible."

We followed directions, Keen's hand slick with nervous sweat as it closed over mine. Then Rakow performed the oath, and we repeated it after him. It was much the same as the oath I took as a soldier and again as a cop. An oath of allegiance to the constitution of the United States, the people of Alabama, and the protection of Delamar County.

Keen's voice tremored as he spoke, but he kept his shoulders squared and his chin up. When we reached *So help me God*, he spoke as clearly as I.

Then the gold star dropped into his hand, and the nervous flash of a smile passed across his face.

I didn't smile, because I knew what that star meant, and

what it would bring. It might be the last badge either of us ever wore.

I pinned it to my belt anyway, and Rakow slammed Keen's tailgate closed, cradling a Mossberg 590.

"Mount up," he called.

We all loaded into Keen's truck.

45

Rakow took the wheel of Keen's Silverado, piloting us down his bumpy driveway and toward the hunting camp. As he drove, he used his cell phone to call the state, advising the Alabama state troopers' office in Montgomery of an impending operation.

He didn't call the adjacent counties, and he didn't call the police force in Muscogee. I was grateful for that. It would be the obvious tactic to call in backup, but if even one cop amid dozens was dirty and tipped off the men at the lodge, our chances of keeping any of their prisoners alive would evaporate.

Better to strike quickly, out of the dark. Take them by surprise and pour violence of action like gasoline on a fire, burning them alive. I still liked my odds.

Rakow pulled the Silverado behind the abandoned service station at Carter's Crossroads and cut the engine. He rolled all four windows down, and we listened for a long two minutes, but this far from the lodge, the only sounds that reached us were chirping crickets and whispering wind.

"Okay," Rakow said. "Here's how this is going down. You're deputies now. Not vigilantes. Your job is to protect innocents and then to protect perpetrators for their day in court. In that order. We'll arrest as many as we can, using lethal force only when necessary. Everybody clear?"

Keen and Willis grunted. I remained silent—not because I disagreed with Rakow's rules of engagement, but because I knew they would fly out the window the moment the first automatic rifle opened up on our position.

I wasn't interested in taking prisoners, and when I met Rakow's cold gray eyes in the rearview mirror, I knew he wasn't, either.

We gathered once more around the tailgate, and Rakow used his phone to call up a digital map of the surrounding area. Everything was pictured during daylight, photographs taken from a satellite someplace high above the atmosphere.

"This is the spot?" Rakow pointed to the lodge.

I nodded. "That's right. Dormitories behind. Gunmen on the porch and possibly scattered around the perimeter. At least thirteen of them, probably more inside."

Rakow spent a long moment inspecting the image, then quietly handed me the phone.

"This is your area of expertise, Sharpe. I'll follow your lead."

I took the phone, a little surprised, but again grateful. This would make it easier.

Panning around the satellite image, we all listened while Keen recounted what he remembered of the lodge from his childhood summer trip. The layout of a downstairs common room, all open save for a trio of bathrooms in the rear, and a segmented kitchen. A rec room and staff accommodations upstairs. Long tables and wide, bright windows.

Any of it could have changed over the past eleven years. Much of it probably had, but it was still a place to start. He finished as I inspected the road leading through the trees, past the gate, and up to the lodge. I thought about the position of all those gunmen on the porch, and more in the dormitories. I wasn't worried about them. I knew where they were, and I could deal with them easily enough.

I was much more concerned about the combatants I *couldn't* see. Without night vision, and with an imperfect understanding of the terrain, I was asking to be shot in the back.

I needed to flush those invisible tangos out of concealment ahead of time. Bring them into the fight on my own terms. And that brought me back to a strategy I had been developing since emerging from Rakow's sunken Ford—the reason I was willing to risk bringing a total civilian into an open gunfight.

I turned to Keen. "How would you like to play the hero?"

KEEN DROPPED RAKOW, Willis, and me at the same pine grove where I had dismantled the Krol boys earlier that same day. The black Raptor still sat abandoned just off the road, front doors open, interior dome light now dead. I found the keys in the ignition, but when I twisted them, I was met with only a click. The battery was dead.

Keen fished jumper cables from beneath his back seat—for once, prepared—and we jumped the Raptor. Then Rakow passed Keen a police radio, and Keen nodded a lot with nervous energy before clambering in behind the wheel and racking the seat back. The turbocharged engine snarled as he piloted the Raptor to that sheltered spot behind the abandoned service station, there to await my call.

The hole in the high fence remained unpatched and apparently undiscovered when Rakow, Willis, and I reached it. Willis struggled a lot to bend and squeeze, but with assistance he made it through. Then the three of us settled into a fast walk, moving amid the damp pine needles with my Mini 14 leading the way.

I walked with one round in the chamber, the trigger guard safety already disengaged, my finger held against the smooth wood of the stock. Six magazines weighed down the cargo pockets of my pants, three on either side, while the Glock 17 rode on my hip, equipped with a total of sixty-nine rounds of 9mm +P hollow points.

Somehow, I still felt undergunned. I knew how quickly ammunition could evaporate in a full-fledged firefight, and that felt like exactly what we were headed into.

We crossed the creek the same way as I had before, wading slowly with our long guns held over our heads. Willis huffed and puffed and muttered grouchy curses, but refused to be left behind. By the time we reached my former position at the tree line, I knew I'd been right about Krol's scheduled event—a human auction, happening even as we knelt in the shadows.

I saw the gunmen as before—at least a dozen, scattered around the lodge porch and across the yard, most of them wielding AR-15s with shortened barrels. But there were additional vehicles now. Seven of them. Joining the Jeeps and old man Krol's Titan, four large, black SUVs and two high-topped vans lined up next to the house, featuring license plates from states as far away as Texas.

The seventh vehicle was more familiar. It was fit with

Alabama plates. A large, fancy, lifted Dodge pickup. Jet black. It was Chief Deputy Owen's ride.

I ignored the truck, pivoting down to the dormitories and finding the row of buildings now abandoned by guards, their doors standing open.

"The kids are inside," I whispered.

Rakow extended his hand, and I passed him the binoculars. He surveyed everything I had, his jaw clenching when he saw Owen's truck. But he didn't say anything—he remained perfectly calm. A trained soldier.

Willis was third in line for the binoculars, offering a whispered tactical assessment as he completed his inspection.

"Tango on the doorstep is your shot caller. He's the only one speaking into a radio. If it were me, I'd place a couple of snipers inside the lodge with access to the second-floor windows, and at least two crawlers in the woods."

I raised an eyebrow. "Not just an old fart, huh?"

Willis lowered the binos, indulging in a humorless grin. "'Nam."

"Meet Charlie?"

"Nope. But he sure as hell met me."

I turned back to the road. With the kids inside, my initial scheme would require modification. Were it up to me, I would have slipped in undercover, torched the lodge, then returned to the woods in time to exterminate the occupants as they streamed out the front door. Like rats fleeing a gassed rathole.

But if there was even a single child inside, that tactic wouldn't be worth the risk.

"What do you think?" I asked.

"We're gonna have to infiltrate," Rakow said.

"Yep," Willis grunted. "And it ain't gonna be bloodless."

"I know." Rakow lowered the binoculars. "This is worse than I thought."

It's exactly how I described it.

I thought it, but I didn't say it. No point now.

"I'll circle left to the far side of the lodge," I said. "Assume a position in the trees. Then we give Keen the go-ahead. As soon as the gunmen respond to the road, you'll both engage from the trees while I look out for snipers on the second floor. Then I'll infiltrate while you cover me. After I take control of the building, you can call for backup from the sheriff's station. At that point, there will be nothing any dirty cop can do."

"Take the sheriff with you," Willis said. "I've got your back."

I hesitated. I wasn't sure I wanted anyone with me. I also wasn't sure I wanted my only cover fire to be coming from an old geezer who, for all I knew, hadn't shot straight since 'Nam.

But there was virtue to the suggestion, also. Once inside, Willis couldn't cover my back. Rakow could.

"He's right," Rakow said. "We should move together."

I shot him a sideways look, unwilling to say what I was thinking. Rakow filled the gap.

"I know what I'm doing," he said.

"Guardhouse duty?" I prompted.

"Only sometimes," he admitted.

That's what I thought.

"All right, old guy. Don't let us get shot in the back, okay?"

Willis snorted derisively. "Mind your manners, young buck. I might just shoot you myself."

46

I assumed point as we left cover, moving down the hill and to the right. Toward the dormitories.

Rakow followed just behind, light on his feet with his Mini 14 riding at low ready. As we reached the edge of the tree line near the dormitory furthest from the lodge, I stopped again to check the perimeter for more of the Albanians or any of Krol's people.

The bank leading gently down to the lake lay empty, tall grass bending under a gentle summer breeze much as it would have the night Delia had disappeared. I wondered which of the dormitories she might have slept in, and imagined her creeping to the window late at night to sneak out.

Sneak out...and meet Keen. It was the kind of thing a good man would never recover from.

"Cover me," I whispered. "I'll signal you when it's clear."

Rakow settled into a crouch behind a tree, shotgun at the ready. I left the tree line, jogging quickly toward the dorm. A light gravel path crunched beneath my feet just before I landed on the front porch built of rough-sawn planks now warping with age. They squeaked a little under my feet as I pressed my back against the wall next to the door and allowed my rifle to dangle from its two-point sling, switching to the Glock 17 instead.

A compact kill zone required a compact weapon.

I tried the latch and found it unlocked. Then I eased the door open and stepped inside all in the same fluid motion, leading with the Glock.

The dormitory might have once been a place for children to sleep happily and in peace, but those days were long gone. Half a dozen steel bed frames equipped with thin mattresses were all that remained of what must once have been dozens of bunks. They were gathered in the center of the room, the windows covered by multiple layers of chicken wire. My nose wrinkled with the stench of human feces, and I glanced down to see a five-gallon bucket serving as a lavatory. There were abandoned clothes stacked in a pile against one wall, and a small table laden with cheap makeup and a cracked mirror.

But no people. No children.

I returned to the porch and whistled softly to the trees. Rakow joined me on the porch three seconds later. I said nothing as we repeated the procedure with dormitories two and three, growing increasingly stealthy as we neared the lodge. From the bottom of the hill, I could see the wide porch that stretched the entire back side of the lodge, overlooking the lake two hundred yards below. It lay empty, illuminated by the soft glow of wide windows covered by more thin curtains. I saw no gunmen.

After clearing the third dormitory and finding much the same as the first two, we completed the short dash to the next tree line, now moving directly opposite Willis's position.

Rakow's disposition had darkened palpably since we inspected the first dormitory, and now brewed with restrained rage. I led the way beneath skinny pines, stopping when we drew even with the back corner of the lodge, the parking lot now hidden behind the bulk of the building.

Rakow slid into position five feet behind me, turning himself ninety degrees to my position so that he maintained a view of the trees behind us—just in case any of the "crawlers" Willis had predicted should sneak up from behind.

"Back door," I whispered. "Signal Keen."

Rakow lifted his radio and powered it on. He flicked the call switch and whispered into the mic, "Keen, move into position."

A short pause, followed by Keen's mumbled reply. It was barely audible with the volume turned down. Rakow reached down for the call switch again.

Then I heard a sound that wasn't the digital chirp of the radio. A sharp snap—a metallic click. I spun in the leaves and saw a shadow rising amid the trees, ten yards away. A tall guy, clothed in all black, lifting the muzzle of an AR-15 toward my position.

I wrenched the Mini 14 into my shoulder, already knowing he had a second's lead on me. Rakow was quicker. His Mossberg belched fire and thunder, and the guy hurtled backward, a grapefruit-size hole blown right through his sternum. The body hit the ground, and Rakow slammed in a fresh shell.

I spun automatically back to the lodge, raising the Mini and sweeping the muzzle across the back windows—on the lookout for the snipers Willis had predicted, flushed out by the sound of the Mossberg.

The old guy was right again. The first curtain snapped back, and the silhouette of a man with a rifle blocked out the light from behind. I opened fire, driving three precision rounds through his chest and gut before sweeping the Mini left and engaging a matching target three windows down. Glass shattered, and bodies fell, my nostrils flooded by gun smoke.

"Call Keen!" I snapped. "We go now!"

47

"Go, Keen! Now!" Rakow shouted. "Willis, call in the backup!"

In the distance, I heard a horn blast, long and hard. It came from the direction of the busted county road—not part of the plan, but a clever improvisation on Keen's part. I pictured the Raptor crashing onto the hunting lodge's drive, engine howling and tires slinging mud. I saw Keen clinging to the wheel, sweat streaming out from under his brand-new sheriff's department hat.

Maybe thinking of Delia. Maybe remembering how he had failed her.

And not about to fail her again.

I measured the distance to the big iron gate in my mind and shouldered the Mini just as the roar of a turbocharged motor was terminated by the wild crash of metal screaming against metal two hundred yards up the drive. Men shouted from the lodge, and boots pounded the ground. I saw at least three gunmen racing for the gate while two others circled to the rear of the lodge to investigate the gunfire there.

They both took rounds to the chest before I slapped Rakow on the shoulder.

"Now!"

We rushed from the shadows, closing on the back porch with rifles shouldered and safeties disengaged. I made the leap to cover the two steps and hit the porch first, headed straight for the back door. It was built of oak and framed by windows. Shadows passed behind the curtains beyond, panicked voices shouting in foreign languages as Rakow closed in beside me. I reached for the door, then caught a glint of steel to my left and pivoted in that direction.

Long before I could raise my Mini to engage the gunman jogging out of the parking lot, the cracking split of a gunshot broke from the forest, and the guy went down with his forehead blown completely off. That gunshot was followed by three more, shattering the glass of a parked SUV and detonating a tire. Boots crunched on gravel, and voices called for a hasty retreat.

Not just an old cop, I thought.

Then I pivoted on the porch, raising my rifle as Rakow placed the spiked muzzle of his Mossberg against the doorframe just left of the lock. Right where the bolt would be.

"Ready?" he called.

"Go!"

The Mossberg thundered, splinters of oak raining over the porch a split second before my boot crashed into the door. It burst open, light flooding our faces as the pounding beat of loud music streamed across the deck.

And then we were in.

The first guy was tall and white, dressed in a western shirt and black cowboy hat. He stood by accident or on purpose directly in our path, a single-action revolver strapped to his hip in a decorative leather holster.

Our guest from Texas, I presumed. I shot him through the face and throat long before his fingers reached the pearl-handled grip. Rakow's Mossberg belched hellfire to my left, another body hurtling to the floor as he screamed through the chaos.

"On the ground! Drop your weapons!"

Whether anybody would comply was a moot point. Nobody could even hear him. I surveyed the interior of the lodge in a split second, finding exactly what Keen had described. One very large room, bathrooms and the entrance to a kitchen on the right-hand side, accompanied by rows of picnic-style tables, all laden with heaping aluminum containers of catered food. A dozen men gathered around those tables, some of them armed, some of them diving for cover behind anything they could find for shelter—including each other.

The left side of the room was cleared of tables, lined by metal chairs that faced a stone fireplace crackling with orange fire...and a group of girls, no less than fifteen of them, twelve and fourteen years old, dressed like twenty-two-year-old pop stars in tight, revealing clothing with heavy makeup. They pressed into a tight knot, some sobbing or shrieking while others appeared barely conscious, subdued under a cloud of narcotics.

But it wasn't the girls who held my eye. I saw something beyond them—another form, pressed low to the ground, inching toward a window. An ugly, weathered face framed by wiry gray hair.

Old man Krol.

Our gazes met, and the Krol kids' father raised a Glock

between two of the girls' heads, a gap no wider than eight inches revealing his face as he brought the muzzle to bear on my chest. My finger flicked across the trigger, and I shot him in the forehead, blowing the top of his skull off as Rakow's Mossberg thundered again.

Everything was chaos. Bodies lined the floor while other men quickly surrendered, small arms raining across the hardwood. Rakow continued to shout, ordering everyone onto their faces. I left him to subdue the room and moved instinctively to my right, toward the kitchen. I kicked the double doors open and was met almost immediately by a blaze of gunfire from around the corner, just beyond a flat-topped grill. Bullets pinged off the door behind me, and I hit the floor, rolling onto my stomach and opening fire. The Mini thundered in the small room, shooting copper-jacketed ammunition right through pots and pans and into the face of an Albanian crouched behind the griddle. His handgun hit the floor, and I quickly returned to my feet, sweeping the room.

Nothing but blood, gun smoke, and my own ringing ears.

I kicked the door open again, finding Rakow standing over Krol's body, shielding the girls as he swept the room with the Mossberg.

"Kitchen clear!" I shouted.

Outside, the gunfire continued. The rapid snarl of AR pistols, joined by the occasional pop of Willis's mini. He was keeping those guys occupied and pinned down, but it was a temporary arrangement. He'd need help, and soon.

"Upstairs!" Rakow shouted.

I wrenched my magazine out and slammed in a fresh one, then took the stairs two at a time. A wide pine landing greeted me at the second level, overlooking the open space below with a hallway stretching out over the kitchen. Half a dozen doors lined that hallway, three on each side. All closed. All featuring brass doorknobs.

I abandoned my earlier stealth, kicking the first door down with my boot and charging in to find an empty administrative office, papers stacked on a desk next to an open laptop. Folders and binders lined a shelf against one wall. A shattered window overlooked the backyard, with a dead sniper lying across the floor in a pool of his own blood.

I abandoned the room and moved to the next. An empty bedroom—just a dresser and a bed. No people. The next room on the left was a storage room, crowded with miscellaneous tools and cleaning supplies, mops and brooms.

I pivoted to room number four, and as I lifted my boot for the doorknob, I saw light flicker beneath the door crack. I dropped my finger onto the trigger and smashed the latch, sending the door splintering and hurtling open. Light flashed across my face, and I dashed straight into another bedroom.

A narrow, twin-sized bed with disheveled sheets and blankets, pushed against the far wall. A window hung with a heavy curtain. A ceiling fan squeaking and spinning overhead, casting yellow light over the small space.

And standing in the middle of the room, a half-naked teenage girl clamped against his chest, his service pistol jammed against her temple, was Chief Deputy Owen.

48

I stopped in the door, the Mini 14 half-raised and hovering over Owen's stomach. Rakow's chief deputy staggered back, dragging the sobbing girl with him. She choked and murmured desperate pleas in something other than English.

Romanian, maybe. Like the girl in the butterfly pants. Or Albanian. Serbian. Ukrainian.

It didn't even matter.

"Let her go, Owen." I kept my voice even, my finger on the trigger but the muzzle still down. I'd never bring the sights to bear over his forehead before he pressed the trigger. It was a mathematical impossibility, and he knew it.

"You know," Owen sneered, half grinning, "I could have sworn I drowned your ass."

"Should have knocked the windshield out. Rookie mistake."

"You have some experience?"

"In exterminating vermin like you? A little. And I'm about to get a little more."

Owen shook his head. “Naw. That’s where you’re wrong. You’re gonna lay that rifle down and walk down those steps with your hands up. Tell Rakow to clear the way to the door. Imma walk out of here with this little bitch. I’m gonna drive out of here, too. And you’re gonna let me.”

“Not a chance, Owen. The only way you walk out of here alive is if you let her go now.”

I stepped forward. Owen stepped back, ramming the Glock against the girl’s face until her neck twisted, and she screamed—loud and shrill. Tears ran down her pale, girlish face.

“Step back!” Owen roared. “I swear to God, I’ll blow her brains out!”

I stopped. Raised my left hand. “Okay. Just chill out.”

“Put the gun down,” Owen demanded. “Do it now!”

“Okay. Okay.”

I bent slowly, laying the Mini on the floor as the girl continued to sob. She’d stopped pleading now. She probably thought it was over.

Maybe it was.

“The Glock, too! Easy, now.”

I drew the Glock with my index finger and my thumb, placing it on the floor alongside the Mini. Owen ran a wet tongue over dry lips, nodding to himself. Then he jabbed his chin toward the door.

“Back up now. Nice and easy. No sudden moves.”

I took a step backward, toward the door.

“Sharpe?” Rakow called from downstairs, a lot of tension in his voice. Eager for me to return and help him secure a load of restless prisoners.

“Turn for the stairs,” Owen said. “Move slowly.”

I kept my hands up, but I didn’t turn. I didn’t move at all.

"Turn around!" Owen said.

"You're not leaving here," I said calmly.

Owen gritted his teeth, wrenching the girl up by her neck. Driving the gun into her head until she shrieked. "I'll kill her, Sharpe! Tell Rakow to stand down!"

I didn't move, hands still up. The girl blinked, brilliant green eyes shimmering with tears. Pleading silently with me. Begging.

"You believe in hell, Owen?" I asked.

Owen's teeth ground. "Shut your mouth, Sharpe. Turn around!"

I took a step forward. Owen twitched in nervous surprise.

"I had a fiancée," I said. "Only woman I've ever loved. She believed in heaven. I think she's there now. But you know, you can't have one without the other."

"Stay right there!" Owen shouted. "I'll shoot her!"

"No, you won't. Because in the split second it takes you to blow her lights out, I'll be on top of you. Long before you get that gun on me, I'll have my hands on your neck. You'll be on the ground. You'll be gasping for air. I'll be closing off your windpipe. Your brain will begin to shut down. You'll kick your feet and grab for my face, but my arms are longer than yours. There won't be anything you can do."

I took another step forward. Barely six feet lay between us now. The length of an average man. I needed to cut that distance in half before Owen moved the gun.

"*Stop*," he growled. "I'll kill her!"

"No, you won't," I said again. "Because the thing about animals like you—you've spent *years* justifying your own depravity. It's not pedophilia, it's just porn. It's not abuse, you just like it rough. And she isn't a kid, she's just a prostitute. You're not a bad guy. Right? But to kill somebody, well. That's an entirely new set of justifications, and you're so married to your moral house of cards you can't let yourself make that leap."

Another step. Four feet now. Owen's heels collided with the bed frame, his arms shaking. The girl sobbed. Spit ran down his chin as he breathed hard. Pressing the gun into her temple until her neck bent.

"You should shoot me," I said. "Now, while you have the chance. Aim for the head—no body armor. Dump the mag. Don't take any chances."

Fear clouded into Owen's eyes. Momentary indecision, and the hint of doubt.

"You wanna throw your life away, Sharpe?" Owen spewed spittle as he spoke.

"Why not? It's worth less than hers."

Another half step. Three feet now. Just out of reach, but not by much.

"Do it, Owen. Do it now. This is your last chance. Shoot me!"

His body shook. He looked to the door, bloodshot eyes darting. Panic overwhelmed his brain, clouding his better judgment. I shuffled another half step. Two and a half feet.

"Now, Owen! Do it now! *Shoot!*"

He flinched. Pressure relaxed off the girl's head. The gun began to move. I shifted another six inches. The Glock rose. His finger contracted over the trigger.

I struck like a snake. My right hand closed over the Glock's slide, wrenching the weapon back against his trigger finger a split second before he fired. The muzzle never made it to align with my face. Ripping, gut-shattering pain exploded in my chest as the bullet made indirect impact with my body armor instead.

And then I was on top of him. The girl fell to the floor as I snatched the Glock backwards, snapping Owen's trigger finger like a twig. He screamed and collided with the bed. I backhanded him across the face with my open left hand, jerked the Glock free with my right, and belted him across the face with the butt.

Owen fell over the bed, his nose exploding with a spray of blood. I followed him, still gripping the Glock by the slide and pistol-whipping him in the face. I grabbed his collar with my left hand and held him over the bed, each smashing impact of the Glock's butt breaking bone and tearing skin. His nose caved in, and he writhed between my legs, choking on his own blood. Unable to fight back. Overwhelmed and dominated before he even knew what had happened.

And I kept going, striking again and again. Smashing in his face and driving shards of skull straight into his brain. Not stopping until his arms stopped flailing, and his body fell limp. I tossed the Glock onto the bloody bedspread next to him just as boots pounded up the stairs and the door crashed open. One of Rakow's deputies barreled in, leading with his sidearm. For the first time, I was aware of wailing sirens outside the lodge, accompanied by shouting voices.

Backup had arrived, streaming through the busted gate Keen had rammed through with the Krol kids' Raptor. Maybe some of that backup was dirty, like Owen. But it didn't matter. They had no choice but to assist in the arrests now. Rakow could sort the guilty from the innocent later.

"Hands up!" the cop said, brandishing his service pistol. I wiped blood splatter from my face, still breathing hard.

Then I looked to the floor and saw the girl curled up and

sobbing. Staring at me like I was a demon of the underworld.

I couldn't blame her.

I moved to the door, sidestepping the deputy as he followed me with his Glock. I drew my badge from my belt and dropped it on the floor. His crazed eyes followed it, and I wondered what he was thinking.

I didn't really care.

"Put it away, Deputy," I said. "We're done killing people today."

49

I used the upstairs bathroom to wash Owen's blood off my hands and face, then stepped to the window to overlook the lodge's front yard. Half a dozen emergency vehicles lay scattered behind the Jeeps and old man Krol's pickup. Blue and red lights flashed, and Delamar County deputies assembled nearly a dozen men on the gravel in front of the cruisers. They were now handcuffed and subdued while Deputy Willis stood watch over them, his Mossberg 590 cradled like an old friend.

Sadie was there, handcuffed among the men. Rakow's backup had discovered her hiding in a bathroom stall, strung out hard on methamphetamine. She looked pale-faced and sick and hadn't stopped sobbing since they hauled her out. I wondered if she understood what sort of operation she was signing onto when she agreed to work the security system at the gate. I wondered if she knew about the sixteen girls held in the dormitories, barely a hundred yards away.

Probably not. Sadie seemed more gullible than evil. But that didn't matter now. Those girls, including the girl Owen had been in the process of raping, sat huddled on the ground near a fire truck. Paramedics and volunteer firefighters swarmed around them, offering blankets and bottled water, speaking into radios and shouting commands to each other. Managing chaos the best they could. Desperately attempting to process the evil they had crashed into. Probably not yet understanding that this night would haunt them for years, maybe decades, to come.

Among the detainees, I counted only two Albanian gunmen. At least four more lay dead across the yard and among the pines—cut down by Willis's sharp eye and quick trigger finger. Add to those the three men Rakow and I had killed downstairs, plus the two snipers and the crawler in the woods...that made twelve, meaning that at least one was missing.

I wasn't concerned. By sunrise, this would no longer be a safe place for child traffickers who slunk among the shadows. Every good cop in the region would be on the lookout, and the citizens would rise up, also. The straggling Albanians might stumble onto a crazy old veteran's moonshine operation, where trespassers would be shot, and survivors shot again.

I turned from the window and stepped into the hall, standing for a moment and reviewing my mental film reel of everything I had seen since breaching the back door. And, perhaps more importantly, what I *hadn't* seen.

And *whom* I hadn't seen.

Rakow shouted orders on the ground level as I crossed the hallway to the first door I had kicked in after climbing the stairs. That makeshift office, with desks laden with paperwork, and a dead sniper on the floor.

I found it just as I remembered it, and closed the busted

door. Pocketing my hands, I stepped carefully around the body and touched nothing as I surveyed the stacks of documents, reading the headings and whatever was visible beneath.

I wasn't surprised to find plenty of documents printed with Krol Industries letterhead. I thought back to the bauxite mines and the train hauling boxcars across the county and down to Georgia.

On to the coast, maybe? It made sense, not only for bauxite shipping, but also for human trafficking. Bring children into the ports, smuggle them aboard rail cars, and then you could move them all over the country with relative ease.

The old summer camp had become something of a distribution hub. Or maybe a temporary sales center. Rakow would know for sure once he interrogated the survivors. Based on the license plates I'd observed across the backs of their vehicles, many of them had driven a long way to be at the lodge that night. Come here to bid, it seemed. To evaluate and purchase.

To fuel brothels in New Orleans, Jackson, Dallas, Little Rock.

The system made sense...yet, in the back of my mind, I still knew something was missing. Something...and someone. Someone who had somehow threatened this operation from the start, so much so that the Krol kids and their Albanian associates were willing to move mountains to run me out of town. To shut down my investigation.

I dug the Victorinox out of my pocket and rotated the three-inch blade open. Then I used the tip to sift through the documents, preventing any risk of contaminating evidence with my own fingerprints.

They were purchase orders from Krol Industries. Shipping receipts. Cargo manifests. All kinds of complex, corporate documentation that I barely understood, but strongly suspected was flush with innuendo. *Crate* might refer to *human*. *Item* to *girl*.

The FBI would need months to sort that out, but my gut still told me that the piece I was missing should be a lot more obvious. A lot more blatant.

Where was Delia Crawford?

The door groaned open next to me, and Keen crashed in. He was red-faced and muddy, still wearing the sheriff's department body armor and ball cap. He looked hypercharged with adrenaline—a reasonable side effect of being shot at for the first time, but he seemed to have survived it. He gave the body on the floor barely a glance before turning straight to me.

"Mason! I was looking for you. Did you find Delia?"

The energy in his voice failed to disguise the desperation. Wide eyes paired with a half-open mouth, sweat trickling down his forehead.

I looked up slowly. Mind spinning. Barely seeing him. Fully focused on the question that somehow formed the nucleus of my entire week in Delamar County.

Where is Delia?

"Did you find her?" Keen asked again, eyes rimming red now. Voice faltering.

I looked back to the desk and slid a document aside, exposing yet another shipping manifest. My knife tip scraped the paper, tracing halfway down. Leaving a little scratch line across the sheet.

And then stopping.

Crawford Imports, LLC.

I closed my eyes. One long, heavy breath. The last piece clicking into place.

"Where is she, Mason?" Keen whispered, his voice turning soft with restrained emotion. He took a half step toward me. "Where's Delia?"

I opened my eyes. Closed the knife. Turned for the door.

"Where she's always been, Keen. Find Rakow. We've got one more place to go."

50

I waited next to Krol's lifted Titan for forty minutes while Rakow established control of the situation. He didn't want to leave at all—but he didn't have a choice. This wasn't something I could do by myself. It was something I didn't want to do at all.

But the job wouldn't be finished until the bad guys were behind bars. And that meant all of them.

At last enough state, county, and city cops had arrived for Rakow to step away, and he climbed in behind the wheel of a Delamar County Tahoe, looking exhausted and overwhelmed. I took the front passenger's seat, and Keen rode in back, still silent and shifting nervously. I hadn't told him what I knew—I wanted to prove it first. Or maybe I hoped to disprove it.

But I knew I wouldn't.

"This had better be damn important, Sharpe." Rakow slammed the door and started the Tahoe.

"Just drive, Rakow."

"Where?"

"Muscogee."

That was all I would say, and Rakow piloted down the long drive. The Raptor lay in a bent and smashed mess next to the obliterated front gate, shoved aside by the volunteer firefighters. The hood was buckled, the windshield shattered. All the airbags deployed.

Dog hair absolutely everywhere.

Rakow spent a lot of time on his phone as we drove, speaking to everyone from the FBI to state police to sheriffs in adjoining counties. Warning them of the Albanian gunmen on the loose. Obtaining an emergency warrant for the investigation of Krol Industries, along with the search and seizure of documents and computers found in their offices.

It was an absolute mess, and Rakow was at the center of it. The state investigators already had questions and a lot of complaints. The bloodbath at the hunting lodge wasn't a palatable thing for civilized society. Rakow had explaining to do, they said.

Rakow told them to take a long walk off a short pier and hung up.

We rumbled into downtown Muscogee, and I directed Rakow toward the historic home district and then to the tall antebellum house resting just off the street. Overgrown shrubs and dusty windows. Most of the second floor darkened...except for one window.

"You're kidding me," Rakow muttered.

"She was here from the start," I said. "She was here when we were here. Here right after she fled the crash scene. The Crawfords hid her."

"How could you possibly know that?" Rakow demanded.

"I should have known it when we first visited. Look at the

windows and the lawn. All overgrown and unmanaged. The whole place is unmanaged. But when we were here before, the maid was washing sheets. Remember? She had bedclothes and one pillow under her arm. A tray of lunch in the other. But the Crawfords were eating lunch outside."

Rakow surveyed the property without comment, and I detected an excited hitch in Keen's breathing. He was starting to believe.

What I said next would crush him, I knew. But I had no choice.

"Bring your handcuffs, Rakow."

I kicked mud off my boots as I approached the door. Rakow and Keen followed, one quiet and reserved. The other breathless and hopeful. I knocked on the door and waited for the shuffle of feet on the hardwood beyond. Mrs. Crawford answered, dressed in a night robe and looking startled and confused.

But not sleepy, because she hadn't been sleeping. She hadn't slept all night, and neither had her husband.

"Sheriff?" she said cautiously, leaving the screen door closed.

"Where is your husband, Mrs. Crawford?" I spoke before Rakow could. She squinted at me, confused and edgy. Fingers kneading the edge of her night robe. A nervous tongue darting across her lips.

"He's asleep," she said, her words piling together.

"No, he's not," I said. "We need to come inside."

She looked to Rakow. He stepped alongside me, shooting me a demanding look. I nodded once, and Rakow faced the door.

"Get Thomas, Cecilia."

She nodded a few times, gaze still darting. Then she

pushed the door open and admitted the three of us, barely giving Keen a second glance. I didn't think she recognized him. That didn't surprise me. She hadn't seen him since he was a kid. I doubted she wanted anything to do with his book.

Cecilia guided us to a parlor near the front of the house, where stiff and fancy furniture served as a landing zone while she went for Thomas. It took less time than it would have if he were sleeping, but longer than it should have considering that he wasn't. He arrived minutes later fully dressed in slacks and a button-down shirt. Polished dress shoes and disheveled hair. Black circles beneath his eyes.

Looking edgy and unsure. Cecilia at his elbow.

"Sheriff?" He acted surprised. I knew he wasn't.

"Have a seat, Thomas," Rakow said, motioning to a chair. Thomas hesitated; then he sat. Cecilia stood behind him, her fingers rubbing the back of his leather chair.

"What's this about?" Thomas said.

Rakow didn't answer immediately. I noticed Thomas's quick eyes scanning our muddy pants and the blood on my sleeves. Both Keen and I had removed our bulletproof vests, but I still wore the duty belt with the empty Glock holster and the one pair of handcuffs.

"Why are you here?" Thomas's next question was directed at me, and it carried an edge.

"Deputy Sharpe has a few questions for you," Rakow said.

"Deputy?"

Rakow gave me a go-ahead nod. I cut straight to the heart.

"Where is Delia, Mr. Crawford?"

A lightning flash passed across his face, come and gone

in an instant, but mirrored in his wife's eyes. Telling an awful lot in that split second.

"What are you talking about?" Thomas spluttered.

"You know," I said. "And so do we."

He shifted. Looked at the floor. His lips twitched as he chewed his cheek, and his eyes rimmed red. But he didn't answer.

"It was hot the day we visited," I said. "Brutally hot. But you met with us in the sunroom, both of you pouring sweat. I guess you didn't want us around any longer than we needed to be. Looking back, I assumed you were in denial about Delia's reappearance. That's how I wrote off all the hostility. But it wasn't denial, was it? It was fear. And maybe a little panic. Because she was here the entire time."

Thomas's eyes watered, and he blinked hard to stop a tear from slipping down his face. "I don't know what you're talking about."

"You do, though," I said. "And you've been dreading this day for a long time."

Another protracted pause. Thomas opened his mouth and closed it twice. Cecilia openly sobbed.

"Thomas?" Rakow's voice was stern, but he didn't shout. He was just loud enough to cut through the room. Thomas faced him, tears sliding down his cheeks now.

"Sheriff...you have to understand. I can't...I just..."

"It's okay, Daddy."

The new voice was soft and female, coming from the hallway. All five of us pivoted in that direction. A shadow fell across the living room floor. Thomas half stood, then collapsed back into the chair as a woman stepped into the room.

Dressed in sweatpants and a sweatshirt. Petite and slender, with long blonde hair and an elegant face.

And two different-colored eyes. One deep brown. One brilliant blue.

"D...Delia?" Keen whispered.

"Hello, Eli."

51

Nobody spoke. Delia stood just inside the room, hands clasped over her stomach, offering the shadow of a smile to Keen. I heard the writer swallow hard next to me, but I didn't take my eyes off Thomas Crawford.

Delia's father sobbed. Her mother simply looked dead—white-faced and detached. Like a shell-shocked foot soldier. I'd seen it before.

"Why don't you sit down?" I said, speaking to Delia, but still facing Thomas.

Delia did sit, settling onto a couch with elegance and looking at her hands. Not speaking. Not displaying any particular emotion in her peculiar eyes.

She was shell-shocked also, I realized, but in a very different way. She was shut down in a way a person could only become after years of emotional artillery detonating right over their heads.

"The girls?" Delia said.

"We got them," I said. "They're safe."

She nodded slowly. "And the Albanians?"

"Dead," I said. "Or in custody."

Delia's cheeks flushed just a little. Rakow shot me a look, but I ignored him. He turned back to Delia.

"Somebody should start talking," he said simply.

Thomas opened his mouth. Faltered, and swallowed hard. Delia looked up.

"It's okay, Daddy," she said again. She faced Rakow, and her shoulders squared. I saw nothing in her eyes. Not fear. Not pain. Not panic.

But not light, either. Not life. She looked as dead as her mother.

"I'm sorry about your father, Luke. I heard what happened. He was a good man."

Rakow said nothing. Delia smoothed her pants legs. Drew a deep breath.

"I know he did whatever he could to find me. I read about his investigation."

She looked to Keen, and he opened and closed his mouth a few times, but didn't speak. Delia smiled, but there was no warmth in the expression.

"What happened?" Rakow said.

"I was kidnapped. At the summer camp. Some foreign people...I really don't know. Everything went black pretty quickly. The next thing I remember, I was in the back of a vehicle. We drove for a long time. And then there was a ship. A long, long ride...days, I think. They kept me in a wooden box someplace in the hold. I only knew it was a ship because I could hear the water sometimes. And seagulls when we reached port."

Mr. and Mrs. Crawford trembled, eyes clamped shut, tears flowing as Delia spoke, but their daughter remained perfectly calm. As though she were reading the newspaper. Telling somebody else's story.

"I don't know where they took me. Someplace in the Middle East, for a few years. A lot of Arabic people. Then north. White people. Some sounded Russian. I learned a few words, but I never knew what the language was. For a while, I would live in one house, with one man. And his friends, sometimes. Then I would be traded or moved along. Lost in a gambling bet, maybe. It was..."

Delia broke off for the first time, staring at an imperfection in the hardwood floor. Crying silently, without any racking sobs. Reliving horrors now years removed, but I had no doubt they felt as real as the day they happened.

I had some experience with reliving horrors.

"I ended up in Albania. I was...well, no longer a prized commodity at that point. But I had developed an ability to talk to the new girls. To calm them. To help them cope. I thought it was a good thing, at the time. I thought I was helping them. But really, I was just helping our captors. Making it easier for them to get what they wanted. The man in Albania who bought me was named Alteo. He owned what they call a stable—a group of girls for hire. Mostly children. He wanted me to be his stable keeper. I was given a nice room and any kind of food or clothing I wanted. He even let me have books and watch movies. In exchange, I was expected to manage the stable. Keep the girls calm. Discipline them if they acted up. Enforce proper hygiene and teach...technique."

Delia's tears flowed a little faster. She sniffed for the first time. Swallowed hard.

"I knew it was wrong. But by their mid-twenties, most women in my situation were sent to Asia to work in the massage parlors, or farmed out to cheap brothels. The horror stories of those places were nightmarish. I was afraid. So...I did what I was told."

The vacant stare Delia fixed on the floor now grew so distant, it was as though she left the room. Mr. and Mrs. Crawford continued to sob. Keen cried silently.

Rakow and I just listened.

"When did you come back?" I asked.

Delia looked up slowly, as though she had forgotten anybody else was in the room. She blinked. Ran a tongue across her lips.

"Don't," Thomas whispered.

Delia looked at her father. Then she looked back at me, and she seemed to return to the room.

"Alteo was a businessman," Delia said. "An importer... and an exporter. His gangs gathered girls from across Eastern Europe. Sometimes they were told a better job was waiting for them in the New World. A better life. Nice clothes, and beautiful pictures on magazine covers. Other times they were simply kidnapped. Then they were exported to the United States. Sold to brothel keepers and slavers in every major city. The largest sex market in the world, Alteo used to say."

"You went with them?" I asked.

"Not at first. But...eventually. I earned Alteo's trust. He sent me with a shipment to Boston. My job was to manage the girls, as always. I planned to escape, and I almost did, but..."

Delia trailed off. Her eyes blurred, and she blinked a lot. I turned to Thomas.

"But she couldn't," I said simply. "Because of you."

Thomas seemed to collapse, falling into his own hands.

Sobbing like a child. Rakow stiffened next to me, but I held up a hand. I knew Thomas would break. I knew he already had. The whole story would gush out like a geyser.

Given another three minutes, it finally did.

"They first contacted us three years ago," Thomas choked.

"The Albanians?" I asked.

Thomas nodded. "They sent us pictures...of Delia. Told us she was alive. I thought they wanted money, but they didn't want anything. Not at first. They said not to tell anyone, or they would kill her. They said to keep very quiet and wait. Then, for a year, they disappeared again."

"When did it start?" I pressed.

Thomas stared at the floor, fingers dug into the arms of his chair. "Two years ago. They knew I ran a logistics company. That I arranged shipments around the world, on container ships. So they...asked me to arrange a shipment. From Durrës to Boston. They said if I did what I was told... Delia might come home. I didn't know if I believed them, but I felt I didn't have a choice. They wouldn't tell me what the shipment contained. I just...arranged it."

Thomas choked out. Delia resumed the story.

"When I got to Boston, they showed me my father's photo. They told me he was working with them, to keep me alive. And that I should keep working with them to keep him alive. They were very...clear about it. About what would happen to him and Mama if I tried to escape."

More watery eyes. More gargled voices. They both stopped talking.

"How many trips?" I pressed.

Thomas shook his head, but I knew he knew. I repeated the question.

"Seven," he said at last. "Including this one. The Albanians liked to keep things moving. One town to the next, never the same distribution hub twice. It was getting complicated and expensive. So they partnered with the Krols to use the summer camp. Repurpose it as a hunting camp. A distribution hub. Someplace where they could repeat operations…right in my backyard."

Thomas choked. "That's when I knew it would never end. I knew Delia would never get away. But I thought, at least if she were close, I might see her…"

"So you helped them set it up," I said.

Thomas didn't answer. His face dropped into his hands, and Delia resumed.

"When I found out we were going to Alabama, I knew the arrangement wouldn't last long. I'd seen them do it before, whenever they set up a rural hub. They would tap into local police and try to make it last as long as they could, but eventually they would have to move on, and when they did…they cleaned house. Everybody died."

Delia shook her head. Inhaled slowly. "I couldn't do it any longer. I couldn't…I couldn't help them. I made a plan to bust the last shipment. As soon as we got off the train in Delamar County, I was going to get the girls out. Take the risk."

"Did your father know?" I didn't bother addressing Thomas directly. The man was a wreck.

"No," Delia said. "There was no way to reach him. I waited until we reached the hunting camp. I hadn't spoken to the girls yet. Most of them didn't speak English. But there was one girl, from Romania, who seemed to trust me. She smiled a lot. She liked butterflies."

"You got her the pants," I said.

Delia nodded. Smiled sadly. "Cristina. I know you found her. I saw it on the news."

"What happened?" I pressed.

"We tried to escape," Delia said simply. "It was raining heavily that night. The previous week I had stolen a pair of pliers from a toolbox—to cut the fence. I got Cristina up, and she helped with the other girls. Not all of them could understand her. We got near the door, but one of the girls panicked. She just started screaming. She wouldn't stop. She pounded on the wall and wouldn't go. She woke up the Albanians...we had no choice but to run. I told the girls to scatter. I figured they might have a better chance that way. But we had no idea where we were. We were so far out in the woods, and there was still the fence. I think only Cristina escaped. She had the pliers."

"And you?" I asked.

Delia's shoulders dropped. "I almost made it. I used the creek to cross beneath the fence; then I fled all the way back to the highway...headed for Muscogee. I flagged down a van and...wouldn't you know it." She shook her head. "It was one of the Albanians."

I thought back to that night, now four days prior. The driving rain. The overturned van on the side of the highway, wheels still spinning. The gathering smoke and growing fire.

The dead driver whom nobody could identify. Another Albanian, slipping into the country. Leaving his passport in his luggage.

A smart criminal.

"I'm sorry," Delia whispered, facing me. "I know you were only trying to help. I knew if I went back to the police station, they would know. I knew the Albanians had people working there. I knew they would go for my parents. I…I had to run…"

For the first time, Delia broke down. Her body shook. Her head dropped. She cried like a little girl, rough and long, not even stopping to gasp for breath. Keen got up and settled onto his knees next to her. She leaned against his shoulder and kept crying while he placed a gentle arm around her back and sobbed with her.

Mrs. Crawford only stared. Completely dead inside.

Thomas lifted his chin, eyes bloodshot. Swallowing hard. Then gritted his teeth.

"You can never understand. You don't know the horror of knowing your baby girl is alive…and held by those monsters. You…you would do anything. Whatever they asked. Whatever it took."

His chin shook. Then his shoulders dropped, and so did his face. He placed both hands on his knees, then rotated them palms upward.

I stood slowly, my stomach a mess of hot, molten lava. My legs heavy as iron. My body aching.

There was no right answer here. No solution to make the pain go away. Only a cold reality that, despite my most primal instincts, would not be ignored.

I thought of Cristina. I thought of the dozens of other girls Crawford had helped to traffic into the United States. Then I reached for my cuffs.

"Thomas Crawford…you're under arrest."

52

If it had been up to me, I would have left Delamar County that same day, placing Able and all the sadness that consumed it in my rearview mirror and driving in the first direction my headlights pointed.

But despite the emergency nature of my deputization, I was still a bona fide officer of the law, and that post carried obligations I couldn't in good conscience abandon. I remained in Able for another week, undergoing one interview after another with the state and federal investigators who swarmed the county like ants out of a wrecked anthill.

The busted trafficking operation in rural Alabama was now headline news across the nation. Everybody wanted a slice—from national media to a slew of true crime writers and enough FBI agents to establish a Delamar County field office. The feds took custody of Thomas Crawford and even arrested his wife, but I knew that neither would remain in jail for long. Thomas would cut a deal with a US attorney—something that required him to detail everything he knew about the Albanian operation in exchange for a shorter prison sentence. Cecilia would probably get off with no jail time at all. After all, what judge or jury would seriously convict a mother in her situation?

Both Crawfords would return home to their daughter, who now spent her days alone in the upstairs bedroom she slept in as a kid, crying herself to sleep. Refusing to talk to the media. Only coming downstairs when Keen rolled up in his maroon Silverado with the balding tires. A new pane of tinted glass covered the back of the cab with a fresh sausage-dog sticker in one corner.

An army of Chiweenies yipping from the back seat.

Willis told me that a major publisher had offered Keen a six-figure book deal to tell his story. Keen had turned them down cold. Said he wasn't writing anymore. Told them to leave Delia alone.

It made me smile when I heard the story, but I didn't have a lot of time to think about Keen or Delia or what would become of them. Some jackass from Montgomery had come down to launch an investigation into the practices of the Delamar County Sheriff's Department, and he had questions. A lot of them—the most difficult of which included Owen's death and the two smashed Krol kids.

Skinny and Muscle had eventually found their way to a Muscogee hospital, where no less than two dozen bones were set, and extensive facial reconstruction surgery was called for. The jackass wanted to know if their condition had anything to do with our investigation, but in the end Rakow and I decided to feign ignorance as to their misfortune, betting on Skinny and Muscle to act in their own best interests and keep their wired mouths shut. After all, they couldn't explain the beatdown without explaining how it started, and with old man Krol dead and the Albanian operation burning to the ground, there was nobody left to bail them out.

It turned out to be a good bet. They cut their losses, said nothing of their wrecked Raptor, and said nothing of me.

Owen's death wasn't so easily swept under the rug. The killing was ruled to be justified, of course, but the nature of his caved-in face gave the squeamish among society second thoughts, and the jackass from Montgomery wanted to make a stink about it. As sheriff, Rakow wasn't really accountable to the state unless laws were broken, but he couldn't afford a scandal either, so he neutralized the situation by launching his own investigation.

I was found guilty of using excessive force and was summarily terminated from the Delamar County Sheriff's Department, ineligible for rehire. I flipped Rakow my star without any heartache, as ready to get rid of it as he was to take it.

After the interviews and paperwork finally wound down, I visited Cristina in the government facility where she was being housed up in Montgomery. I brought her a little mesh enclosure I'd bought at a sporting goods store. Inside were three Monarch butterflies I had spent the better part of an afternoon capturing along Delamar's pothole-infested county roads.

Cristina smiled like the sun when I entered her room, her bright child eyes fixating on the butterflies.

"*Fluture!*"

53

As the investigations wound down and the media finally began to lose interest, I felt a strange itch returning to the back of my mind. Kind of like a nervous tic or an odd restlessness. Rakow's guest bedroom had served as my home for the better part of a month, and it was comfortable. But one Thursday night long after Rakow had gone to bed, I wandered outside and found my GMC nestled in dewy grass beneath a star-filled sky. I used the little battery pump to inflate my air mattress; then I flopped out in the truck bed and spent a lot of time just enjoying the gentle music of rustling grass and distant cicadas.

By the time the sun broke through the trees and Rakow appeared on the front porch, shirtless, scratching Mossy with one hand and cradling a cup of coffee with the other, I knew what the itch meant. I knew that it originated in my feet, not my mind, and there would be only one way to scratch it.

Settling onto the porch next to Rakow, I accepted the coffee cup he passed me and leaned back into the creaking rocking chair. The wooden arms were smoothed by a few thousand such mornings, and I wondered if Rakow's father had favored this chair. Or maybe his mother.

It was a comfortable place to relax. But it wasn't my own.

"Bailey's coming over tonight," Rakow said. "I thought we'd throw some steaks on the grill. Maybe you could bring out the violin again."

I nodded slowly, but I didn't answer. I sipped coffee, and Rakow shot me a sideways look.

"You're going, aren't you?"

I rotated the cup on the arm of the chair and enjoyed the growing blaze of Alabama sun. It was barely seven a.m., and already the demon heat of a Southern summer was on its way. It would be suffocating in a couple of hours.

But with my windows down and the crackling old radio of my GMC doing its best to maintain a connection on rural back roads…I'd be okay.

"I'm starting to think that's what I do," I said softly.

"Hit the road?"

I nodded.

A pregnant silence fell between us, lingering so long I began to wonder if Rakow was going to ask me to stay. Despite my termination from the sheriff's department, a sort of relaxed friendship had developed between us. An easy familiarity, born maybe from combat, or more generally from the Army. Who the hell knew? We didn't have that much in common, but somehow it seemed that Rakow felt he owed me something.

Maybe it was just guilt talking, for kicking me out of town when I had been right all along.

"I…" Rakow started, then stopped. I hoped he wouldn't start again, but I also knew he couldn't leave it alone.

"I want to apologize," he said at last.

"Don't. You were just doing your job."

"No, not that. About the other thing."

I looked at my coffee, and my eyes stung. Not because it really bothered me that Rakow had pried into my past—he was a cop. He was just doing his job.

My eyes stung because things had been too quiet for too long, and I was losing my own ability to bury the past. Maybe that was why my feet itched. Maybe I was ready for another distraction.

"If you ever wanted to talk about it...I mean..." Rakow trailed off. I knew what he meant, and I appreciated it. But it wasn't a door I wanted to open.

"Do you ever talk about how you earned that Silver Star?" I asked.

Rakow's face twitched. He looked into his coffee and grew very quiet. I extended my mug.

"To life, Rakow. To loving good people and burying bad ones."

Rakow met my gaze. Smiled, ever so slightly. Then he touched his mug against mine, and we both drank. The coffee was good—strong and black. Just the way the Army made it.

After another long beat, Rakow cleared his throat, and I knew he'd let it go. I was grateful.

"Where you headed?"

I shrugged. "South, maybe. I'd still like to see Florida."

"You should. It's gorgeous down there. Lots of good seafood."

"I'm not much on seafood."

"Really? Well, try some anyway. It's better than whatever they catch in the desert."

That brought a smile to my lips, and Rakow rocked his mug back to finish the last gulp.

"You gonna keep sleeping in the back of that truck?" he asked.

"Probably."

"Well, come with me. We gotta do something to keep you dry."

We left the mugs on the porch and followed Mossy behind the house, past the firepit, and down to the barn. Rakow led me around the sagging structure to a hog-wire enclosure about twenty feet square, with a truck bed camper shell propped up on blocks right in the middle. It was constructed of aluminum, dirty white in color, with dusty windows and a metal rack on top. Old school.

"That damn goat used to sleep under it," Rakow asked. "Lord knows I'm never getting another. Reckon it'll fit your truck?"

I gauged the length of the shell, then helped Rakow to lift it out of the enclosure and carry it to my GMC. It fit almost perfectly, maybe an inch short, but it covered the bedrails just right and matched the two-tone green and white of my pickup. Rakow pulled the water hose out, and we spent half an hour scrubbing the dirt off, cleaning the windows, and using C-clamps from his barn to affix it to the truck bed.

When I admired the setup from a distance, I liked it a lot. There was nearly four feet of space between the truck bed and the roof of the shell, leaving plenty of room for my air mattress and gear. It would be loud when it rained, but it beat getting wet, and I felt better about my gear, having it at least a little secured. If I dropped the tailgate and slept with my head poking out, I could still see the stars.

"What do you want for it?" I asked.

Rakow waved a hand dismissively. I nodded my thanks, and we stood for a while in the baking heat.

"Well," Rakow said at last, "I'd better get to the station."

We shook hands, and he wished me well. Then Rakow returned to the house, and I returned to my sagging bench seat. The weary old inline six fired up with a rumble, and I gave it a minute to warm before I eased toward the driveway. Rakow waved from the porch, and Mossy followed me all the way back to the dirt road, barking once in farewell as I turned away from the house.

I sifted through the radio stations as I hit the highway, driving past the crash scene of a month earlier and thinking about Delia. Thinking about her parents and those girls at the summer camp.

It felt like an empty victory when I remembered the thousands of other girls who would never be found. But even so, I'd left Delamar County better than I found it, and there was a little satisfaction in that. At least enough to carry me into Florida, where I'd find another place to camp, another place to watch the sunset.

Another week to let grief work itself out—the slow way. It wasn't a perfect solution, but I wasn't looking for perfect.

I was just looking for another day.

Mason and trouble have had a long relationship. They're about to renew their vows.

"Ladies and gentlemen, this is a robbery!"

Two heavily armed gunmen crash into a quiet Florida bank, and army veteran Mason Sharpe is caught in the middle of a deadly heist.

Later, the cops describe the robbery as an act of senseless violence, but something seems off to Mason. Was this really about the money? Or is there something else going on here?

When the two gunmen are revealed to be fellow veterans from the Army's famed 75th Ranger Regiment, Mason's doubts only grow. The bond of shared military service is strong, and Mason can't let these questions rest.

He starts to dig for the truth - and finds himself on a headlong collision course with a governmental conspiracy big enough to bury him.

But he won't go down without a fight, and this time, he won't be fighting alone. He's bringing a band of fellow warriors who understand the call of duty.

He's bringing a Fire Team.

Get Fire Team now.

Please enjoy this preview of Fire Team.

CHAPTER 1

"Ladies and gentlemen, this is a robbery!"

The front door of the bank blew open, followed immediately by a string of rapid rifle shots cracking like firecrackers inside the sprawling building. I spun around in the office chair, my vision snapping toward the main entrance.

Two men, both dressed in all black from head to toe, faces obscured by ski masks. The first held a shortened AR-15–style rifle pressed into his shoulder, the muzzle sweeping the lobby. The second dangled a similar weapon from a one-point sling, an oversized backpack riding his shoulders while he bolted the doors. People lined up at the teller counter screamed and ducked for cover behind the credenza. The banker sitting across from me choked and dropped the phone pinned against his ear, fumbling beneath his desk for the silent alarm.

But it was much too late for that.

"Stay calm," I hissed, my own heart accelerating as the second man in black finished with the doors and brandished his own rifle.

"Everybody on the floor!" Number One said. "Hands up, cell phones out. Let's move!"

"You hit the alarm?" I asked.

The banker nodded like a bobblehead, his face chalk white. I held up a hand to calm him while I tracked the two men toward the credenza. Number One kept his rifle at the ready while Number Two corralled the bank customers into the lobby—maybe ten of them, now all lying facedown on the dingy carpet, hands and legs splayed. Cell phones spinning into a pile.

I kept my voice low. "They're not here to hurt you, they're just here for the money. Don't panic."

The banker might have nodded again, I wasn't looking. Number One saw us through the glass panel of the recessed office and pointed his rifle at my face.

"You two! Out of the office. *Move!*"

We complied, stepping through the open door with hands raised.

"On the floor. Join the others. Hustle, fat ass!"

The last comment was directed at the banker. He stumbled, tears streaking his jiggling cheeks as he reached the pile of hostages. I dropped to my knees and lowered myself slowly onto the floor, measuring my breaths. Recalling SERE training in the Army.

A special hell of a school, dedicated to teaching soldiers how to survive capture by the enemy. Easily my least favorite portion of my entire stint in the military, but the lessons it taught came flooding back. Lessons about remaining calm. Humanizing yourself to the enemy. About not doing anything stupid.

I hit the carpet as Number One stood over me with his rifle, his companion clearing the other offices and the teller line in short order, driving the bank staff to join us on the lobby floor. The pile of cell phones grew rapidly, and the bank manager mumbled a plea for the safety of her staff.

A brave woman, but speaking at the wrong time. She caught a backhand across the face, not all that hard, but sudden enough to earn a gasp from the knot of people on the floor.

"On your stomach, sister!" Number One ordered. "Keep your mouth shut."

The manager went down with the rest, and the two men circled. I twisted my face toward the main door, looking beyond panels of glass, past a bank of elevators, to another row of glass doors that faced out over the parking lot and the street beyond. The bank was situated on the first floor of a fifteen-story building, the other floors presumably still accessible by elevator.

If the silent alarm hadn't worked, an office worker exiting the elevators would see us soon enough. This wasn't a well-conceived robbery.

I remained loose.

"All right! Here's how it's gonna go down," Number One shouted through his ski mask. I noted an East Coast accent. Definitely American by birth. Not New England. His tone sounded more central, but still carried that snap and pop of big-city energy. "Anybody who's caught with a phone gets my boot in their face, so if you held one out, you'd better toss it now. We're not here to hurt you. We just want the money. Am I clear?"

No answer, just a murmur of panic, followed by another string of blaring gunshots directed at the ceiling. Three of them, not automatic, but pressed together by the rapid use of a trigger finger. Brass rained across the carpet, and a woman shrieked.

"When I ask a question, you answer. *Am I clear?*"

This time a murmur of agreement rose from the crowd. I kept my mouth shut, focusing on what I could see of the men. Just black boots and black pants, joined by an oversized black bag I hadn't noticed before.

"Okay." The leader spoke again. "That's better. Now work with me, and we'll be out of your hair in time for lunch. Where's the head teller?"

Another hesitation. A foot landed hard on the carpet, right between my nose and the nose of a young woman with raven black hair. She faced me, her cheek pressed into the floor, one panicked eye visible over the toe of the boot. Late twenties or early thirties, maybe. Aging another five at present.

"Stay calm," I mouthed.

"*Where is the head teller?*"

"R-right here!" somebody choked. "That's me!"

"Great. On your feet. You too, Wonder Woman."

The bank manager was dragged to her feet alongside the head teller—a skinny Hispanic guy. They both looked ready to faint, but they had nothing to worry about. I figured the vault worked in halves, like the missile codes on a nuclear submarine. The captain and the executive officer were both needed for a launch to occur—or in this case, for the vault to open.

"Let's move!" Number Two took over. He propelled the two bank staff toward the vault while Number One kept the muzzle of his rifle sweeping the crowd. The faint smell of gunpowder still hung in the air, mixed with the infrequent moan or whimper of a strained voice choked by tears and panic.

I rolled my head an inch, just enough to stare up Number One's pants leg. He was shorter than his companion, but stood straight, holding his rifle at low ready, trigger finger stiff against the receiver. Shoulders loose. Eyes up and moving.

From the vault, Number Two snapped an unintelligible command, and something clanged. I pictured the bank manager and the head teller scooping cash out of the dual-access vault. Probably less of it than the gunman expected. I doubted banks carried all that much cash anymore. Why take the risk in a cashless society?

This wouldn't take long. With every passing second, the value of *just one more dollar* would be offset by the increased risk of being caught. They would take what they had and split for the white panel van parked under the portico outside, leaving the bank staff and patrons alike to clean out their pants. A terrifying but relatively harmless experience.

"Back to the lobby!" Number Two shouted from the vault room. The manager and head teller stumbled out of the vault room, back into the open lobby. They dragged a duffel bag between them, half full and not that heavy, dropping it as they reached the knot of bank staff and customers.

"Back on your face!" Number One ordered. The pair complied, returning to the floor. But I didn't see Number Two. Number One now looked toward the vault room.

Rotating my face in that direction, my view was blocked

by a pair of desks resting in the middle of the expansive lobby. But in the momentary stillness, I thought I heard a sound. A dull scratch, followed by a whoosh. Vaguely familiar to me, but not in a firsthand way. Like a sound I had heard in a movie.

Number One's body remained loose, dark eyes perfectly calm behind the ski mask. Lifting his wrist to his mouth, he spoke a calm word into an invisible mic.

"Sitrep?"

Whatever reply he received must have been channeled through an earpiece. I didn't hear a voice, but I did hear an intensified whooshing from the vault. I remembered the oversized backpack Number Two wore, and suddenly the noise made sense.

A blowtorch. The guy was going for the safety-deposit boxes. Was he out of his mind?

I twisted my arm to look at my watch, guesstimating how much time had passed since the two men had burst into the building. Not less than six minutes. Maybe eight.

The police would be here in no time. They could be screaming this way even now. And that *wasn't* a good thing. The moment cops arrived, this would become a hostage situation. A standoff with no clear resolution. A potentially lethal predicament.

"You should go now," I said, keeping my voice calm. "Somebody on an upper floor will have heard the gunshots. The cops will be here soon. Take the cash and leave."

I braced myself for a boot to my exposed ribcage, but Number One didn't even flinch. He calmly checked his own watch and remained silent. I lifted my head an inch and surveyed the pileup of people gathered around me. It was a hodgepodge of humanity if ever I'd seen one. Young bank tellers in pants suits. A Hispanic guy in a dirty T-shirt with a landscape company logo, clutching a cross necklace with his eyes closed. A fat guy in a sweat-soaked white dress shirt, heaving and red-faced.

And the raven-haired woman next to me, clutching her purse for dear life, her face still streaked with drying tears.

"Hey, asshole! Head down!"

Number One toed me in the ribcage, and I dropped my face. The whooshing continued from the vault room, hissing now and again as the oxygen lever on the torch was depressed to make a white-hot cut.

And then I heard another sound. Distant at first, enough so that I hoped I had imagined it. But ten seconds later it was louder. Screaming toward us, wailing like a hurricane wind.

A police siren.

Get Fire Team now.

ABOUT THE AUTHOR

Logan Ryles was born in small town USA and knew from an early age he wanted to be a writer. After working as a pizza delivery driver, sawmill operator, and banker, he finally embraced the dream and has been writing ever since. With a passion for action-packed and mystery-laced stories, Logan's work has ranged from global-scale political thrillers to small town vigilante hero fiction.

Beyond writing, Logan enjoys saltwater fishing, road trips, sports, and fast cars. He lives with his wife and three fun-loving dogs in Alabama.

Did you enjoy *End Game?* Please consider leaving a review on Amazon to help other readers discover the book.

www.loganryles.com

ALSO BY LOGAN RYLES

Mason Sharpe Thriller Series

Point Blank

Take Down

End Game

Fire Team

Made in United States
North Haven, CT
03 December 2023

44970647R00207